-Worlds Apart-

Ruination

Amanda Thome

Athena Alley Press

Athena Alley Press Book

First Edition: March 2014

ISBN 978-0-9960608-0-6

This book is dedicated to my family and to all those who have shown me support before, during, and after this process. A special thanks and dedication to my husband Clint, without him I wouldn't have found my inspiration.

ACKNOWLEDGMENTS

There were so many hands and minds that helped to create what you see here today. I was just the initial step and I am so thankful for all those who helped get me to the finish line. A special thanks to my husband Clint for his constant support. I couldn't have done it without my family, they are great supporters. Thank you so much to all the friends I trusted to read the drafts and whose feedback made the book all the better for it. Those trusted friends are Emily W, Lori G, Ginny Z, Clint T, and two of my biggest supporters Katie R and my wonderful mother Lori. A special thanks to Janet Thome and her husband Mike for their support. Lastly I would like to thank my very talented editor Cassandra. Without all these people my book wouldn't be where it is today.

Chapter 1: Nessa

Emma's spending her first night in this world howling inconsolably. I'm not mad at her for keeping me awake all night, I wouldn't sleep anyway. Not with Mama's lifeless body lying in the next room. I pace endlessly in the pitch-black living room, blood still trickling from my knee. I gently rock Emma in my arms. My thoughts bound so fast that my head can't keep up. It's losing ground the same way I do when I try racing the shuttle.

My head cramps and hurts as it tries to organize and contain my thoughts. I'm reminded of the post, the way the supplies are all labeled and stacked. So structured and clean. I wish I could contain my thoughts, I wish I could organize and store them away somewhere, anywhere, so I don't have to feel them beating inside my head. I keep thinking there is no way the sun will ever rise again, positive that light and goodness will never reach us now that Mama's gone.

My eyes flutter briefly then snap open as night is fractured by hues of orange and pink. Bright bold colors that are meant to symbolize a new beginning, a beginning to another day here in the Inner. Oranges and pinks, colors that are good and pure, nothing like the darkness I feel inside. I stare through the fogged window, amazed that somehow earth continues forward and life continues without her.

The sun just breaks the tree line as the hovercraft from Central arrives. My chest squeezes as the ramp drops from the bottom of the craft, time freezes. The reflecting sun blinds me but I can't turn away.

These are the last moments I've got, after this everything will change. I know it all changed yesterday, but somehow having mama's body here makes it seem so indefinite. I know she's gone, that her body is empty and cold. I don't feel her spirit in the air like I did yesterday but even still, I know it will only be harder once they've taken her.

The Central representative is an indifferent woman, neither impolite nor inviting. To her this is purely business, nothing personal. She paces around the sitting room; her steps are hollow and echo straight to my chest. I involuntarily sink with each step, I feel like a wounded animal that is too scared to trust.

Her job is twofold today, she has to initiate Emma into society and usher Mama out. Her steps fall silent and I slowly straighten my knees trying to regain my strength. Why am I so weak? Is it fear or maybe the grief? It might be because she's from Central, she's in a league higher than me. Higher than anyone here in the Inner. My arms shiver, not because I'm cold, they shake in anticipation I suppose. She brings her head around, staring from wall to ceiling then landing on me. Her smile, one of indifference squeezes between her lips as she dislodges the bag carried under her arm. It's the paperwork validating Emma's Inner sector citizenship and the first in a series of grey clothes that all children under the age of six are required to wear. I brush my grey sleeve off; I hadn't noticed the blood on it until now.

She opens her arms directing me to hand Emma over. I hesitate, it just feels wrong. It should be Mama that hands Emma over, not me. I place Emma in her arms and step back as the representative opens her briefcase. Cradling Emma in one hand, she deftly uses the other to plunge a syringe into Emma's shoulder. My hand instinctively grasps my own shoulder; my immunization scar feels more prominent now than ever. Emma's shrilling scream reaches its peak just as she pulls the needle from her shoulder. Something inside me crawls and squirms hearing her cry. It turns my insides around like the washing machine does to our clothes. Her crying breaks just as fast as it started and my gut relaxes itself.

She hands Emma back to me, "You can go store the documents and then we'll begin the next order of business." I nod, turning toward the back of the room.

The representative waits patiently for me to return from storing Emma's papers. I'm taking extra time locking the safe

Central provides for documents, delaying the inescapable moment of letting my mother go. Avoiding that final moment when this will all become reality, the point of no return. I stare ahead hoping I'll hear Mama call to me. It's silly I know but I can't help hoping I'll hear her voice again. Maybe this was all a mistake, maybe she'll come back to life and hold me.

The hollow sounds of the representative's boots echo from the sitting room again, I can tell she's becoming anxious to leave and I can't delay any longer. I know what I need to do, I just don't want to.

Hesitantly, I lead the representative back to Mama's room. My eyes are fixed to the brown floor. I'm terrified they'll reflexively travel to the red sheets covering her lifeless body. I let my eyes travel there last night, I let my evil mind play tricks on me. If I stared just right it looked like her stomach was moving. Like maybe there was still breath in her trying to push its way out. Countless times I went to her, grabbed her hand and shook it but Mama was gone. No breathing, no life, just gone. I keep my eyes cast down now. I'm afraid I'll see the breathing again and be left crushed as I learn it was all just a trick.

"Any last words for her?" the representative asks as Mama's body wheels by. All I can do is shake my head 'No.' I am ashamed, like I've let her down. Mama was always so good with words. I never met a person she couldn't converse with for hours. She would have wanted something said, I should've had words prepared.

I shrink again as the representative takes her scan card and work articles. I wish things were like it was before the divide when they buried their dead and had funerals to honor them. If they had funerals I could have prepared something to say. I wouldn't have let her down. Now Central disposes of the bodies and mourning is private and short-lived. There are always work quotas for the living to meet.

The echoing steps intermingle with the grinding wheels as Mama's body rolls towards the craft. It's a horrible noise, insulting to the ears. The last noises of my mama's life, nothing like she would have wanted. The representative loads mama's body into the craft and takes-off like nothing happened.

I sit outside for hours, waiting to hear Mama's forgiving voice echo from the sitting room. Maybe to hear her soft footsteps against the floor. Her steps wouldn't have echoed like the representative's did. I never want to go inside again. It's over now, it's done for me. Mama is gone and while I'm not alone in this world, it sure feels that way.

Soon gusts of arctic wind whip my face, biting hard into my bare skin, pushing me inside. Into the house that's no longer a home. I walk through the doorway; but I don't want to go to bed. It reminds me of her. I lie on the ground next to Emma's crib instead. Loss consumes my heart. I could tolerate little pieces of my heart being taken away bit by bit but this is too much. It was torn apart with such haste and fury that it feels like the fragments have been tenderized to oblivion. It's too much pain for a child to endure and I'm not sure I can.

Papa's at work, he left this morning just before first light. His body looked weakened, like he was shattered from the inside out. Our eyes met as he bent forward to kiss Emma. I saw the raw pain inside and I saw it melt for just a second as his eyes met mine. I know he would have stayed if he could but work called, it's a duty Central requires.

A relief worker is scheduled to come provide assistance with Emma. I think of their uniforms, black, the color Central issues to all retired citizens, with a single grey arm sash signifying their role assisting children.

I hear the sound of feet traveling our walkway. I imagine the relief worker's boots making their way along our drive, unknowing of all the horrors that happened only yesterday. Then a knock sounds. I slowly rise from the floor reaching my hands in front of my small body. I try navigating by memory and touch. With every step towards the door my swirling head fogs like mist creeping and rolling inward. The mist parts as I see myself opening the door, welcoming Mama home. Every fiber that holds me together wants to believe that she will be on the other side.

Deep down I know that the mist will never part, that mama will never come home, but I need to open the door, just to be sure. My puffy eyes don't allow much clarity of vision but I reach the door, pulling it open. The mist rolls back, it's not Mama. Through the fog and broken hope I realize it's not the relief worker either. This person's far too small, my size just bigger. I blink, the cloudy tears escape and I see a golden haired boy my age.

I wipe my eyes and see his acorn-brown eyes looking into mine, his face twists with pain. He fists flowers in his small hands. They're blooming in yellows, purples, and blues. Once I spot them I can't take my eyes away, I follow them all the way to the ground as he places them at my feet. I've seen those colors in my mind before, laid out in front of me, all of them beautiful and bright.

"I wish I could've helped more" he says.

It wasn't his mama, he doesn't even know me. I want to ask him why he cares and I actually feel the words tickle my throat as I try to get them out. He turns his eyes down just before he runs away. I lift the flowers and take them to my room.

Over the next three months I care for Emma with the help of the relief worker. I don't know what will happen to us when I turn six and start education. Papa said other families cope and we will too. His words are somewhat comforting but even they can't ward off my lonesomeness.

It's mostly during the nights when I get crushingly isolated thinking about Mama. I lie questioning if I'd made her die. I wish she could sing to me as I hold the withered and fading bouquet of flowers that crumble under my touch. I just stare at them through the darkness until they turn into endless brown eyes staring back at me.

The thought of any respite from the pain gives me hope. Hope, it's a four letter word that holds more weight than the longest word in any vocabulary. With hope all things are possible. I can hope for a better life, I can hope for my chance to leap to

Central. With or without Mama, no matter the isolation or despair, I can always hope.

Chapter 2: Nessa

Seasons have come and gone since then but fall will always be my favorite. It's like nature purges itself of all the needless weight that pulls it down. The hot blanket of heat shatters and cool crisp air settles in its place, the lush green forest explodes into color just long enough for me to appreciate the change.

My blue boots crunch through the leaves that have just started to fall. I let myself trace back to childhood and kick a rock as I pick my way along the twisting road. Today was the last day of education. It still hasn't hit me yet that it's all over and in three months I'll turn seventeen. I've spent half my life consumed by this one thing, then 'poof' it's gone. Gone like the leaves that corkscrew in the breeze.

"No more education…" I let myself say it, if I speak the words maybe they'll sink in. It's no surprise I'm lost, it's one of the most fundamental things we're required to master in life. Education will lead to the leap, which in turn decides my entire life.

I've still got the three months of prep time before the leap, three months to absorb all the changes. I square my shoulders and keep walking headfirst. I line my foot up to kick the rock again but at the last moment I step to the side, leaving the rock whirling. I can't linger on juvenile things anymore, no more education, no more leisure, this is life…

"Nessa!" I hear Gwen's raspy voice well before I perceive her bounding steps.

I turn, stunned to see her on the abandoned road.

"G! What are you doing out here?" I ask. She wraps her arms around me.

"Umm…same question?" She cocks her head before we break apart.

"Good point." I say. She links her arm in mine as we walk forward, her black hair bouncing.

She clears her throat, "Wait, I know why you're out here, you've just finished education." I nod confirming it. "Say no more." She smiles hugging our arms closer together. "I remember my last day of education. I felt so lost. I just plopped down in the first snow bank I could find and stared into space for hours."

"Gwen, that sounds terrible."

"Yea, wasn't one of my best moments."

"Probably not even your top ten." I smile at her. "It's good to know I'm not alone."

"Well at least you don't have to deal with this limbo crap. Every week since the leap finished I've shadowed a different job. Every week it's a new face, place, new everything."

"It's that bad?" I ask and she nods pitifully, making me appreciate her suffering, "I guess I am lucky. Being born in December does have its advantages. I don't have to deal with limbo, plus I don't have to wait long for the banquet." I say shrugging.

"And why else would being born in December be good for you…" Her eyes narrow into that mischievous look that drew me to her in the first place.

"What are you talking about?" I ask teasingly. She shoves me off course but I stumble back. "Oh you mean because *Garrett's* a December baby too?"

"You think? Like you haven't thanked your lucky stars nightly that he was born in December too."

"It will be a nice advantage." I shrug my shoulders.

"Have you two hooked up yet or what?"

"Gwen! We're just friends. It's not like that." I flush as my heart skips thinking about hooking up with him. She drags me to a fallen log, tapping the cold bark next to her until I sit.

"You mean to tell me you don't like him even a little?"

"I didn't say that…" I roll my blue eyes. "I would be lying if I said I wasn't attracted to him, in a superficial sort of a way."

"Uh huh, details."

"Don't you have somewhere to be?" She shakes her head until I continue, "I don't think of him that way, we're *too* good of friends." I say as she rolls her eyes.

"Well you two have been inseparable since infancy but there comes a day when childhood is over and something called hormones kick in."

"Not infancy, but a long time, a very long time." I temporarily trance out, thinking of him at five with flowers in hand. "We've been good for each other. We've helped each other through education and other stuff. Life stuff."

She shoots a sidelong glance. "Helped you through education? The way I remember it there was one day your whole life that you didn't know the answer to the educator's questions and that was like your third day."

"Second day" I cut her off.

"Right, second day of education. Since then you've been one of the top in the class, and don't get me started on skills, you dominate."

"I can't take all the credit, he's helped me." Gwen's eyebrows drift north as she fires me that pressing look coercing me to continue, "And yes, I've helped him too."

"Now that we've cleared that up, get back to the good stuff, you know, about liking him."

"I really thought I'd sidetracked you."

"Nope, feed me, I'm bored to death, only child syndrome."

What do I even say here? Finally I tell myself to stop overthinking; it's a habit of mine that I'd like to break.

"I don't know what to tell you. He's handsome, funny, and actually pretty sweet but I still don't think we're right for each other."

"Handsome is an understatement." She grins ear to ear.

It's true, he is gorgeous. He's average height but after that there's nothing average about him. His eyes are a warm acorn-brown that make me melt when I look into them. The sheer size of his physique is intimidating, he barely fits into our uniforms, his muscles press to the fabric. And then his tanned skin is perfectly flawless, the hue reminds me of autumn. I picture his strong hands smoothing down his hair, a nervous habit of his that only makes him look sexier than ever. The way his blonde and brown flecked hair looks after he works his hand through it always makes my stomach turn. The only thing that's not perfect is his smile, the one that lifts the right side of his mouth, exposing dimples on that one side. I can't picture him smiling any other way; in fact, I think his smile is imperfectly perfect. Gwen interrupts my trance.

"So you're telling me you don't want to get with him because you're both brilliant and attractive people that happen to get along bizarrely well? Yeah sounds like a rotten match."

"Horrendous," I smile. "No, I have my reasons. For starters he's from a different sub than me. Our families aren't from the same lineage sectors. Plus we're just *different*." I answer robotically, like it's something I've rehearsed a million times before. In reality it is, I've told myself those things for years as a way to protect myself from falling for him.

"Put the lineage scores aside because you're gonna test high enough to marry into his sub. What do you mean by 'different'?" She asks but I hesitate, deciding if I'll answer.

"Ugh, Gwen." Do I tell her?

I haven't told anyone my secret. I've never been strong enough to bear the consequences. Maybe it's time to let it out, to see what ill comes of it. Or perhaps I should hold it in a little longer, protect it close to my heart where nobody can get to it. I don't know why but I resolve to tell her. Probably because I want to talk about it, and it'll never be with Garrett.

I swallow hard and continue, "I have visions. Like 'I'm a freak' visions." I say it knowing she won't understand but I can't bring myself to describe it all right away. She shifts in her seat then leans back to me.

"Nessa you're gonna have to elaborate."

I exhale, thinking of what to say next.

"When I was five I had a vision one night. It was bizarre, like multiple blurred images flashing all at once but the eventual picture was my mother's death." I swallow, "I saw the entire thing a week before she died."

"Wow," she shifts uncomfortably, "Just that once?" She asks.

Somewhere in my brain, in the part that stores memories, tragic memories that I try to press down hoping that with enough weight they'll sink forever into oblivion. Somewhere in that part of my brain I have memories from the visions I've seen. I shake my head no.

"There's been more. I saw the attack on our sector too." Gwen's eyes engorge. "I didn't know when it would happen, it was blurred but I saw the foreigners' hovercraft and the bombs. I saw all those people murdered." I blurt it out, trying to defend my innocence.

"Geez Nessa, did you tell anyone?" I snap my head around to hers.

"No, never! Nobody knows, just us." I sit, burrowing the heel of my boot into the brown mud that's molded around the base of the log. "The worst part is I didn't do anything about it." Her eyes meet mine; they're kind, telling me to go ahead. "I can almost forgive myself for the vision with my mom. How was I supposed to know what it meant? It was my first one. I thought it was a bad dream or something."

My heel sinks further into the lax ground.

"But I can't forgive myself for the attack. I saw the pavilion and the bombs. If I'd told someone, maybe a regulator or an educator, they could've done something. I had a full five days to tell someone and I didn't."

"It's okay Nessa, it's not your fault." I let her words wash over me, attempting to cleanse my guilt.

"You're right. I didn't fly the craft over that pavilion and bomb innocent people, the foreigners did that. But I didn't try to stop them either. I was selfish. I didn't want anyone to know about my visions. I was too afraid they'd call me a freak or exile me."

"You were just a kid Nessa, we were fourteen. You're allowed to be young and naïve and selfish when you're a kid. I would have done the same thing." She sits, her eyes gaping absently ahead, "I'm sorry Nessa. That had to be awful."

"Yeah," I lower my chin momentarily.

Awful doesn't come close to capturing it. There is no word to describe seeing your loved ones taken from you, to have a warning and yet do nothing about it.

"It's something I don't think Garrett would understand, that's why we're different."

"I think he'd make an exception for you" she smiles taking my hand. "Let's head back, dinner's soon." I take her hand as we head toward the pavilion.

I believe in the leap, I believe in Central and my family. There is a lot in this world that I believe in. I wish I could believe Garrett would understand but I know he wouldn't.

Chapter 3: Nessa

I walk home from third line, my fingers tingle in the cold. I had gotten there earlier than usual and somehow beat Papa and Emma. I ate alone thinking about a million things at once. Gwen stirred up questions in my head. My prattled brain beat itself trying to justify why I won't give into Garrett's attempts. It's obvious he's been trying to win me over for years now, but I won't give in. Why? I keep asking myself. He's my best friend, someone I can count on. I'm pretty sure that's what you should want in your partner but still I resist. He's gorgeous by anyone's standards and his personality calls to me. I guess it's because there's still so much unknown.

The leap test is three months away and all the uncertainty that surrounds it grips me too tightly. Three months and I'll take a test that's so protected, that once we've taken it we're never allowed to talk about it again. Nobody knows what exactly will be on the leap since it's against the law to discuss it. We don't break the law, if we were caught we'd get a mark. It takes three marks to ruin your chances. All I know is I've spent the last ten years in education, learning and practicing the skills Central says I'll need to take it. Top in my class or not, there's still the unknown. What if I fail something, even if it's just one little thing, it could ruin my life.

At seventeen I will take this one test that will decide my fate. It will tell me who I'm eligible to marry, it will determine my profession, the sub I'll live in, and for one boy and girl from my year it will take us away from our sector forever. Two of us get to cross the concrete walls that divide us from Central and start a new life over there, a better life.

I suppose there's just too much pressure mounting lately to bother giving into Garrett's attempts. Too many worries drive me away, worries that we won't test into the same sub, won't get to work together, or worse, only one of us will make the leap.

I stumble up our walkway into our modest home. Papa and Emma already left for third line. I must've just missed them. I unzip my blue jacket and lay it across the table. My hands work out the knots in my long chestnut brown hair. It's unruly but still one of my best features. I shed my clothes as I walk toward the sleeping quarters. It's a simple room Emma and I share. One bed, one dresser and a single closet. We don't need much. Emma has a single spiraling shell she's kept since childhood, it sits on the dresser. Margaret, the relief-worker that cared for Emma since she was a baby had given it to her. She told Emma that if she held it to her ear she'd hear the ocean.

I always liked listening to Margaret's stories. She was in her late seventies when she came to care for Emma. She had lived a full life, with more experiences than I'll probably ever have. Margaret was born in the Outer sector. She used to tell us stories about the ocean that bordered her home. Emma and I would sit in awe as we'd strain to picture endless blue water. We are landlocked here in the Inner, chances are I'll never see an ocean. Margaret told us stories of her fishing with her father, pulling nets out of the water that swelled with glistening fish.

The shell was the only thing Margaret had from her former life. As is customary in the Outer sector, they take their leap when they turn fifteen. All those years ago Margaret had been top girl. She'd made the leap from the Outer into our Inner sector. She got herself a step closer to Central. Sometimes when she'd talk about the Outer I'd sense she was sad, I could almost feel the sadness inside her. Life over there was harder, it was different than ours here. I think the adjustment was a challenge for her even after living here for sixty years. I couldn't help feeling sorry for Margaret, it had to be hard never seeing her parents or sisters again.

I pick up the shell and hold it next to my ear, I let the whooshing sound take me away as I close my eyes, picturing the ocean that lies across the concrete walls separating us from the Outer. It calms me as I imagine sitting on the grains of sand

Margaret said bordered the ocean. I can almost feel the sand creeping between my toes as I sink into the tan grains. I open my eyes again, setting the shell back on our brown dresser. I make my way over to the bed, sitting down on top of the grey covers. I lower myself back to my elbows. Out of the corner of my eye I see a folded piece of paper sitting on my pillow.

I grin, snatching it up. Another one of Garrett's creations. This one's a swan. He spends days turning sheets of paper into these little animals. He knows they make me smile which is why he gives them to me when he's done. I turn it over in my hands; its wings stick out from the sides as it sits in my palm. I carefully pull it open stretching the paper to see his messy writing centered on the sheet.

'Nessa, congrats on ending education today. It's a big deal and I'm proud of you. Don't spend your night like a ball of nerves (I know how you are). Just breathe. Tomorrow we start preparing. Before you know it we'll be at the banquet accepting the leap together. See you tomorrow at our spot.'

I grin as I fold the paper back into the swan. I swing my long pale legs off the bed and walk to the dresser. My fingers wrap around the worn knob as I open the top drawer and set it next to the other folded notes he's made for me. I listen to the shell one last time before I crawl into bed for the night.

Chapter 4: Ty

My family called me Tyler in the Outer. I always liked Ty better but my mom wouldn't let me shorten it. It didn't take me long to change it though, I was on the hover for all of ten minutes before I decided to leave Tyler behind and go by Ty. I set my mind to it and when that happens there's no turning back. I was going to be a new me, I had to change and grow up.

The move from the Outer seems like a blink ago, mind blowing to think it's almost been two years. It was the hardest thing I've ever done. At fifteen I had to leave my parents and brothers behind. My mother bawled when I made the leap, it wasn't happy tears either. I know she was proud and all but that wasn't it, she was broken. I could hear it between her sobs, sorta like an empty straining noise.

The day my uncle Dan died in a mining accident my aunt Ginny cried like that. She just sat in the corner, cradling his work-jacket, wailing like an animal. That was the last day I ever saw her. Central took Dan's things the next day and she went ballistic, I mean crazy.

They said she'd lost touch with reality. Central said she was unfit to be a citizen so they sent her away, beyond the walls. Sometimes I wonder how she's doing, wonder if she's still alive. I think about Ginny and my family a lot, more than a lot, almost all the time.

My youngest brother Sammy will take the leap next year. Michael didn't make it otherwise he'd have been transferred to the Inner last year. The day the newbs were coming in last year I sat at the hover pad waiting, hoping Michael would walk off the hover, but he didn't. I'd hoped but I didn't really expect he'd make it. I doubt Sammy will either. They don't have 'sight' like me. Not like I know what that means, it's just what my mom called it. All I know is it gives me a leg up during the leap.

It was my 'sight' that got me out of the Outer in the first place. Doubt I would've accepted the offer without it, probably not even scored high enough to worry about being offered the leap anyway. Back then I couldn't imagine leaving home. I didn't care about going to the Inner, average was fine with me. That's not how we are programmed to think but I couldn't force myself to want to leap, not till I saw her.

I had six months ticking away before my birthday. Three months of classes and skills training before I'd finally be left alone to prepare for the leap. My other classmates were brainwashed with the leap. Not me, all I had to do was make it through those three months and then I was going to basically do whatever I wanted. I was going to 'passively learn' as I call it. I could sleep late every day, go swimming and fishing, or do nothing at all. It was going to be awesome.

Then bam, just like that it all changed. I was diving off the cliffs that June. I leapt straight into the water and I'd taken four or five pulls down when I felt the pins and needles. I knew I was going to have sight so I booked it in the opposite direction, pulling my way to the surface but I was too late. I was paralyzed, dropping like a stone.

That's when I first saw her, it wasn't clear but my sight never is. It comes in patches and it's my job to put it together. I saw her lips, full and pink. Cold air was pushing between them. Her brown hair was dancing in the wind. It fell past her shoulders, curling at the ends. Her deep blue eyes stood out against her pale skin. She was gorgeous. It wasn't so much seeing her that got me hooked, it was feeling her energy. I could *feel* the history between us, even though I'd never met her. I fell in love with her on the spot.

More patches flashed and I saw her on stage with me, gorgeous and proud. More patches flashed and then we were in the woods, she was walking away from me. Flash after flash filled me and I knew she was what I needed to find and protect. My sight became more ballistic as images flashed in a fast string and then she was on fire. Screaming and shrieking.

Just as fast as it came, it was gone. I pulled myself to the surface, coughing and choking for air. I dragged myself to the rocks and I cried like my aunt Ginny had. I was just a kid, only fourteen but in a blink I'd found the love of my life and lost her. Love and pain bashed through me. I had to find her and save her. Maybe my sight wasn't a curse. I decided if I could use it to keep her alive then maybe it was a blessing.

So that is what I did. I made it through the three months of education and instead of passively learning I studied and prepared. I had motivation; I had to get to the Inner and save her. Leap came and went and before I knew it I was at the banquet accepting the offer. I don't know what I thought would happen when I transferred to the Inner. I guess I'd assumed she'd be there waiting for me.

It was dumb, I'll admit, but I was just barely fifteen and naïve. I was housed with the other Outer-transfers in a separate subdivision than the native Inner citizens; I couldn't meet her at education either since we were separated too.

That gave me two years to cover all the skills and education they'd taken a decade to learn. I don't mind the challenge; I know I have to get on stage with her at the banquet just like I'd seen in my sight.

Last year I hardly slept. When I wasn't in education I was studying or practicing skills. During the first winter I snuck out every night, wandering the streets looking for her. It was the first thing I'd seen in my sight. She'd been bundled in her blue uniform, winter air between her lips. I looked for her every night that winter and every night I came home empty, but I knew I had to keep trying.

Chapter 5: Nessa

Garrett and I have been capitalizing on our three months before we turn seventeen, the time when Central absolves us of all obligations other than preparing for the leap-test. The closer we get to the test, the faster the time goes. Days that once seemed lengthy and endless now come and go in a blink of the eye.

His voice startles me, "You must be kidding. You call that a *concealed* snare?" He laughs as he heaves a stick, triggering my hunting snare. I'd painstakingly veiled it amongst the thick trees and grass; certain he wouldn't find this one.

"Ok, no more snares today. What else do you want to practice?" I ask.

"Nessa, I don't need to practice, I need to *perfect*. Get it right!" He's kidding, but it's true.

"Fine, let's *perfect* healing." I've always 'dominated skills' as Gwen says but healing is my shakiest area and he knows it too.

"Okay." He pauses momentarily. "It's the night of the banquet and you're looking pretty amazing, by the way." He flashes his crooked smile, making me blush. "Naturally I'm top boy. I'm standing on stage ready to accept my offer." I roll my eyes; he can be so narcissistic. He crosses his arms behind his head, "I look at the crowd, everyone's envious of my superb self and then I see your face. You botched your test because of your *awful* healing skills." I shove his arm but he carries on. "I'm seriously distraught by this point, thinking of never looking into those eyes again, hearing you, or having you around, so I decide to eat churn berries in a shot to snuff myself." He looks raptly at me. "What would you do?" He asks.

"Boil root of bine and force you to drink two cups," I say with a smug look on my face. "Then kick your butt for being so dumb."

Who's he kidding? There's no way he'd eat churn berries. He flashes a smile and I temporarily forget his penetrating eyes. He thuds down in the grass and I position myself next to him.

"Tell me something I don't know about you" I ask.

"You pretty much know it all Nessa, except for my hygiene routines which I'll keep to myself, thank you very much."

"Tell me something I don't know. Seriously."

"Using dangerous words like 'seriously' could get you in trouble little lady." I shoot him a sideways glance before I push harder.

"Come on, I really want to hear something new, anything to take my mind off the leap." I turn on a flirtatious smile to soften him.

"Okay..." He finally breaks. I roll on my side to cradle my head. "Our family has a mark." He says.

"Don't most?" I interrupt

"Yeah. Except *I* got the mark."

"When?" I can't believe he's never told me.

"It was actually right after we met." I instinctively lower my eyes, our first meeting carries so many emotions, most too painful to think about. "That afternoon after I found the healer I went to pick you flowers." I smile remembering him holding them, the way the colors captured my eyes was like water capturing the sun. "I'd seen my dad bring my mom flowers before, it made her happy." He laughs. "I'd gotten the bunch and was on my way back when I saw a den." He pauses to remember. "I heard whimpering, so I went to it. There was this starving kit, it had been abandoned."

My heart unexpectedly aches for the abandoned fox, like a part of me could relate to it. The isolation and fear, the loss that comes with being alone without your mother. I really could relate.

"I couldn't just leave it there to starve so I went back every day to feed it. It ate just about everything I put down. Eventually it got stronger and walked and then it played and ran." I picture him at five-years-old playing with the little animal. "It would come when I whistled, all sorts of dumb stuff, but to me it was awesome. I had a friend and something that needed me." He pauses briefly, "I'd been going there for months, and my best guess is that one of the retirees told a regulator I'd been pocketing food during second line, because one day a regulator followed me. He was real sneaky; I never knew he was there until I was already at the den." His eyes soften and his voice cracks, "I whistled and the fox came out, I fed him like always and then everything was a blur. I heard a twig snap and I saw the red hairs on the fox stand straight up, but it was too late. It tried to run but the bullet was too fast."

"Garrett that's terrible."

"The regulator took me home and explained the situation to my parents. He said he was being 'lenient,' since technically I could've gotten two marks, one for lifting food from the pavilion, the other for interacting with animals outside of hunting."

"How come you never told me?"

"Don't know. It's one of the only times I've really been mad at Central. I don't like thinking about it. Reminds me that the place I'm supposed to idealize may have flaws."

I can't find the words he probably wants to hear, something along the lines of agreeing with him. I don't have the anger he has, I idealize Central. It's one of the few things I truly believe in. When you believe and trust something so totally, it's hard to find faults in it.

"So why all the studying and preparing? Would you even accept the leap?"

"Of course, it would be stupid to turn it down. I figure everything's better over there. Who knows, maybe they're allowed to keep animals." He laughs. "Plus someone has to keep an eye on you when you're over there."

"Right! Cause I'm so pitiful that I need constant supervision." I roll onto my back and think about Garrett with his fox. I wonder what it would have been like to have someone care for me during the time my heart was healing. Papa did his best but he couldn't take the pain away. Either way, I made it through that darkness. I gathered my shattered heart and piece by piece put it back together. Part of it was through hope, part of it was believing in something better.

The sun strikes its highest peak when Garrett breaks the silence.

"Why won't you go out with me?"

I snap my head to look at him. "Not this again." I smile.

"It's been a couple weeks since I asked. Figured it was worth another try. I'm patient; I'll keep waiting for a moment of weakness." He grins, nervously combing his hands through his hair. Man does he look good when he does that.

My eyes trace a path across our bodies to my pale arm. I look down seeing my skin turning red. I should cover my arms I think. The last time I let them get this red my skin blistered and peeled like a snake shedding its skin. My absent thoughts get interrupted by his breathing. "You sound like the shuttle when it hits a loose rock" I joke. Garrett turns to me, shrugging his shoulders.

He grins and I find myself staring at his lips. "I bet I can swim to the northern embankment and back before you even get wet" he says. I barely have time to question that possibility as I briefly envision him running for the water. Suddenly there's a rush of air and his strong hand taps my shoulder.

"Tag," he yells.

I sit up, supporting my weight on my elbows in time to see him lift his blue shirt up and over his head. My eyes narrow as I stare at his muscular back. Garrett hits the water, tossing his blue shirt to the side, emerging wet and dashing for the northern embankment.

Water splashes across his waistline and awakens me from my dream state. This was a challenge I realized, pushing to my feet. I peddle my bare feet through the warm grass sprinting towards the water. Should I go in with my dress on? It will weigh me down and take hours to dry. The thought of being without it embarrasses me. I'll jump straight into the water, he won't see me, I decide as I lift my blue dress over my head. My brown hair sweeps side-to-side, dancing across my shoulder blades. By the time I hit the water he's already halfway back. I instantly freeze as the arctic water strikes my thighs. I hadn't expected it to be this cold. He notices my weakness and attacks. Fountains of water splash towards me, soaking every inch of my bare skin.

"Stop it!" I squeal.

The wintry water feels like a whip striking my body but he doesn't end his assault. I pivot on my foot, turning toward the warm hillside. He scoops the water, spraying it at me. My legs splash water along my ribs as I try to retreat. I'm closing in on the muddy embankment when Garrett wraps his arms around my stomach, dragging me back into the frigid water. My legs kick in all directions as he carries me backwards.

"Put me down!"

I'm about to find my voice again and scream louder but I feel the heat from his body radiating to mine. His skin is so soft but his body feels strong. How can someone be so soft and strong at the same time I wonder? My legs stop kicking. I feel his solid chest pressed against my back and streams of electricity course between us. Where does this come from? Is he making it or am I? Electric sparks prick my skin, it isn't unpleasant, it actually feels good. I want to feel more of this electricity, more warmth, more of him. He dunks me under the icy water, letting me refocus my thoughts as I'm submerged.

I stand up brushing my hair from my face. "I made it to the water before you got back, so technically I won."

"I wanted to see you freeze when you hit the water." He smiles. "I know what a baby you are when you're cold."

He smooths his hair back from his face. I can't stand him right now, I can't stand how good he looks, how he bet me at my expense, and mostly I can't stand him for taking the sparks away. I launch at him, dragging him underwater. Our bodies twist and turn rolling underwater. I get pinned beneath him and just like that, the fiery sensations return. I reach my hands linking them around him as he lifts to his feet. I let him wrap his arms around my waist, pulling me to my feet.

I stand thigh deep as the water breaks around my legs. I strain to catch my breath. He strokes my back with his sure hand. My body involuntarily tenses. It shouldn't, it feels unnatural to be tensed. Instead I wish I would relax into his touch and melt into his hands. Sensing my awkwardness, he stops. He closes his strong hand around mine, walking with me back to the hill.

Garrett recovers my dress from the wilting bushes it landed in, flashing a smile as he throws it back to me. I spread it across my lap as our bodies splay close to each other. We don't touch as the sun dries our shivering skin. When the sun reaches the top of the trees to our west I know our day has ended. We head for our separate subs before curfew hits. I crawl into bed that night and fall asleep thinking about him. Thinking about the years we've spent together and the countless hours and minutes that have led us to where we are today.

Chapter 6: Nessa

Seconds tick at a steady rhythm, sixty seconds to a minute yet each minute seems faster than the last. The weeks whittle away, shaving what little time we have before the leap. Garrett and I meet at our hideaway daily. Each day there's more excitement and nerves wound into our meetings. Wound tight like the sewing thread the relief workers unravel before they begin patching our torn uniforms. Excitement that maybe I'll feel the sparks again, nerves that I'll feel them and won't be strong enough to stop them.

I sit on my half of the hill writing then desperately erasing. Today we're creating a dry run of what we think the leap test could be. We'll design a test that incorporates all the areas the leap coordinators could be looking for.

That would be too easy for him, I think. He's never been great with a spear and I know I have to find a way to work it into my test. I think about our skills lesson years ago, the one in the open green field. The crisp spring air still fills my nostrils and I can almost feel the warmth across my back. The sun hung low that day. I remember staying late watching Garrett heave his spear over and over, always missing his mark. It was the first time I'd seen him fail at something, I think it surprised us both. I stayed and watched him sweating and exhausted, either too proud or in too much denial to admit defeat. The skills instructor waited in the background, too tired to give direction. Just as Garrett's legs buckled from exhaustion he hit his mark.

I keep working on my test. From time to time I glance over to see him either feverishly writing without once erasing or sprawled on his back with his arms crossed under his head. When the sun begins extending its blinding fingers toward the highest peak it's time to collect our things and head for the shuttle. If we're going to make it to the post and home before curfew we have to leave our refuge now.

"Thirty minutes." Garrett says as we ride the shuttle.

"Thirty minutes, what?"

"That's how long it'll take me to beat your test." He smiles.

"Is that so?" I shoot him the evil eye. "I guarantee I'll beat your time."

"Nessa, if you could see how darn cute you look when you're wrong. It's adorable."

I stick my tongue out as my free hand winds up to swat him. I'm propelled forward as the shuttle comes to a standstill at the post. His eyes narrow to mine just as a smirk pulls at his face. I can almost feel my pupils constricting as I size him up. There's no need for words, we've been together long enough to know what's next. We exit, battling to be the first to the attendant. We're tied neck and neck but at the last second I kick my foot out making contact with his ankle. He yelps as he hits the ground and I victoriously strut to the post attendant.

"Scan card" the attendant demands. I hand it over quickly; they don't like their time wasted. "Needs?" He barks, his sunken eyes have defined lines streaking from the junctions like a spiders legs. He looks irritated and slightly frightening.

"Vanessa Hollins here to check out leap-training weapons. Bow with quiver, three arrows, and one spear."

Garrett lets out all the air held in his barrel-sized chest.

I stare at the bins stacked behind the attendant. It's like rectangular puzzle pieces, none are the same size yet somehow they all fit perfectly together, stacking side by side and on top of each other. Everything is labeled, contained, and clean. The attendant hands the weapons under the glass window that divides us. The routine is repeated with Garrett selecting a hatchet and a spool of string. My brow furls, what does a hatchet and string have to do with a challenge?

He collects his materials, tapping me on my shoulder. "Race you!" He shouts, bolting off. I don't delay; my feet pound the ground as my supplies smack hard against my back with every step. I fall behind and watch him reach the platform with ease.

"I let you win. It would be embarrassing if I beat you twice" I shout. "Especially since I have twice as many supplies!" He victoriously pumps his fists in the air.

We board the shuttle, quietly riding the twenty-minutes to my sub. I think about the post. I wonder if I could organize my life into neat compartments. Label and stack my feelings. Maybe I could store them away and keep them from growing for Garrett. Protect them in a rectangular box in the corner until I'm ready. I step off the platform and race home to finish preparation for tomorrow's test.

Chapter 7: Nessa

Morning finds me stepping out of the bathroom straight into Emma's frantic pleas, "Nessa, braid my hair. I need to look extra pretty today and my hair looks so awful right now. Pleeeeease, Nessa!" She whines.

I debate saying no just to hear her whine some more but I don't have the heart. I guide Emma to our sitting room, directing her into the chair. She hums and lazily swings her legs as I make a winding braid that weaves around her whole head. I finish before first light. Curfew's lifted at first light and I'm free to join Garrett. I tuck the last pin into her hair just before the first rays fall. I lean over, wrapping Emma in my arms. She giggles when I kiss her cheek, she's always been ticklish. She hugs me back before I leave for our hideaway. I run and I run, carrying the provisions I'll need for his test. I think about his challenge, wondering if I'm about to push him too far. The air is cool as I cross the log onto our hillside. The culmination of Garret's test will be the moment he spears the last clue, which is partially made from my grey play clothes I saved from childhood.

I break onto the hill just as Garrett slips past the southern embankment, swallowed up by dying trees. I'll meet him back here later, after I set up his challenge. It takes practically two hours to set up the challenges and when we meet back at the hill we're both sweating. I'm doubled over with my hands pressed onto my knees as I try catching my breath. He stands to my left laughing.

"Shall I go first while you gather yourself?" He taunts. While I want to say no, he's right; I need time to recover. I hand him his first clue.

'Find the bed that neither animal nor man lays in, where water once stood but has since gone dry, yet animals still travel to wet their lips and find there, the way to cross.'

He freezes briefly before he's off running toward the overflow bed I was hinting at; it's about a half-mile through the brush. It's a dried-up streambed that's always the first to flood when the rains are heavy and the first to dry when they've stopped. Over the hundreds of years of wetting and evaporation, chemical sediments have developed into salted formations that draw the deer and other animals to it. I follow closely behind him, sure he knows of my presence but he doesn't say a word, he's on a mission.

He reaches the bed and instantly spots his next clue attached to a large sediment rock. I painted it bright red and marked it with a piece of tattered grey cloth. The entire streambed is smattered with red and brown rocks positioned in a seemingly random fashion but it's anything but accidental, it's a puzzle.

'To cross this bed you must dance above rocks that are red. Many paths you may make, but rest assured there's only one you should take. Use these two boards of different lengths to navigate from bank to bank. The boards are all that can touch down, and must be moved from red to red and never touch brown.'

Garrett works the puzzle in his mind. His handsome face scrunches in deep thought. I shift side to side enjoying minutes of watching him agonize over his plan. I've seen him look this way before, confused yet unrelenting. I love watching him plan and struggle, it brings him to everyone else's level, even if it's momentary. Finally he springs into action and I watch him lifting and swiftly moving board to board. At first he chooses the right path, forcefully placing the small board forward, long board left, small board backward and then he moves off course by setting the long board left not forward.

He's a board length away from the clue when he realizes he's out of moves and has squandered at least fifteen minutes. The frustration is obvious and I relish in watching the ultra-cool

Garrett sweating, exasperated, and lost. Right when I'm starting to enjoy my fine work he figures it out.

He's tearing up and placing board after board so fast that he must have it. He places the long board forward, short board right and continues meticulously assigning the boards until he crosses over the bank. His face cracks wide open with his stunning smile.

He turns his head looking over his broad shoulder and smiles, shaking his head as if saying, "Well played." He swings back into action. Positioned next to the final rock are the bow, arrows, and quiver. Picking them up he scans the ground, systematically skimming higher and higher until he sees the braided rope high above the ground where the next clue is secured.

I nearly died setting this clue up, my foot slid once down the ridged bark. I almost fell a full twenty feet, sending my stomach into a twisting flip that lodged itself in my throat. As my gut untwisted I made my way back up the winding tree. I'd purposefully attached the clue to a branch that could support my weight for placement but would snap under his physique. He has no choice but to make all three shots. He strides to the highest ground and strings the first arrow. He pulls it back and releases as he exhales, just like we've been taught.

That lesson feels like a lifetime ago. The targets were all spread in front of us just begging to be hit. My arms shook as I drew the string back, mounting tension built as my muscles felt ready to snap. I wanted to stop and rest like the others in my year but I wouldn't quit. I needed to build strength, not so much in the muscles that run from bone to bone, but strength of mind and character. I drew the string back over and over again until I'd found that inner strength. My character, my drive.

His arrow skims through the air contacting the middle braid. He doesn't hesitate as he draws the second arrow back and releases it into the left braid, the clue sways from the assault. He lines up his final shot. Light breaks the trees hitting his sweat-specked skin. His arms and back pull taunt with his muscles tensed, his golden brown hair shines the way it did the first time I saw him. He discharges the arrow and me from my trance.

He runs for the clue before he bothers to see if his arrow made contact. It buzzes through the air and strikes the last tether just as he strides under the clue catching the next challenge.

'You may want to run to the next and final stop for you have to travel north 440 feet once then twelve times more before you have reached the cure. Now take these berries and be on your way, pace your run or else there may be no more days.'

He shoots me a sideways glace and I half expect he won't accept my dare. Putting it together yesterday I thought it would be something we could laugh at. I'd make him see how foolish he was for even suggesting eating churn berries that day. But really what's so funny about this? I've seen death before, had it dig it's long and jagged claws into my heart. Maybe death has a plan, or maybe it strikes at random, all I know is I shouldn't be mocking it. I shouldn't be toying with something so harsh.

The blood red berries look striking against his tanned palm and I realize what a stupid idea this is. If I didn't prepare enough of the cure last night, or if the container spilled into the river he'll die. He only has thirty minutes to drink the bine root.

I scream, "Garret NO!"

But it's too late. I watch horrified as he tips his head back throwing the blood red fruit down. He swallows and my stomach turns. He wipes his forearm across his red lips. A dark and heavy blanket coats my heart, like deaths preparing to tear it to pieces yet again.

"Are you coming or did you wanna just stumble across my body later?" He hollers over his shoulder as he bounds rock to rock down the river bed heading one mile due north.

I break into a cold sweat realizing that in thirty minutes he could be gone. Images cross my mind of his blond hair bounding down my walkway when he was no more than the acorn-eyed boy. My chest lurches as my heart slowly crumbles like the dried flowers that sit under my bed. I run to catch up with him, counting my steps. Two hundred and one, two hundred and two, two hundred and three. It's a nervous quirk of mine.

The branches along the riverbed reach across my path and whip my face, striking me so hard I look like I've been seared with a whip, but I keep running. My feet and heart pound in unison. If the cure isn't right he will die. There's nothing I can do to stop it. What would I do then? I need to think of words to say when Central comes for his body. I won't let him down like I did Mama. My throat clamps down, squeezing its way towards my chest. I can't think of words to say. How could I? He feels as much a part of me as my own breathing does, as my own heartbeat, which I'm sure pumps in the same rhythm as his. My being is too intertwined with his, without him a half of me would die too. How do you say words for a death you're bound so closely to? I'm frantic to keep him safe. He's ahead of me, closing in on the final clue.

The mile run over the rocks and through the trees only leaves fifteen minutes to release the cure. Without it his stomach will heave and he'll be doubled-over in pure agony as his insides work from his stomach into the world outside, and then he'll die.

He reaches the clue and with shivering hands unfolds it…

'The Outer wear blue when the Inner wear grey, when Inner wear blue Outer wear green, when Inner dress in green Outer take this color. With this color come their jobs. The missing color tied to the final letter in the second most coveted job of those that wear blue when the Outer wear green is where the spear must strike.'

Dozens of submerged river rocks lay in front of him. I painted them blue, green, and grey with the letters 'R', 'T', and 'P' for healer, attendant, and develop. Just some of the jobs assigned to us in the Inner. He needs to find the grey rock with the letter 'R' and spear it to complete the riddle and release the cure.

Garrett struggles with the puzzle as sweat collects on his brow. I hear a loud scream escape his mouth. I turn seeing him doubled in pain; the churn berries are taking effect. Water hits my thighs before I realize I'm running. Out of the corner of my eye the spear buzzes past my head falling a full twenty feet short of the grey rock.

Garrett has never been great with a spear but he generally wouldn't miss a shot this easy. He has failed and is dying. My legs spring into action as I lift my knees trying to break the water's surface. I run for the spear as Garrett falls on all fours coughing and gasping. I reach the spear as the coughing stops. A loud thud sounds from behind me. Death's blanket rips at my insides, pulling my chest like it's playing a game of slow torture.

The spear is mired in the mud, I tug and twist and still it won't come loose. Sweat pours out of me as I throw my full weight behind my final pull, just then the suctioning mud releases. The force knocks me on my back and I lay disoriented. Water rushes over my face; there's a dull buzzing inside my head. I blink, water blinds my eyes. I latch onto my inner drive, that character I've built to be strong and fight. The end of Garrett will mean the end of me, and I won't end yet. The buzzing stops and I push to my feet with seconds to pinpoint the target. I cock my arm back and pitch the spear watching it pierce the target exactly where it needs to.

"Drink! Garrett drink!" I coax as I try tipping the cure to his lips. I cradle his head in my palm looking into the same glassy eyes my mother had just before she died. Bile rises into my mouth.

"Nessa," he whispers. He's barely alive but there's hope.

"Drink, Garrett. Drink." I tilt the cup, hoping he'll sip.

His strong body that looked so oversized earlier now looks frail as I cradle him. I sing to him the way my mother used to do for me. I can't let him go, not like this.

Chapter 8: Ty

I wish I would stop wasting my time wondering what she's doing. I can't count how many times I've played my sight over and over in my head. I've gotta have faith. That is what I keep telling myself. I've gotta believe that whatever she's doing, it's something to get her to me.

No matter how I order the flashes I saw during my sight, I know that our time is coming. I take my leap soon. In just a few weeks I'll test again. I've got no choice but to test at the top again. I've got to get on stage like I saw. I bet the banquet in the Inner is even more outrageous than the one we had in the Outer. It has to be, everything in the Inner is better.

I bet they feel more pressure to make the leap here too. Of course the people in the Outer wanted to leap to the Inner.

Getting here puts you one step closer to the perfect life Central offers. But it wasn't Central that we were leaping to. It was still leaping into a less than perfect sector. We could never leap directly to Central, not without coming here first. Here in the Inner they get to hope and know that if they leap, they go straight to Central. That had to be intense growing up with that pressure.

Sometimes I imagine her studying; dealing alone with the pressure she must have felt her whole life. I picture her next to me as I practice my skills. I pretend she's with me, helping me learn. I've gotta find her. One of these nights I'll see her and then I'll know that I'm not crazy. I'll know what I need to do and that it is right.

Chapter 9: Nessa

It's almost like I'm having an out of body experience, I see Garrett lying across my legs but I can't entirely process it. My mind takes me away like a shuttle rocketing off course. I'm transported to a time years ago, a time different than now.

I remember standing in front of our window, watching the sun break the hilltop east of my home on the first day of January, I knew I'd finally be starting education. I turned six the day before but was still wearing my grey play clothes, not the blue uniform that children six to sixteen wear.

Papa still had his family quota at the factory to meet and with Mama gone he had to work twice as hard to fill it. Either way, the end result was a mark against the family, one mark if a regulator caught me without my blues, one if Papa didn't meet his quota.

I still hadn't learned how to use the shuttles to get to the post where I could collect my Central-issued supplies. On our sixth birthday we're supposed to learn how to navigate the shuttles and collect the tools we need to begin one of the most important tasks of our lives, the leap.

On my first day of education I watched jealously as the other kids stood in their blue uniforms. Their hands gripped the Central issued blue bag swollen with supplies they needed to succeed. The other kids waited on the platform dancing foot to foot in excitement, holding the hand of a proud parent. I was so envious of them and hysterical that I had to take the one item I'd wanted to preserve. I wished I had anything but the bag I was holding. I wanted to keep it untouched as a way to remember mama.

I'd searched our home for anything to carry what few supplies I had. All I could find was Mama's burlap bag. It was the one she carried her work provisions in. When Central took her body they took all her materials except the tattered bag. In their opinion it wasn't salvageable.

I had wished I had my mother's hand to hold but the thought suddenly sickened me as I remembered how cold it had been in her last moments. When the sleek white shuttle pulled up, I turned waving good-bye to the family that wasn't there and I blew a kiss to the mother that was just a memory.

The other kids laughed at me as I walked along the darkened aisles. I didn't blame them. The shuttle operator made me scan my card to prove I was actually six. Of course she believed everyone else was old enough to ride the shuttle unaccompanied, they were all wearing their blue uniforms.

I walked straight to the back, taking an empty seat. The black seats looked cold and uninviting. I folded my legs to my chest. I wanted to make myself dissolve; I tried collapsing within myself by wrapping my slight arms around my legs. I jammed my eyes against my knobby knees, letting tears escape the corners as I listened to the others laughing. Why me, and what I wouldn't give to be in any of their shoes I thought. If they only knew how delicate and vulnerable my heart was I wonder if they still would have laughed.

The shuttle made its final stop at education and I purposefully exited last. My legs tingled as I uncrossed them, dropping them sluggishly to the floor. I took three hesitant steps off the shuttle and was overwhelmed by the sight of swarming children.

Kids my age all smiling, some doubled over laughing at one person. I spotted the acorn-eyed boy folded in laughter too and realized they were laughing *with* him, not *at* him like they did to me. Strange that the same act can evoke such different emotions. The joke from a friend's lips brings cheerful laughter, a sound of pure joy. Yet the same sounds, the same laughter from the lips of those against you, from those laughing at you can be so hurtful and so harsh. My anger was mounting when the education chime sounded, breaking me from my rage.

The chime indicated the start of education. A sea of blue flowed into the building like water breaching a dam. Once inside, several kids including myself stopped in our tracks. The lights were nearly blinding and brighter than any lights we'd ever seen. The education building was strikingly bright white. I followed the sea of blue into our room, feeling a lurch in my stomach as I realized it was time to pick my seat.

Mama always told me to sit front and center. She said it would "keep you focused on the educator. The more focused, the more engaged, meaning the better you'll do on the leap."

Everything revolves around the leap. When I was very young mama would place our only chair in the front of the room and clap her hands, practicing for this very moment. I'd race to beat her, gliding gracefully into the seat. That was then and I couldn't sit front and center anymore, not without my supplies or uniform.

I had to hide the best I could, I picked the seat in the back corner. The educator entered, the entire class sat at attention. She was a slender women dressed in all white with her brown hair drawn neatly into a tight knot at the nape of her neck.

It took her less than ten minutes to spot me in the corner. "And whom do we have here?" Her sarcastically sweet voice was piercing like her eyes. "I refuse to believe you've come to education out of uniform."

I swallowed, preparing to speak. "I'm sorry ma'am...I'm Vanes..."

"Enough." She cut me off. The others giggled. "You'll leave my classroom immediately and won't return until you're prepared to follow the rules."

My cheeks blazed as the others snickered, all except the brown-eyed boy sitting front and center. I bolted from the room, tears threatening to fall. In my embarrassed rush I left my mother's burlap bag with my scan card inside. I had no way to prove I was six. For minutes I braced myself outside the classroom door debating if I should go back to get it. Finally I gave up; I'd find a way home.

Rolling clouds passed lazily by as I waited on the shuttle platform. Finally the sleek vessel arrived. The shuttle attendant shot me a nasty glare. She half-barked at me.

"Where's your supervision?"

"I don't have any, but I'm six..."

She closed the shuttle door, leaving me alone on the platform. I was angry at Papa for making me look foolish and forcing me to break the rules. I remember thinking we could get a mark against the family for this, and three marks meant neither Emma nor I would have a chance to make the leap when we turned seventeen.

It took me almost two hours to walk home. My legs were no bigger than miniature twigs and they were shaking with exhaustion when I reached our entrance. I scarcely had enough energy to open the creaking door and once inside I fell to the floor next to Emma's wooden crib. I slept so solidly I imagine I looked like a discarded pile of grey clothes.

I slept for hours next to the crib; Emma apparently sensed my exhaustion because she didn't stir. After hours of sleep I was awakened by the jiggle of the doorknob. I shot up immediately.

My heart bounded with alarm as I tiptoed across the room. I backtracked a few steps, collecting an umbrella to use as a weapon. I reached for the door, flinging it wide. I grunted something unintelligible hoping to startle the intruder away.

There was no intruder, just my mother's burlap bag wrapped around the doorknob. The bag was brimming. I pulled it open exposing my blue uniform and education supplies. I snapped my head up to see the blonde haired boy rounding the corner, walking into the horizon. Why? That's what I wanted to ask him. I wanted to know why he would do that for me. Why give me the flowers and now the bag. That night I dreamt of flowers turning into acorn-brown eyes and for the first time I could remember, I was happy.

Chapter 10: Nessa

Garrett twitches, momentarily breaking my mental reflection. His body relaxes and I continue to seek refuge in my memories.

I recall sounding accusatory and angry without meaning to when I saw him at education the next morning. "How'd you get that?" I asked. His eyes stared straight into mine.

"You left your bag; it had your scan card in it. I knew the way to the post, plus you needed your card to get the supplies so I did it for you." He shrugged his shoulders. "Now they can't send you home. Hey, I didn't know your name was Vanessa. I like it."

"I go by Nessa. I don't know your name at all so I can't say if I like it."

"Garrett" he answered.

"Garrett?"

"Yup." He answered with his smile.

The bell curtailed our conversation. The sea of blue repeated the routine like the day before. The educator walked into the room, craning her head sharply to the back expecting to see me in grey.

She singled me out twice with probing questions I didn't know the answer to. I've been told that before the divide school wasn't taken as seriously, but here in the post-divide, education is one of the 'BIG 3' that decides our life. The other two factors are skills and lineage scores. The leap is a combination of all three. I remember thinking if I didn't catch up I'd be assigned a job like trash disposal.

I can imagine my small six-year-old self pretending to sit calmly at my desk, though all the while I was mentally fixated on my imminent failure. At days end I waited for the shuttle with my mind racing to devise a way to catch-up. I heard his voice.

"We could work together." He paused as I dumbly stared at him. "Study I mean."

I expected him to be kidding, possibly mocking me like the other kids. My immediate reaction is to say '*no*' but all I could think about was trash disposal. Maybe a partner was what I needed, maybe we needed each other, I tried telling myself. If I didn't make the leap I'd never know what lies beyond the concrete walls where the regulators patrol. I accepted his offer.

From that day on Garrett and I meet here, at the river between our two homes. Together we've played, studied, practiced, and mastered the skills essential to cross the concrete walls into Central.

Chapter 11: Nessa

Garrett's coughing shakes our intertwined bodies as I cradle him along the riverbed. Between his earth-shaking coughs there is a horrible gurgling sound from deep in the back of his throat. He hasn't said another word and I don't even know if he can.

My fingers comb through his golden hair just as his coughing silences. I watch the rising and falling of his chest, I'm cast into a trance watching the rhythmic breathing. Rise and fall. Rise and fall. Rise and fall. Over and over it repeats.

His raspy voice snaps me out of my trance. "I wasn't serious." I don't know what he's talking about; maybe the churn berries affected his mind. "Yesterday," he half chokes. "On the shuttle. The thirty-minute thing, I was kidding." He clears his throat, flashing his smile. "You didn't have to kill me to prove your test making skills."

"Garrett, I'm sorry." I sound desperate.

"It's ok. *I* took the berries."

"Why did you do that? It was stupid!"

"I knew you'd save me. At least I did at first. There *was* a little doubt when I was on all fours dying. I remembered what an awful healer you are. I thought for sure I was a goner." He playfully jabs his elbow into my stomach.

"Very funny. Honestly, it was so stupid. I'm an idiot."

"I'm fine; I knew you'd save me."

I had to save him, without him I would be lost. A part of him knows that too. It hits me just how exhausted I am. I lower his head and lay in the mud next to him, holding him close. It feels right, like our bodies fit perfectly together.

Water rushes over the rocks and swells form along the water's winding route. A twig snaps underfoot of a passing animal as the sun crests to its highest peak. I take it all in, both him and our hillside and imagine never leaving this moment. We could just stay here forever, becoming part of the ground. All I want is to hold him and hold onto these moments, to pluck them from time and keep them forever. His voice interrupts my thoughts.

"We should go" he says.

I don't want this moment to end but he's right. We need to leave to get the weapons collected, returned, and home before curfew. The entire right side of my body has fallen asleep making rising to my feet practically impossible.

"I'm sorry I didn't do your challenge" I say brushing the mud from my legs.

"It's fine. It would've been boring compared to yours. You know, since no one was supposed to die in mine." His hands comb through his hair, "I can think of a way you could make it up to me though."

"Nice try Garrett."

"Man, you're frigid." He grins, the corner of his mouth draws at his dimple.

I roll my eyes before we separate, running towards our supplies. I move as fast as I can gathering my equipment. I break the tree line, hands full of weapons when I see him already waiting at the platform. Even after almost dying he still beat me.

We ride the shuttle in silence. Small beads of sweat break across my forehead, the supplies feeling heavier than yesterday. I try my best to hide the trembling in my arms. Just as they begin to give out the shuttle stops. Unlike yesterday we don't race to be the first at the attendant. The mood is different now.

"Scan card," It's the same spider-eyed man from yesterday. "Needs?" He barks at me.

"Nessa…. I mean Vanessa Hollins, returning leap-testing weapons sir." His eyes dart to his clock. A look of annoyance crosses his face.

"Cutting it close." He says curtly.

We're only allowed to have training weapons for twenty-four hours. A minute longer would've resulted in a mark against our families. After what the educators told us about life in the pre-divide, I understand why Central controls all weapons.

We glide up the hill toward the station, neither of us talking. On the shuttle home Garrett stands close. I can hear his gentle breathing in my ear. My brown hair flutters, tickling my neck when he exhales. Without touching him I feel heat radiating, like he's reaching out to me. The shuttle stops at his sub. I shift to get out of his way just as his hands land on my shoulders. He squeezes them; it's like steam where he touched. I glance to look at him; my unruly hair covers my eyes.

"See you tomorrow Nessa." He brushes the rogue hairs from my face, tucking them behind my ear.

That night I still feel his touch across my cheek. It's not normal to spend so much time thinking about someone, or actually trying *not* to think about one person. His body, his touch, his *everything* keeps me awake until at last I fall asleep. Once again I dream of him.

Chapter 12: Nessa

Emma's tossing body abruptly interrupts my dreams. I follow her into the bathroom as she crouches over the toilet. My free hand strokes her shaking shoulders.

"It's ok Emma. I'm here, I'm here." I collect her long blonde hair, holding it clear from her face.

"Nessa I..." She's cut off by another surge of wrenching vomiting. Her tiny body quakes under my arms. Wave after wave lays assault to her insides.

Most of the night we alternate from the toilet to the floor. Emma can hardly open her beautiful eyes that are now rimmed with red. It's been at least an hour since the last wave hit and I scoop her tiny body from the floor, carrying her to bed.

"First light's almost here. I'll take the shuttle to education and tell them you're sick. I'll let Garrett know I can't come today but I'll be home right after" I reassure her. He's only got two days left until his leap but Emma needs me more.

"No, I'll go. I'll fall behind if I don't."

Education's supposed to be every citizen's top priority but I never thought she took it as seriously as she should. Maybe she just hid it, or maybe she's finally seeing how important it is.

"I'll get the lessons from the educator, we can do them together."

I watch out the window until the light over the eastern hills severs the grey landscape, releasing me from curfew. I close the creaking door as quietly as possible and enter the cold December air. It constricts like a vice on my chest. I force my breaths around its icy grasp. The rhythmic left, right of my legs pumping warms my body until I can finally empty my mind and become a vacant vessel. My breathing becomes less erratic as I pump my legs toward our hillside.

I sprint through the sub-two neighborhood and automatically turn left leaping across the fallen tree that's been unhurriedly rotting since before I was born. I've taken this route almost daily since I was six. It feels like home to me. I hop foot to foot across the scattered rocks that lay at the base of the log.

I keep running through the canopy of trees along my trail that's been pounded down from years of travel. I memorized every rock, stump, and tree along the way years ago and my body responds automatically. I cut through the thick forest until I see the glittering water of the river peak through the trees. Garrett isn't here yet.

Our hillside's open, all except for the oak tree that stands just left of center. Countless days I've sat on the hill gazing at the tree in awe. The dark arms reach in all directions; some wind and curve upwards while others dip and twist toward the ground to hover just above the red soil. The soil gives way to a massive trunk that I could lay at the base of and be hidden from sight.

This tree is the reason Garrett and I chose this spot. It provides shade in the summer and shelter from howling winds and heavy rain. For years we've tied messages to the low hanging branches for each other. I tie my brief note to one of the sagging arms knowing he'll look here once I haven't made it to the hill.

I have to hurry if I'm going to catch the shuttle to education before class begins. I clear the tree line crossing the log as the shuttle approaches the platform. I duck my head letting my chin nearly hit my chest. I swing my legs fast racing to the platform. I leap onto the shuttle just as the doors seal shut.

There is a sea of blue when I arrive at education. Blue clothes, bags, even blue socks. I make my way through the sea to find Emma's educator.

"Nessa Hollins. Emma's sister," I say with a hint of unease.

Educators have always made me marginally uncomfortable and I'm certain she hears it in my voice. She looks slightly annoyed by my presence and probably offended by my unkempt dress and hair that's mixed with mud and leaves from my run to the hill.

Educators are always immaculately groomed with white clothes pressed and unpolluted, they're Centrals. They know what lies beyond the wall. At day's end they take the hovercraft across the barrier and return to a life I can't imagine.

"Yes, Miss Hollins?" Her dark perfectly shaped brows sit over her fair green eyes. Her black, shoulder length hair falls to the side as she asks her question.

"Emma is unwell today, ma'am. I've come to collect her assignments."

I try rushing through our awkward interaction and wait while she collects and organizes a stack of lessons. Tucking them into my bag I dash from the education building, relieved to be free from the white walls and judging eyes.

Darting through the streets back to Emma, I can't help but recall my first day of education so many years ago, when I walked home in my grey uniform. It only takes thirty minutes to run the route now. Once I round the corner to our sub my mind switches to Emma. I sprint twice as fast up our walkway and reach the door, swinging it open.

"Nessa?" Her voice is weak.

"Hey, little miss. How are you?" I stare at her, curled into a tense ball.

I try comforting her. I crawl in bed arranging the grey sheets over our heads. She rolls to me half smiling. I sing to her while her eyes flutter open and closed in a battle to fight exhaustion.

"Sleep, Emma. I'll wake you soon," I say between songs.

She lets sleep conquer her. I hold the covers above us and partly sing, partly hum as images of my mother and Garrett flash through my mind. I picture mama holding me, her soft voice a hum. Mama fades into the background and I imagine Garrett with me, surrounding me in his arms. I let my attention and voice wander for the better part of the morning before I find the heart to wake her.

"Emma, it's time to wake up." I comb my fingers through her hair, coaxing her awake. She yawns, stretching her limbs in all directions. She stares at me through refreshed green and gold eyes. "Let's see what we're learning today," I usher her out of our room to the open table. I pull out the stack of papers. Her eyes fly wildly open and alert.

"All of those?"

"Yes, it's not bad really. We have to learn moon cycles first."

"Why?" She asks with a hint of whine to her voice. It makes me want to laugh.

"Because it's what the educator gave me. Plus, moon cycles are important to know for farming." She gives me an absent look. "For instance, harvest moons are in September and October, the moon is so full and bright that it casts light into the darkness letting the farmers reap until late in the night. Or May is the planting moon. Everyone should know when to plant and when to harvest, even if you don't become a farmer." I poke my bony finger at her stomach, making her giggle. We spend the better part of the morning learning the different moon phases and cycles.

"Full, waxing gibbous, first quarter…" On and on she repeats, proving she has them memorized.

"Ok show off. Let's move on." I smile at her across the table. I pull out her skills lesson, "It says you're supposed to work on trapping today." She curls her top lip in a sort of snarl. Skills instruction has never been her favorite but it's mandatory. "You're learning the twitch-up snare today." She cocks her head, giving a disgusted look. "I hope you're feeling better because we have to go outside to do this."

I fold her in my arms, hugging her before we dress in our warm blues. We march towards the woods bordering our home. Emma snaps nearly every branch that litters the forest floor.

"In case you were wondering, hunting isn't your thing," I mutter over my shoulder. "When you're tracking and hunting you have to be quiet. Animals have a keen sense of smell *and* hearing. Each branch you break takes you a step further from reaching your prey."

"Ok." She says, focused on my words.

I give her more instructions, "Look for signs of animal activity. It can be broken twigs, foot-prints, even flattened blades of grass showing where animals have bedded down. Once we find an animal trail we'll begin construction."

I look over my shoulder, her eyes scour the ground. We walk through the thick forest sweeping the land in a diagonal pattern. She lifts and lowers her feet gingerly; her eyes focus on the ground in the duel task of finding an animal trail and avoiding making noise. I haven't heard a twig break since I told her miles ago.

"There!" She shrieks with excitement. Her eyes land on an animal trail.

"What kind of animal is it?"

"Rabbit?" Her response sounds more like a question than an answer; obviously she isn't confident.

"You're right. *Why* did you say rabbit?" I patiently wait several minutes for her to piece together her reasoning.

"The trail is low to the ground... The tall grass is unbroken and larger game would've broken the tall grass or even the twigs. Also look," she points to the tracks, "two long prints in the back for the hind feet and two small in front. Definitely a rabbit." She finishes with a smile.

"Exactly right. Okay Emma, now we need to cover our scent." She shoots me a puzzled look. "We have to coat our hands and trapping materials in mud from a creek bed."

Her puzzled look turns into one of pure disbelief. I imagine the thought of voluntarily covering her skin in mud is absolutely preposterous to her, but she eventually agrees. We walk through the woods to the nearest creek. I stare at the mud, tracing my eyes around the swirling shades of brown. Squatting down I sink my hand into it, mixing the colors and lifting them to my arms. I've covered the right half of my arm when I feel a cold splat against my thigh. Emma has hit me with a muddy projectile. My eyes turn to hers. She's laughing, her dirty hands point at the matted mud she just threw at me. I reach deep into the brown, retrieving an overflowing handful. Cocking my arm back I aim and fire, throwing the projectile at her. It slaps her hard against her shoulder. This means war.

Her next mud rocket lands square against my jaw. Wiping the mud away I fling the excess back to the ground. I pause, deciding my next move. I could end it here maybe tell her we're wasting time, or I could follow my automatic response and teach her a lesson. I grin in just the wrong way, giving my choice away. She tries to run but she's no match for my long legs. I catch up to her, tackling her. She emerges, face and front of her body covered in the thick brown filth. For a second I'm terrified she's going to be furious, worried she can't handle my retaliation. She stares at me shocked and then breaks into hysterical laughter, her body shakes as she folds over, grabbing her waist as she laughs. Her slick hands slide down the front of her thighs and she nearly falls face first again. Within ten minutes we're layered with mud, laughing uncontrollably.

We head back to the rabbit trail, along the way I teach her which twigs to use for the snare. "Don't use the green ones" I bend down snapping a green twig in half, exposing thick syrup. "The sap will bind the materials together and once that happens your snare's useless." Emma nods as she absorbs my instructions. "We need two forked sticks, one long, one short," I instruct.

Within five minutes she's back with two textbook sticks. We crouch together as I show her how to position the forked sticks along the rabbit path. It takes Emma close to an hour to mimic my snare but eventually she's mastered it.

"Let's try it out" I say. She looks at me like I've grown three heads.

"But that's against the law. We aren't hunters…we'd be poaching." She says.

"I know silly, I meant we'd set it off ourselves." Game is only for the hunters, everyone knows that.

I lay on my belly in front of the noose. I know where the snare is but we've concealed it so well that I have a difficult time finding it. I run a thick branch through the noose and just as it would with a rabbit, the snares triggered. The branch goes flying into the air. It dangles, swinging like a pendulum. For a moment my mind morphs it into a rabbit and I recognize that our snares are effective and deadly. I hear Emma hooting and hollering behind me. She leaps in the air doing some silly celebratory dance. I teeter on my heels for a few seconds, laughing at her display.

"Alright, alright, let's head back, third line is coming and we both missed the first two."

She stops her little jig. Freezing momentarily the same way a wild animal does when you first stumble across it. I lunge for her and just like a startled creature, she takes off. We race home to clean our mud-coated bodies. We weave and dance between the trees as we chase each other. It carries me back to times with Garrett. Days spent chasing each other by our streambed. It usually started innocently; a simple game of describing clouds would morph into a foot race in no time. I'd see a rabbit while he'd see a groundhog, before we knew it we'd be arguing and ultimately end up chasing each other around.

I run now with Emma in front of me, twisting her way through the brush, her hair swinging all the way to our front door, right up to the bath.

The dried mud forms crevices along the length of our skin. We look like scaled brown beasts as we stand in the bath. Flakes of mud drop to the tub from our furious scrubbing. We dress, giggling as we leave the house and our tub coated in a layer of filth.

We walk to the pavilion where all meals are prepared and delivered. It's a large faded grey and blue rotunda just a short jog from home. Each sub has their own pavilion where three meals a day are provided. The food's always simple but it is filling and nutritional. Central designs a balanced diet plan so nobody has to worry whether they'll eat, or be distracted with preparing food like they did pre-divide. When I was young I'd imagine eating the way they did pre-divide. If I focused all my energy I could smell the food cooking, the smell of hot meats and vegetables drifted through the house, permeating. My ears would perk-up as I'd hear pots and pans scraping and mama shuffling. I always pictured Mama there, making dinner and singing to herself. She was already dead but she was still in my imagination. She'd sit with us and we'd eat together in our own home, like a real family.

Four lines run through the left section of the pavilion where we eat. There's a line for citizens five and younger where swarms of children in grey grab at food haphazardly. Then there's our line for the school aged citizens six to sixteen, all of us wearing blue.

I glance to my right toward the third line looking for Papa. My eyes trace the trail of green uniforms until I find his worn face. Sensing eyes on him he lifts his head, meeting my stare. He signals to a table in the corner, I nod. The hunters must have taken down deer for tonight's meal. The retirees in black dish the venison onto our plates in appropriate proportions. I smile and nod as I go down the line collecting dinner.

Emma and I take our seats next to Papa. His worn face reminds me of the mud we rinsed from our skin earlier, the wrinkles wind through his face like the crevices the mud made just before it flaked off.

"How was education today?" His voice is tired.

"I couldn't go. I was sick." Emma sounds guilty. She shouldn't, I can vouch for her.

"Hmm." Papa mutters.

"I got her lessons. We covered them all." I smile at Emma. "She learned about the moon cycles and trapping." Papas eyes light and for a moment he looks years younger.

"Oh yeah? Which trap?"

Emma launches into a detailed description of the twitch-up snare. I chuckle. She actually sounds like she enjoyed it. The way she describes everything it's like I'm actually back in the forest searching for the rabbit path and fastening the noose.

Part of the reason she's so animated is because of me. She learned these things from me. A jolt of excitement rushes to my stomach. I could do this; I could be an educator if I make it to Central. If Emma can learn and love it then I can teach anyone. My mind wanders as I see myself standing in front of dozens of eager children. I am dressed in pressed and perfect white. I've made the leap and am an educator.

Eventually my mind makes its way back to the present and I see Papa and Emma both laughing. Small tears collect at the edges of their eyes and I laugh too. I'll miss them when I make it to Central. I can't think of missing them though, it hurts too much. Instead I hold onto the mental images of me in my pressed white uniform.

Soon our laughter slows as fatigue sets in. The sun is dropping fast, painting the sky in pinks and oranges as it sets. The colors are dull and beautiful as they cover the western skyline, but the hues are also a warning for Emma and me. Soon curfew will come. Papa is the first to push away from the table. We follow. We walk with the sun setting behind us. Twice I notice Emma look over her shoulders to appreciate the colors.

Walking through the door I see the exhaustion conquer Emma. I rinse the tub one last time, banishing the mud that coated its white floor. Emma and I crawl into bed and she slides her hand in mine. I'm happy I had my day with her but I'm also aware of a void that hollows me.

I haven't seen Garrett all day and it's like a part of me is missing. I don't think I'll feel whole until I see him tomorrow. How unfair is it that I've kept my composure for all these years and am now falling to pieces so close to the leap. I've watched day in and day out as the other girls in our year try to win him over, never once was I jealous or even thought of sharing their same affections, not until now. Maybe it's the leap that's making me crazy, or maybe it's the hormones Gwen talked about. All I know is he consumes my thoughts like a rolling fog; he's all I think about. I lay in bed trying to wrap my cloudy head around my emotions. It seems less than coincidental that I've fallen for him this close to the leap, but I think I have.

Chapter 13: Nessa

I wake just before first light, Emma's hands still in mine. My body is stiff from my heavy sleep. It's miraculous that I even slept considering my test is only two days away. It's my last day to train with Garrett. This realization makes my stomach spiral.

I tug at the corner of the blanket covering us and slide stealthily off the bed. My toes touch down and involuntarily retract, trying to escape the frigid floor. I set my feet down again, this time prepared for the cold as I tiptoe toward the bathroom. Emma is still asleep when I exit dressed in my warm blue uniform. I'm leaving my hair free today, hopefully it shields my ears from the December winds.

"Have a good day." I whisper, kissing her pink cheek. She stirs but goes back to sleep.

I stand at the front window and stare into the grey landscape, staring and waiting for first light. Hurry up, hurry up, I keep repeating. My mind fights an internal battle.

'I should go now, its close enough. Nobody will see.'

'Maybe he's already there waiting for me.'

'No, you can't go, you'll get caught. He isn't there yet anyway, it's too early.'

I keep echoing the circular thoughts until finally the first pink and gold rays break the eastern trees. Without pausing I lunge for the door and sprint toward our hill.

The air is cold and my breath materializes in a hazed cloud as I exhale. For once I don't feel the cold; my body is too preoccupied with the crushing desire to be near him. I run through the streets along the same path I've taken a thousand times before, but now with each step I feel my need growing stronger. It's like a magnet is pulling me toward him.

I reach the fallen tree and cover its length in three leaps instead of the usual five. I land on the jagged path I've beaten down and bound rock to rock until I see the water breaking through the wilted trees. I tell myself he's not going to be here, it's too early. I crash through the wooded tree line onto our frosted hillside.

I see him. His strong and oversized body sits soundly on the lowest branch of our live oak. My heart lands in my throat. I restrain my urge to run directly to him. I slow my steps and my erratic breathing. My heart is pounding so strongly, I'm certain he can hear it from across the field. I slow my approach as I try mastering my breath. *Breathe in, breathe out, breathe in, breathe out,* I repeat until I finally get control.

Garrett turns to me, his deep brown eyes stare straight into mine and I lose it. I run toward him, my eyes fixed to his, watching him stand to meet me I leap into his arms.

"Whoa." He says, as my weight knocks him off balance.

"I'm sorry, I just…" He pulls back to look at me.

"Are you blushing?" He asks. I instinctively fix my hair.

"I'm just warm from my run."

"Nessa Hollins is warm in the middle of December?"

"Maybe I am. I don't know. I just…" I trail off. "Hey wait. What are *you* doing here so early?" His face flushes as he runs his hand through his hair. "Now you're blushing!" I shout. "When did you get here?" I ask.

He shifts before he answers. "I stayed here last night."

"What! That's against the law! What about curfew?"

"My mind kept racing about the test. About a lot of things." He swallows. "Part of me wanted to rebel a little. You know, break a rule before I came of age." His voice sounds strange and muted. "Another part hoped you felt that way too. I thought maybe I'd find you here. Your note said you would try to come later." The red drains from his face as he stares at the ground like its a thousand miles away. "It was stupid but I waited all day and when you didn't come I thought maybe you would show up at night. I thought 'later' meant after curfew." He looks back to me. "I was convinced you'd be here too. It was dumb, I know."

I shift awkwardly, suddenly embarrassed. "I had no idea. I…" He cuts me off, pulling me into his arms.

"It's okay. It was a stupid thought," I hear him deflate. I curl my arms around his waist, folding them across his back. I imagine staying like this, holding him here so close to me. He releases me to sit back on the oak branch. "How's Emma?" He asks. I hide my disappointment with a smile.

"She's better now." Awkward silence settles, finally I tell him about yesterday's lessons. He laughs as I detail our mud fight at the creek. Silence falls again and I have to break it, "What do you want to *perfect* today?"

"I don't wanna study today. I think I'll go home. I'm just tired from last night, that's all." He adds trying to ease the hurt written across my face.

"That's ok. I understand."

He leans in, pulling me into his arms. He inhales at the nape of my neck; I feel the electricity between us. His hands drop, releasing me.

I force myself to say something. "Good luck tomorrow," I try to smile.

"I'll see you later." He turns, walking away.

I wait until his steps carry him past the trees before I stare vacantly ahead, holding back the tears. Hours pass and the entire time I beat myself up for my overt weakness. Maybe *these* are the hormones Gwen was talking about. If that is the case they make me irrational and frustrated. I stayed up half the night last night rehearsing our day together. We were going to do some skills training, maybe some Q&A on farming and healing. At some point I was going to take his hand and hold it, or maybe even lay against his chest if I felt brave enough. Maybe he would ask me out again and this time I'd say yes. All I know is sitting here alone wasn't what I had envisioned.

The day seems so long without him. It hadn't occurred to me how long a single afternoon could stretch. Eventually my shaking limbs force me to stand. I need to go home and warm myself.

I meet Emma and Papa at third line for dinner and sit vacantly at the table as they talk. Twice Papa asks me questions I completely ignore. When the orange and pink rays hit the pavilion my stomach jolts as I think of Garrett.

I follow several lengths behind them on our walk home. I don't have enough energy to undress before falling into bed. My arm is flung over the edge with my fingers resting on the bouquet of crumbling flowers. My eyes feel just as heavy as my heart until finally the weight of both carries me into another night of restless sleep.

My stomach is turning circles when I wake well past first light. Today is his day. He's probably testing right now...tomorrow that will be me. Both thoughts terrify me. I want so badly to leave and find him, watch him test, or at least be there when he finishes.

I scoot myself to the top of the bed and curl into a ball. My eyes cry for reasons I don't totally understand. I should practice but I can't study, not without him. My mind jolts realizing I could leave him a note. I jump out of bed, running to get paper and a pencil.

'*Garrett, I hope you did great today! I am sure you did…*' No that sounds too fake. I erase it.

'*Garrett, I was lost without you these last two days.*' I immediately erase.

'*Garret, I wish I could have seen you today, I am sure you did great. Happy birthday. I'll see you later.*'

That sounds good. There's only two hours of daylight left to attach the note, get to third-line, and back home before curfew. I scramble from the table so fast that I actually forget the note. My mind screams as I reach the door, reversing I snatch it off the table. I travel the worn path to our secret spot, tying my note to the branch we sat on yesterday.

'Please let him come tonight, please let him find my note and stay,' I say over and over in my head as I bound toward the pavilion.

I join in the conversation at dinner. I have to act normal or Emma or Papa will suspect something. When dinner is over I change out of my day clothes into my blue nightgown. While Emma gets ready for bed I quickly bundle my day clothes into a tight ball, tucking them under the loose wood paneling at the side of the house.

"Good luck tomorrow, Nessa," she says from across the bed.

"Thanks. Let's go to sleep, it's getting late." I watch her eyes flutter until they close. I wait for the quiet sound of her snoring. At last I hear it and I creep lightly out of the house into the night.

Chapter 14: Nessa

I close the door so gently that the creaking is hardly audible. I enter the dark night with the wind cutting across my exposed legs; it's a struggle to move. I crouch into a ball and run. I try staying hidden from regulators that might be patrolling for people like me. That would be our second mark, I could still leap but if we got a third before Emma's seventeenth birthday she wouldn't have the chance. I'm being careless and selfish but my guilt is overruled by my needs.

I move to the side of the house, holding my arms outstretched as I search the frosted ground for my clothes. My hands sweep back and forth while I try coaxing my eyes into night vision. On my fourth pass I feel the bundle. I unroll the blue clothes, hastily throwing them on over my thin nightgown.

The usual path to the hillside is too dangerous after curfew; I have to alter my route. I keep my posture low, pumping my feet on my detour around my neighbors' homes. I wind and weave between fences and trees. All the houses are silent and dark; my only compasses are the stars that glitter in the black sky and the road I keep to my left.

I make it through the sub-three neighborhood and eventually I'm weaving through the larger sub-two homes. Some of them have their electric lights on. It must be nice to have electricity like that. I can't imagine flicking a switch and having electricity surge through and brighten an entire room. Our oil lamps in sub-three aren't so bad though.

Thirty minutes pass before I'm finally at Grove Street. Once I cross it I will be at the fallen log. And after that, I'm safe. I hold my position, crouching at the side of a sub-two home. I scan the street that separates me from Garrett. My head turns left and right scouting the empty road. Three times my torso lunges forward to run but my feet stay grounded. My heart and mind are at war with each other. My heart wants to sprint across Grove Street onto the hill with him. My mind is in self-preservation mode, trying to shield me from exposure.

I scout one final time. The road to the left is vacant. I look to the right and my stomach immediately drops. I see the silhouette of a man running straight for me. My body instinctively sinks into the wall. I pinch my eyes closed until the sound of his approaching steps are nearly on top of me. I wish I could stifle my breathing but my chest heaves and air spirals as I pant wildly.

My chest lifts and falls rapidly, in sync with my beating heart that is ready to burst. I've been caught.

Chapter 15: Ty

Every night I searched for her and just kept coming up empty. I did get pretty good at dodging Borgs, but that wasn't my aim. That first winter went in a blink, but spring and summer dragged. Fall was brutal. Every leaf that fell was a tease, tiptoeing me into winter when I could look for her again.

It is my second winter and I'm more reckless. I can hear my mom scolding me, "Tyler Mitchel, you're gonna get yourself put in lockdown." That doesn't faze me though. I go out every night anyway. It's coming to the end of the year and I still keep turning up empty. Panic starts creeping in, what if my sight was wrong. It's never been wrong before but what if this one was, maybe I threw my family and life away over some misfiring neurons.

My breath smokes between my lips as I run. The regulator's boots echo, they're over by Quincy Street, a full three blocks from me. Boredom builds till I need to blow off some steam. I pick my way toward Quincy, timing my route to theirs. They are a few meters away so I prop myself against the post and prepare for my rush.

"Hey you, Borg!" I shout.

The regulators stop in their tracks. If there is one thing I've learned it's that they hate being called a Borg. When I was younger some foreigner propaganda made its way over the wall, it called the regulators Borgs. It compared them to bionic robots that were a fad years ago. I guess they're pretty pissed about being likened to metal pieces of shit that basically self-destructed. They turn their lights straight at me, guns slung across their backs. The booming voice of the first Borg sounds out.

"Surrender Citizen, we have you in sight."

"Oh shit," I shout as the lights settle on my chest.

"Raise your arms and walk toward us slowly!" The one hollers as the other shoulders his rifle.

I step toward them. The first relaxes his arms, letting me make my move. I bolt through the ally between Quincy and Walsh. The Borgs are on my tail but I'm not worried, I've done this before. I hurdle a silver trash can bordering the street. I clear it and stop, turning it on its side. The regulators are close but I'll lose them I think as I roll the barrel towards their feet. The first clears it but the second fails.

"Shit!" He yells as he falls to the pavement, grasping his knee.

The first regulator stops, momentarily torn but ultimately stays with his downed mate. I keep tearing through the subs, heart pumping from the rush. I turn the corner into sub-two with my feet pounding. Somewhere a few streets over the Borgs are rallying themselves for the hunt.

Suddenly it hits me, everything's so familiar. The moon, air, even the stars are like I remember from my sight, and then I see her. She's crouching beside a house, looking terrified. I head straight for her, this is it.

Chapter 16: Nessa

I force my eyes open and see his tall silhouette coming at me.
This will be our second mark, one mark away from being banned
to leap. What was I thinking? My heart drums as my stomach
knots and twists in a shameful dance. I'm guilty of this, I'm the
one that's compromised Emma's chances. One mark after this
and she will never have the chance to leap. I'm just about to give
myself up when he takes form. He isn't a regulator from Central,
he's dressed like me. He comes to a sudden stop, eyes staring
directly at mine. At first he looks alarmed but then his shoulders
relax, seeing I'm in blue, I guess. He's lean and strikingly tall. I've
never seen him before. I would have noticed green eyes like his.
He strides to me and I instinctively rise to meet him. He waves
his hand, signaling me to crouch again, I immediately obey.

His voice is deep and commanding even though he whispers, "Hey, gettin' on alright?" I hesitate. What an odd introduction I think, but I answer.

"Fine, you?"

"Good." He pauses, like he's waiting for me to say more. He breaks the awkward silence, "It's notta good night to be out, Borgs are going ballistic."

"Borgs?" I ask.

"Regulators." He shakes his head, "I call 'em Borgs."

My voice cracks, "How many? Where?"

"Don't know. More than usual." He shrugs his shoulders. Usual? That means he breaks curfew a lot. I'm stunned that someone could be so careless as to break curfew more than once. "Where you goin'?" He asks, looking around as I point.

"Across the street, toward the river."

"You have two, maybe three blinks before they come, you should bolt."

"Thanks." I smile as I try hiding my confusion.

He smiles back. It pulls the corners of his mouth at perfect angles. I hear the crunching ground under his feet as he runs towards the woods behind me. I find myself suddenly overcome with curiosity. Who is he? Where did he come from and how don't I know him? His retreating steps distance themselves from me but the farther he runs the more I want to know. Shaking my head I focus and scan the road ahead. The coast is clear. My guilt-ridden stomach unknots as I stay crouched and cross the street, hurdling onto the log.

My feet slam down just as I hear the regulators' heavy boots marching from the street to my right. There is more than one of them and they are close. I cover the length of the log and dive stomach first to its base, just as the regulator's sweeping lights fall across the rotting tree.

My insides are in my throat. Sweat forms across my forehead as I lay prone with rocks and leaves pressed against my face. The regulators march in rhythm as their boots slam the pavement closer and closer to where I am. Gravel crunches beneath their heavy boots. The sound of crunching gravel and crunching leaves pressed against my head fills my ears. My pupils dilate in the darkness then suddenly snap and constrict from the glare of the regulators' lights that pass along the top of the log. I roll to the left to conceal myself behind the fallen tree. It only takes a second but in that single moment I land in the path of their lights. The powerful beams hold where I'd been laying only seconds ago.

"Did you see that over there?" The one says in his deep and husky tone. "I know I saw something move." I hear him draw his gun.

I shake, or maybe it's the ground that shakes as their steps vibrate the nearly frozen soil. Step-by-step they march their way closer to me. Just ahead there's a boulder that I might be able to make it to. With shaking hands pushing against the shaking ground I inch my way toward the brown boulder. Maybe I can hide behind it if I can make it there. I follow their lights like a child watching a meteor shower. I track them left and right as I time my moves. The lights sweep left as I crawl toward the boulder. The regulators swing the lights back toward me and I drop to the ground while the beams dance over the top of my back. I move forward again until the next beam bounces toward me. I hardly progress as I stop and go, pulling myself inch-by-inch closer. All the while they steadily close the space between us. The regulator nestles his gun to his shoulder as I hear the tick of metal snapping. My breath quickens as I imagine them shooting me on the spot.

"Come on out. We know you're in there!" The regulator hisses. "We might even go easy on you if you turn yourself in."

I swallow and feel my throat closing in out of fear. My chest tightens like my breastbone is being squeezed in a vice. It extends outward along my ribs toward my arms and tingles unpleasantly as I fight the terror. Squeezing chest and sweating arms are all I can think about as I crawl the last foot toward the boulder. My knee jams into a jagged rock and I gasp in pain. The lights land across my back and hold steady.

"Got ya!" The regulator shouts.

Their lights feel hot against the back of my neck. What should I do? Do I stay where I am and let them punish me, or maybe I should just stand up and run? What if they shoot me like Garrett's fox? I tremor as their steps close in the last few feet. With each closing step my chest tightens more and more until it feels like my heart is about to burst my chest wide open. What would happen then? Would Central send a hovercraft to scoop up my lifeless body in the morning I wonder?

Out of nowhere a thunderous crack echoes halting the regulators. My body jolts from the sound. It was powerful and terrifying. My blood gushes through me at an alarming rate; I feel the blood pounding against my skin. Then, another loud crack booms from behind me.

"What the hell was that?" The regulator asks.

I cringe and wait for them to make their next move. One more crack resonates followed by a shout from across Grove Street.

"Hey Borgs! Looking for something?" I recognize that voice, it's the guy from earlier.

"You little shit! We're going to enjoy killing you!"

They run toward the sound. I roll to my back and watch their lights bouncing in all directions as they track him down. I catch a glimpse of the silhouette of the boy from earlier. He runs from across Grove Street drawing the regulators into the woods. Did he just save me? I push to my feet and hurdle across the rocks, pushing the close call from my head.

I sprint toward our hill. I'm almost to Garrett. I hope he's there. I break the tree line and see the moon's light glittering across the river. I can't help but think our hilltop is even more beautiful at night compared to day.

I run from the tree line heading toward the black silhouette of the live oak. It looks ancient and alien standing alone in the blackness of night. I reach the tree and search the lowest branches for a note from him. My heart plummets as I come up empty. I move around to the front of the tree and nearly trip over Garrett as he sleeps on his back.

"Garrett," I whisper as I lay down next to him. He stirs, opening his deep brown eyes.

"Nessa, you came." He looks straight at me, flashing his crooked smile. "Your test is tomorrow. You shouldn't have come."

"I had to see you first. I've been miserable without you."

"You missed me then?"

"I missed you enough to evade regulators and meet you here," I say with a hint of smugness at my bravery.

"Did you really see regulators?"

"Two of them. They almost caught me but I…" for some reason I stop myself, I don't want him knowing about the boy. "I hid behind that giant log."

"Who would've thought that rotted old thing would save you. I've spent years waiting for it to cave in and break your legs." He briefly laughs at the thought. "So since you missed me," he pauses, "does that mean I've got a chance at asking you out?"

"Nobody's stopping you from asking." I inch closer to him.

"I don't think I can handle more rejection. Not on my birthday, at least."

"I wouldn't let you down on your birthday."

He slides closer to me. My stomach turns as he cradles my cheek. I let him keep his hand there; I shiver as he moves it along my face. I want him to keep moving his hand, to take his fingers across my skin. I can imagine his fingers tracing their way across my neck to my collarbone and then further down. I imagine feeling the heat from his fingertips as they graze along my chest. I can almost feel the tingling as he traces circles along my shivering skin. His fingers will graze further down across my stomach until he reaches my thighs. I squirm, imagining his strong hands wrapped around my legs, squeezing the fleshy parts of my inner thighs. I'll let him move his hands upwards just a touch until he reaches that perfect spot. I push my cheek into his hands hoping he'll take them further.

His touch alerts me as he takes his hand through my long hair and wraps his arms around my back. Electric sparks ignite. My body becomes all sensation.

"You've always been beautiful" he whispers.

He closes the last few inches between us, tilting my head to meet his. His breath is warm across my lips. My mouth bursts as his lips find mine. He draws our mouths together.

Somehow his touch, his lips, and his mouth melt away the nerves and fears that bashed through my body earlier. It's like the regulators never existed, like there never was a risk at all. I'd risk a mark any day compared to losing this moment, to ever risk losing this feeling ever again.

My first kiss, this is it I think. Matching his moves I yield myself to his kiss. I exorcise anything that's left of the girl in me and morph into a woman. I'm aware that I'll never get this moment again, never get to have another first kiss. I make the most of it, relishing every instant and every sensation. I've spent so many years avoiding this moment, too afraid it could lead to heartache. Finally my walls are starting to come down and I let myself enjoy this. Warm wetness bursts with fire as his tongue touches mine. I withdraw for just a second. It feels strange having someone so close and intimate but I push myself deeper. I drive myself into his kiss, swirling my tongue with his, feeling the wetness.

I shake as he traces his thumb down my stomach, swirling it around my hips. I hold my arms steady against his back as his leg rolls over mine. He pins our hips together and my body moves to an unheard rhythm. The whole time my body grows like fire and I can't get enough. He's the first to release our tangled bodies. He breathes heavily as his chest rises and falls like he just finished a race.

"I've wanted to do that for so long. I fell for you the first time I saw you. I've loved you from the start" he says.

"Love?" I whisper. Funny that my head screams the question yet my throat only allows a whisper to escape.

"Yes. I love you." He kisses me.

I want to say it back. I think it's what I feel. How am I supposed to know what love feels like? I've spent too much time building walls to protect myself; I'm not prepared for all of them to fall yet. How could I? They are the very walls that have gotten me here today. Ones built at the age of five when my mother was taken so fast. Walls constructed from a practical place, not an emotional place. I had to look at things practically, investing emotions might lead to heartbreak. The only thing I had was Emma and Papa, everything else was a risk.

"What does this mean?" I ask.

"That I want to be with you. Not just at our hillside, but always." Always hardly seems like enough time. He tucks my hair behind my ear, "I've been thinking a lot about it. We could make the leap. Once we get to Central, we'll start our lives together there."

"And if only one of us can leap?" I ask knowing the possibility exists.

"If you don't make it then I don't stand a chance. We'll stay in the Inner together. We'll test high enough to be in the same sub and we'll start our life here." He brushes the stubborn hair blocking my face, "If you don't leap then I don't leap. I won't go without you."

I push my mouth to his. Our bodies move, dancing together until it finally feels like I'm where I belong. When the signs of first light emerge over the treetops we wake in each other's arms.

"Happy birthday Nessa."

"Thanks for reminding me." I joke, rolling to my stiff back. He positions his chest onto mine, kissing me. "Sorry, I bet I have morning breath," blushing I run my tongue across my teeth.

"Didn't notice, but now that you mention it…" He grins.

"Oh stop!"

"I was kidding Nessa." He pulls a twig from my hair, "I'll walk you to the platform."

I nod, collecting myself at the base of the tree. We leave the woods hand-in-hand and he holds me as I wait for the shuttle.

His body protects me from the wind, protecting me like I always knew he could.

Finally the shuttle arrives and I board it alone. I feel bare without him. It's an hour's ride to the leap center but I'm not anxious about anything, I'm just lightheaded from love sickness.

The cool black seats look brighter than ever in my flustered state. I stare at the seat ahead of me with a dumb smirk across my face. Finally the shuttle squeals to a stop and I'm snapped out of my trance. I see the enormous white dome. For the first time all day my stomach churns as I realize the gravity of this moment. I've arrived for the leap, the test that will determine both our lives.

Chapter 17: Nessa

The mountainous white gates leading testers in and out of the facility virtually block any ground level view of the colossal dome where I assume testing will be held. The gates extend as far as I can see. They're covered with green vines inching their long tenuous threads at odd angles in an attempt to extend themselves over the highest peaks of the walls.

My eyes are carried from the spiny green vines and pulled to a massive concrete tower. It sits just adjacent to the front gate. I see two regulators dressed in white uniforms with their heavy black boots laced around their muscular calves. Their black and white helmets are secured tightly around their neckline. They could be looking at me but I can't tell, their visors hide their eyes from view.

Their imposing figures are intimidating enough but when my eyes connect with their guns my stomach immediately somersaults. I remind myself that they're here to protect me, not hurt me. The guns look so complicated. I'm thinking about all the intricate details when a loud buzz snaps me back to the present.

I'm twenty feet from the entrance when it becomes obvious that some sort of alarm is sounding to notify of my trespass. The alarm continues, growing louder the closer I get. At the ten-foot mark the sound is almost ear splitting and I wonder if I should keep going. I'm just about to turn around when the alarm silences. I freeze, waiting for a sign telling me what to do next. The December air bites across my face making my eyes well with tears. I squint looking up to the regulators. My heart's squeezed into my throat as I automatically cower, taking two steps backwards.

I've done something wrong, I must have. Maybe they recognize me from last night. Maybe I've been caught after all. They're pointing their guns directly at me. I lift my foot to take my third step back as a booming voice resonates over the speakers that are housed in the corner of the regulators tower.

'State your name and purpose' the echoing voice directs.

"Nessa. I mean VA-nessa Hollins, here for leap testing." I swallow hard, holding my recoiled posture. The speaker booms again.

"Scan your card."

My eyes dart left and right as I look for the scanner that is nowhere in sight. I fumble with my documents trying to get my ID. My fingers find it just as a scanner materializes. I was certain it wasn't there moments ago but I must have missed it. It couldn't appear out of thin air.

My hands tremble as I bring my card to the scanner. It connects with the red laser and beeps three times, verifying my identification is valid. The regulators lower their weapons in unison as the large gates swing open toward me.

One of the most strikingly beautiful women I've ever seen comes toward me from behind the gates. Her shining jet black hair is collected neatly in a braid that falls down her back. Her skin is olive. Her deep, dark eyes stare directly at me. She carries herself with such poise that I'm stunned and immediately jealous.

"Miss Hollins, a pleasure to meet you." She says, throwing her hand forward to take mine.

"Likewise" is all I can answer.

"My name is Natalie, sorry for the little scare at the gate. Central has instructed us to follow red-alert protocol today."

I'm instantly uneasy. Central hasn't issued a red alert since the foreigners attacked our sector years ago. I immediately worry about Emma and Garrett. Who will be there to rescue Emma if another attack happens, and what if something happens to Garrett.

"Let's get you started, shall we?" She asks in a sweet singsong voice that sounds forced.

She ushers me out of the December winds through the expansive front gates. I had expected the gates to lead into an open landscape and I'm surprised as we enter immediately into a narrow circular passage. Our steps echo against the concrete floor as we travel through the downward sloping tunnel. We must be going underground. My unease is mounting the further we walk and I distract myself by counting my steps. We walk two hundred and fifty steps before I see the first fracture in the tunnel, a forked divide Natalie steers to the left of. The next fracture is only one hundred and two steps from the divide. It's a door to my right labeled OS1-2. She walks much faster than I'd expected and soon I've taken another one hundred and two steps. I see a heavy dark door labeled OS3-4.

Natalie's gait slows and finally we're walking up a long and steep ramp. I try muffling my breathing; I'm embarrassed she will assume I'm out of shape. My eyes catch a small door to my left, I should take it I think, hoping it might lead me back home. I force the ridiculous thought from my head and walk the final one hundred and eighteen steps into a large circular room.

My eyes take in the features of the room. In the center sits a large semi-reclining black and silver chair with numerous cuffs to lock the occupant in place.

I take in the rounded walls where screens are flashing with numbers and symbols that are foreign to me. The Central testers are accessing numbers and equations from the wall and pulling them directly into their handheld tablets. I've never seen technology like this before.

"This way Miss Hollins." Natalie says with a sweeping hand, indicating I'm to sit in the black and silver chair.

I hoist onto the leather chair and cross my legs, swinging them nervously in hopes that this is the extent of my encounter with the chair.

"Lay *all* the way back, Miss Hollins." Natalie instructs in that sweet voice that officially annoys me now.

I can't help but cast a hesitant look in her direction but ultimately I do as I'm told. The chair feels cold and unnatural. I lay down with my head and neck held at an uncomfortable angle.

"We need to conduct some simple examinations before we take you to the official testing room. Its standard protocol, I assure you," she says narrowing her eyes as she forces a tight smirk. I really don't like her now, she sounds condescending.

The cold metal of the first cuff tightens around my wrist and I instinctively try fleeing. She thwarts my progress with her steady hand slamming into my right shoulder.

"Miss Hollins, I assure you this is all for your safety. It will be done before you know it." Her smile does nothing to ease the pain in my right arm. Each restrictive cuff locks around my limbs.

"Hello Miss Hollins. My name is Dr. Glidden. I'll be completing the medical intake testing."

I try snapping my head to the right where the doctor is standing but I'm stopped by the metal ring thrusting into my temple.

"This will be brief. I'm just going to inject a benign substance into your bloodstream to ensure you respond appropriately and are fit for the demands of the leap test." He pauses momentarily, "You won't feel a thing. In fact, you won't even remember this encounter."

He sinks his needle into my right arm. Icy fluid dances up my veins. The ice is traveling through my body, encompassing me like the green vines covering the walls of the facility.

I try lifting my head one last time but the metal halo stops me. Someone, probably Natalie, places goggles over my eyes. Hands hastily begin attaching sticky pads over the base of my skull and chest.

Total darkness falls as my eyes search the lenses of the goggles seeing windows to utter blackness. Something is wrong. Maybe I'm failing the intake. What if I can't test? What if the medicine kills me? Panic sets in. What if I am stuck in blackness forever? My thoughts are stopped instantly by a loud alarm.

It grows louder and nearly shatters my eardrums. I can't concentrate or hear anything but the alarm and then suddenly a thunderous explosion sounds from the hallway we just passed through. The alarm continues to thunder in full force. I hear a popping noise that's totally foreign to me. Is this part of the test?

The loud speaker sounds a warning, 'Our walls have been breached. I repeat, our walls have been breached.'

What does that mean? The panic is sickening and I throw my body in all directions, trying to free myself from the metal bindings.

"We have to wake her. She's not safe here!" The doctor shouts to Natalie.

They begin frantically pulling the pads from my chest and neck. My head gets released from the halo. A woman releases my right arm and ankle and then my left ankle's freed. I pull the goggles from my face and am immediately blinded by the overhead lights.

Central testers are running in all directions carrying armfuls of papers and computer equipment. Some are destroying their tablets in a giant machine that looks like a meat grinder. It's total chaos when the loud speaker sounds again…

'Total breech. I repeat, total breech. Initiate RAZE protocol.'

"This isn't good." Natalie says as the massive door leading to the circular room begins descending from the ceiling. The door drops painfully slow.

I hear the muffled screams from the approaching intruders. "Quick, throw a frag!" One of them shouts from the corridor.

I don't even have time to wonder what a 'frag' is before the tiny oval ball bounces into the room. It looks non-threatening.

The tiny ball explodes at the entranceway to the dropping door. My ears ring and everything sounds distant from the concussive damage to my eardrums. My throat and lungs fill with smoke. I'm as good as dead if I stay here. I have to get free. I frantically pull at my left cuff.

My fingers shake around the complicated lock. They dance over the levers but I can't control them. Again and again my sweaty fingers hover around the levers but I can't get free.

The popping noise comes closer as two Central testers drop to the floor, and blood spills from their stomachs. It's gunfire and I'm only fifteen-feet from where they just died.

Natalie crawls to the back of my chair, pushing herself off the floor to free my left cuff. Her hands shake as her dark eyes fill with tears. The lever releases just as a bullet buzzes past my left shoulder, landing squarely in her chest. Blood pours from her white shirt. The stark crimson against the white is striking. She gasps once as blood bubbles from her mouth. She died saving my life.

Another intruder points his gun at me. I've got a split second to react. I dodge his bullet, rolling backwards off the table. I have to get out but the exits are surrounded. The room is filling with intruders, foreigners dressed in dirty mismatched clothes with sashes of bullets draped around their chests. They smile as they fire round after round at the defenseless Central testers.

"Take me to the controls!" One of the foreigners yells at Dr. Glidden, pressing the barrel of his gun to the doctor's temple.

Dr. Glidden is sweating like Natalie was but at least he isn't shaking. His eyes dart side to side until he makes eye contact with me. I'm crouched in a concealed position behind the black chair. He jerks his eyes towards the corridor. He's trying to tell me something but I don't know what. I can't take the corridor, it's too dangerous and there's no exit. Then I remember, there was one door, one hundred and eighteen steps away. I could try to make it there. For once I'm actually thankful for my nervous quirk, it might save me. I nod at Dr. Glidden.

"Okay, okay." Dr. Glidden's voice is collected. "You'll need the code first." The foreigner drives his gun hard into the doctor's head. "I can get it for you," Dr. Glidden responds. "You didn't have to kill all these people. You could've just asked. All we had to do was go to the black rock by the river. You would've found what you needed there." He stares straight at me. He's trying to send me a message.

"Don't mess with me!" The foreigner shouts, shaking the doctor by his neck. "You're going to take me to this place."

Dr. Glidden takes one last breath before his scream reaches my ringing ears, "Now!" He shouts.

He raises his right arm so fast that I nearly miss it. He strikes the foreigner against his neck with such force that the foreigner's gun drops to the floor.

The foreigners are preoccupied with Dr. Glidden. He has somehow positioned himself behind the foreigner and is holding the gun to the intruder's head. I stay in my crouched position weaving between the bodies on the floor.

A foreigner cocks his weapon as I jump the jagged floor where the frag exploded. A loud bang thunders from behind me. I look over my shoulder as Dr. Glidden drops to the floor, blood trickling from his forehead.

I keep running through the tunnel as fast as I can, counting as I sprint. The tunnel is in absolute darkness and I have to keep track of how far I've come. My running strides must be twice the length of my steps. At stride fifty I slow.

My hands trace along the cold wall to my right. It has to be here, I know it. Back and forth my hands sweep for the door. I'm stepping forward and backwards pacing like a caged animal trying to locate the seam of the small door when I hear muffled voices shouting from the circular room.

The foreigners employ an enormous light with its blinding rays casting down the tunnel, landing less than five-feet away. I press my chest against the cool wall hoping I won't be seen. The light comes closer as I hear their steps descending the tunnel.

I look to my right just in time to see the door frame illuminated inches from my fingers. I have to expose myself and try for the door.

I lunge my body sideways pushing into the door. It holds steady but on my second thrust it bursts open. I stumble into daylight. Stacks of smoking pillars rise from the walls surrounding me. Bombs rain down from the sky, bursting the walls into cascading jagged pieces.

"Over there!" One of the foreigners shouts from the tunnel.

They saw me; I have no choice but to run. My attempts will be futile; I'm a prisoner inside these walls but I have to fight.

The door slams with such force that the brown soil jolts outside. The blue-sky overhead is mixed with curling grey smoke that travels like the rivers that cut through our sector. The grey smoke dances along the blue canvas and somehow looks beautiful, like it's taken on a life of its own.

The winding stacks are suddenly blocked by a massive shadow. The hovercraft appears swiftly and eclipses my view, thrusting me into darkness. It's just like it was three years ago during the massacre. It's the same black hovercraft I saw in my vision days before the foreigners used it to bomb our sector.

My eyes dance the length of the craft looking for the symbol I saw during my vision, but this craft is void of it. A loud clanking sound like metal striking metal comes from its base. I see the craft expel the barrel of an enormous gun. My heart constricts in terror as the gun slowly rotates towards me.

I hold my position with my feet planted to the ground; the foreigners will be breeching the door any second now. My back's bracing the door as I scan the wooded landscape to take inventory of my surroundings. Three hundred feet stand between me and the protection of the tree line. The area between the tree line and me means certain death. To my left sprawls a mountainous hill with sporadic wilted trees and jagged ledges, terrible terrain for concealment. The center bares thick forest that would be excellent camouflage but the dense woods would be unbreakable, they'd track me down and kill me in no time.

The gun keeps winding its way counter clockwise. It's a quarter turn from setting its sights squarely on me. I keep bracing my shaking back to the door as the foreigners drive at it from inside the tunnel. My feet slip marginally but I hold steady, waiting for the right moment.

I steal one last look to the right. The landscape slopes downward but at the edge of my peripheral vision I see an animal trail breaking its way through the dense woods. I hold my position and focus.

My actions have to be perfect, anything less will mean death. The gun makes its last adjustment, positioning itself directly at my chest. This is it. I release my feet from the ground, pivoting my body to the right. I spin away from the door just as the foreigners slam into it a second time. Without my body bracing the exit, it flies open. I'm shielded by twelve-inches of steel door. Thunder storms from the barrel of the craft and the foreigners are met head on with raining gunfire that was meant for me.

Their screams are wild as sick gurgling noises escape them. Their bodies drop to the ground plagued with bullet holes. Three hundred feet stand between me and the chance of survival. I hear the clicking of the gun as it refocuses its sights.

I have less than a second to act. I dig my feet hard into the ground, sprinting full force toward the animal trail. Thunderous popping echoes from the gun. I run in and out of its path.

Bullets fly by so close that I actually feel the heat against my skin. I weave my path in an unpredictable manner attempting to avoid the bullets. The ground bursts all around me as bullets strike the dirt.

Only one hundred and fifty feet left. I'm halfway there, I just might make it. I veer to the left and unfathomable pain takes hold. Deep searing pain radiates through my left thigh. Hot blood pours down my leg. My instincts tell me to run but the pain threatens to destroy me. I've been hit.

I stumble once, on my way down I see images of Emma perched on the bed as I braid her hair and Garrett splashing in the waters of our secret hideaway. They give me strength. I have to fight, I have to live. The blood's steady but my body is strong and I keep driving myself forward.

Twenty feet until the trees. Rocks and dirt fly around my face. Fifteen feet, ten feet, five feet until safety. I run and limp and scream but finally I'm there.

The animal trail is well worn. I use the path to my advantage. I need to put distance between the foreigners and me but I also need to stop the bleeding.

My fingers tear at the sleeve of my shirt as I sprint down the trail. I fist the fabric in my shaking hand, ripping it off.

I need more time but I can already hear more foreigners running after me. I stop to tie the sleeve around my thigh. I'll die if I lose too much blood. I continue weaving down the path with my shirt secured around my throbbing leg.

My eyes catch sight of a flattened grass bed and I leap from the trail onto the trampled blades. I take the largest leaps my injured leg can manage, carrying myself off the trail. I hear heavy steps of at least two foreigners in close pursuit.

My mind races in search of my next move. I can't hide. I'm bleeding out slowly and won't last a night in my condition. They have guns and I'm wounded. I need to get to water and it hits me that Dr. Glidden knew I'd make it outside and need direction.

He'd said something about a black rock by a river. My stomach jolts as bile rises to my mouth. I replay the last image of him crumbling to the floor with blood running from his head. I can't think of that now. Weakness, even if momentary could cost me my life.

Years of skills training tells me I need to stay close to the animal path, it's my best hope at finding water. I head back toward the trail, following its winding course downhill. The pain in my leg is numbing and the world around me is framed in a hazy light.

The blood loss is affecting my mind and I'm near fainting. I can't stop moving, instead I bear down on my stomach attempting to raise my blood pressure. I need to keep the blood flowing to my brain, the hazy frame maintains but at least it's stopped inching its way inward.

The trees and grass become greener the farther I run and I know water must be near. I brace myself on the trunks of the massive trees and stumble straight over the small saplings. I've become sloppy in my desperation for the black rock. The foreigners are on my heels. I hear them snapping trees as their steps close-in. I draw upon the last of my strength to push forward.

The world hazes and then I hit the cold water. The wetness constricts my vessels and shoots blood to my fading brain. For a moment I have clarity. I frantically search for the rock.

One hundred feet ahead I spot the gigantic black boulder that sits completely alien to this landscape. I crash through the water, crossing the embankment just as the first foreigner breaks the tree line. He doesn't hesitate as he shoulders his gun and opens fire.

Bullets splash water to the shoreline wetting my arms as I sprint. The bullets hit closer and closer as I run. One grazes my shoulder just as I reach the backside of the massive rock. Tucked beneath its ledge is my hope, a bow with two arrows.

"Over there!" The foreigner shouts to the other.

Immediate waves of gunfire rain down, it's now or never. I grab the bow and swiftly fasten the first arrow. Gunfire is closing in from the right much faster than the foreigner on my left. I roll to the right and aim. My arrow flies through the air, striking the foreigner straight in the chest.

It's only a fraction of a second but in that moment I see the life leave his eyes. I realize the gravity of what I've done. I just killed a man. I killed someone's son, maybe someone's father.

The gunfire to my left closes in and snaps me back to reality. I string the second arrow. I have a clear shot but I can't take it. I won't take another life even if it means dying.

Suddenly a veil of absolute darkness falls over me and my body feels like it is plunged into an icy bath. My ears strain to hear but I no longer perceive the sound of gunshots from the foreigners.

The darkness continues to blind me but my ears begin distinguishing a slow and steady beeping. The sound reminds me of a medical alarm, nothing I'd expect to hear in the wilderness. The alarm grows faster in parallel with my pounding heart.

"She's waking up. We have five minutes before she'll be coherent." I hear Dr. Glidden's muffled voice.

"Her results are quite interesting." Natalie says sweetly.

The alarm accelerates in conjunction with my growing confusion. They're supposed to be dead, I saw them die.

"She made it to the black rock and even eliminated the first assailant, but it appears she chose death over killing the second attacker." Natalie pauses, "It's quite unique."

"Is that so?" Dr. Glidden asks, sounding halfway intrigued.

"Oh yes. Only sixteen percent of testers make it out of the facility and of that sixteen percent, less than one percent make it to the river. Let alone to the black rock." She pauses adding a dramatic effect, "The elite few that make it there *always* kill both assailants." Her voice fills with excitement.

"Well it's in the designer's hands to interpret the meaning. Our job is to wake her and put her through the dummy test." Dr. Glidden no longer sounds interested, he is formal and direct again.

The darkness is beginning to take on a hazed quality as the minutes carry on.

"Let's get her to the dummy room before she wakes." Dr. Glidden barks.

Hands reach and pull at the pads stuck to my chest and head. I'm so confused by what is happening. My body wheels across the concrete floor as I feel the heat from multiple hands pushing the giant chair out of the oval room.

"Less than one minute until eyes open!" Dr. Glidden shouts. My chair turns abruptly about face. My body is set free from the shackles holding me down. "Thirty seconds people!" Dr. Glidden booms.

Someone pulls the goggles off my eyes just before draping my limp legs off the corner of the chair. In that exact moment my body is released, I'm awake.

"There, there, Miss Hollins. Everything's alright now," Natalie coos to me as she grazes my back with her hand.

"What happened?" I look to both her and Dr. Glidden.

"Miss Hollins, I'm Dr. Glidden. You had a syncope episode, nothing to worry about. It happens to many testers." He flashes a smile to Natalie before turning his attention back to me. "What is the last thing you recall before you passed out?"

I almost reveal that I remember everything. The corridor, the icy drug dancing in my veins, watching them both die, but I stop myself. I'm not supposed to remember. Even Dr. Glidden had said I wouldn't remember our meeting.

"I remember the shuttle ride over here and that's all, sir." I try forcing confidence behind my words.

"It's quite normal Miss Hollins. Not to worry. You've been cleared to test and I'm sure you will do quite well." He says as his strong arm guides me off the chair.

I'm in a completely different room than before. No more screens or tablets, no more Centrals dashing around in white coats. It's a bright, cheerful room that in no way resembles the sterile oval room from earlier.

Natalie takes me by my elbow, guiding me from the room into a large open arena. To my left I see weapons and trapping materials laid across a long brown table. To my right are stationary and moving targets located throughout the expansive room.

"Miss Hollins, you have a list of skills you must complete and then you'll be free to leave." Natalie says, handing me a sheet of paper.

My hands tremble momentarily. I grab the paper from Natalie, but my mind is still in the other room. Why did I remember everything? Does everyone remember but nobody says anything? A part of me already knows the answer. I know that I am different.

I have to construct a snare, use a bow and a spear to hit three moving and stationary targets and then finally, start a fire. This test can't be serious. I'm angry that I prepared my entire life for these stupid tasks and then I remember, this is a dummy test.

I already had my test in the next room over. The one where the foreigners attacked me and I was in the elite few to make it to the black rock.

I smile sweetly at Natalie, striding over to the bow and arrow. I rapidly fire and hit every target squarely. In total my dummy test takes less than an hour. I've done everything perfectly but that doesn't matter. What matters is how I did inside the oval room and even Natalie said it was unique, but unique isn't always good.

Chapter 18: Nessa

My mind races a hundred miles an hour. I went into today's test light hearted after my night with Garrett. Now I'm leaving confused and anxious. I don't understand how I'm so different from the other testers. I made it to the black rock and even Natalie said only the elite made it there. But unlike the others, I sacrificed myself.

There's something different about me, I'm certain now. I have spent my entire life keeping my visions a secret because I was afraid it would prove I wasn't normal. Now I have proof. I remember my entire leap test despite the serum Dr. Glidden injected. It's clear that I'm different.

The cool leather seats of the shuttle do nothing to absorb the nervous sweat I've broken into. My legs stick to the seat. My forehead flecks with salty drops. Words like 'abnormal' and 'unique' dance through my head, carrying with them a harsh undertone.

The hour-long shuttle ride feels like an eternity. The closer I get to my sub the faster my heart pounds and my stomach spirals. I know Emma and Garrett will ask how it went today. The thought of having to answer makes me sick. The shuttle glides to a smooth halt at my sub and I slowly peel my sticky skin from the seat.

When I step outside the colors look muted compared to when I left this morning. I force my way home, stumbling over rocks and dirt that feel thicker than ever before. I round the corner and see our blue door. I have to lie to them. I can't bear telling them that I may have failed and even if I could, I can't explain why.

My hand hovers over the doorknob for minutes before I gain my composure. Painting a smile across my face I open it. The shouts of Emma, Garrett, and Papa all mingle in a splitting tone.

"Surprise!" They all shout.

I hadn't expected to face them all at once and I'm actually shocked. Emma's the first to move as she dashes across the room, folding herself around my waist.

"Happy birthday Nessa! How was it? How does it feel to be an adult?" She beams at me.

"What's going on here?" I ask forcing a smile.

"We thought you could use a little celebration. It's not every day you become an adult." Papa says as he pulls me into his arms.

Garrett stands across the room smiling at me. His eyes look through me, penetrating me.

"Before you ask a million questions, let me start by saying I don't remember much. The parts I do remember I did really well on though."

"No one doubts that honey." Papa says, clasping his hand against my shoulder.

"Can I get a hug from the birthday girl, I mean woman?" Garrett jokes.

Papa and Emma step clear and let my handsome man stride toward me. He wraps his strong arms around me and I instantly feel a mixture of electricity and guilt surge through my veins.

I'll never reveal my secrets to him. No matter what Gwen says, I don't think he would understand. I wouldn't want my perfect Garrett in a position to judge me anyways.

He whispers in my ear, "You look beautiful."

I automatically blush even before he releases me from his arms. I wanted him to hold me for hours and tell me everything's fine but I let his hands fall. I don't want Papa or Emma thinking there is something between us. I'm not ready to reveal that yet.

Garrets deep voice focuses me, "We got you a present."

He turns, walking into the sleeping quarters. I can't even see his face when he steps back into the room; the bouquet of flowers completely eclipses him. This is a gift from him; they're the same colors from when we were kids.

"They're perfect" I say.

Emma and Papa smile. I'm nervous they can read my mind and my cheeks flush at the thought. I turn my eyes to each of them.

"I'm so happy you all were here." Papa nods and clasps Emma's shoulders before he talks.

"You could probably do with some rest. We're heading to third line. Just make sure you come before curfew, they stop serving at dusk." He guides Emma out the door leaving Garrett and I alone.

Before the door has even closed I feel Garrett's chest against my back. His arms are tender as he squeezes my shoulders, releasing all my tension. He caresses my neck in long steady strokes as I instinctively tilt my head to the side. He wastes no time, his warm tongue traces circles along my exposed skin.

Reaching my hands behind me, I find his arms, pulling them around my waist. His hands run up and down my stomach. Our bodies grow hot as I'm pressed between Garrett and the door. I lean forward, trying to press my hips into his. My head snaps as he turns me around to face him, my backs pinned to the door as his lips find mine. He grabs my leg, lifting it effortlessly as he wraps it around his thigh and pushes himself against me. My body feels like it's set on fire. He moves against me as my leg pulls his hips closer. We hold our positions, swaying our hips to meet each other. With each contact my breathing becomes deeper and my body burns more. He drives his hips hard against mine. I focus on his body as I let my veins rush and my head spin.

"We should stop before we go too far." Did I just say that? I chastise myself. "I'm sorry, I don't know why I said that!" I'm furious with myself.

He pulls his hips away. "Don't apologize. I plan on being with you for a long time. We can do things your way." He smiles, "You're the boss."

I laugh at that thought before wrapping my arms around his neck.

Without warning a jolt grinds in my stomach. I can't imagine living without him and it hits me that it could happen. This is why I fought my feelings for so long. Central could separate us after tomorrow, and there is nothing I can do about it.

He pulls me from the door, leading me across the room. I push him into the chair before folding myself in his arms.

He whispers in my ear, "I missed you today. I couldn't stop thinking about you." He pauses, "That's part of the reason I came over tonight."

"What's the other part?"

"I wanted to talk to you, see if you thought the test was as big of a joke as I did."

He laughs as my eyes dart side-to-side like I'm waiting for a regulator to materialize out of thin air.

He speaks again, "I mean it was just some silly target practice and a few skills. Wasn't it the same for you?"

I hesitate, trying to find the right answer. "Yeah, pretty much. I don't know how they can score on that alone." I force a smile feeling horrible for keeping the truth from him.

"What do you think the chances are we leave together?" He squeezes my ribs while he talks. "I'm not going anywhere without you, you should know that." He relaxes his grip slightly, his brown eyes pierce mine. "I won't go unless you go."

"Don't worry Garrett. We'll either go together or stay together."

I try convincing him of my sincerity but my conscious says otherwise. Natalie said I was unique but it didn't sound like unique was necessarily an admirable quality. I have been with Garrett long enough to know he'd be in the elite few to make it to the black rock, but he wouldn't hesitate to kill the foreigners. He'll be offered the leap for sure.

He lifts me off his lap. His hands run through my hair while he talks, "It's getting late, I should head home. Plus, you need to eat." I smile, trying to hide my anxiety.

"I'll see you at the banquet tomorrow" I say pulling my hair from under his hands.

He flashes his crooked smile. "I'll wait for you out front, we can go in together. We get to start the rest of our lives together tomorrow."

With his final words I let him collect my body in his electric embrace, kissing me one last time.

I fall into the sitting room chair sinking my head against my folded arms. I don't want to eat tonight. The thought of food makes me nauseous. I get ready for bed, falling into a deep and restless sleep.

Chapter 19: Nessa

It's hours before first light and I'm wide awake. I spent last night thrashing in bed. Again and again my dreams threw me back to the black rock. Over and over I sacrificed myself.

I creep out of bed, hastily pulling on my winter greens. It's my first day wearing them and I'm reminded that I'm an adult now. My life's forever changed. I stand in the corner of the room pulling at the hem of my jacket. I want the fabric to tear, to turn blue, grey, or any color but green.

Why do I have to wear this color anyway and who decides such things? Suddenly I am furious that I've spent the last seventeen years being labeled, organized, and contained by a faceless place. This all-knowing, all-powerful entity called Central has dictated almost every move I've ever made. It seems hardly fair that today these same people will tell me where I can live, what labor role I'll pursue, and possibly separate me and Garrett.

Emma's small body tosses in bed forcing me to run from the room. I don't want her seeing me broken and weak. I hit our walkway, the winds cut straight to my chest. My tears are like ice traveling down my cool cheeks as I run.

I make my way through sub-three crossing into sub-two. I cross Grove Street and leap across the fallen log. Even in total darkness my body knows every turn, rock, and tree along the route.

Bouncing from rock to rock I clear the tree line. Daylight is nearly breaking as I rush to the oak tree. My shaking hands grasp at the winding branches as I hoist myself higher and higher toward the sky.

I keep reaching and pulling skyward until I'm at the highest peak. The sky breaks with pink and orange rays reaching their threads in all directions. I sit at the highest peak and cry. I cry because I'm angry, I cry because I'm scared, and I cry because it's so beautiful.

How is it that I'm considered an adult yet this is the first sunrise I've ever been allowed to see outside my own home? It isn't fair.

I sit in the branches for hours. I can't pinpoint one exact thing that consumes my mind. My head is bounding too fast with memories being played in a circular reel.

The sun is breaking the peaks of the hills to my east when I resolve to go home. I've got the banquet tonight and hours of preparation ahead of me.

I lower myself from branch to branch until my feet touch the frosted ground. Collecting myself on the run back, I enter our empty house.

I draw a bath, lowering myself into the water to soak. I let the water wrap itself around my body; filling all my spaces with a gentle warmth. It's comforting and pure as I lay with my eyes closed, letting myself drift away.

Deeper and deeper I drift until suddenly my head's thrust under water. Hands grip around my throat. I thrash, clawing the assailants arms.

My vision is blurred by several inches of water but through them I see a white uniform and Natalie's beautifully wicked face. My legs twist and turn until at last I kick the base of the tub. My head crashes, knocking me unconscious. Her hands release from my collapsing throat and I awake. The bath has long turned cold and my head drapes over the side.

It felt so real but I immediately orient myself, realizing it was just a nightmare, or maybe a warning. With my heart pounding I scrub myself from head to toe, rinsing the foaming soap from my waterlogged skin.

My hands shake as I reach for my towel. I hardly manage wrapping my fingers around the rough fabric as I draw it over the length of my body.

In the pre-divide women wore makeup on their faces to accentuate their features and clothing of all styles. In the post-divide such clothing and grooming is permitted for leap night only. I've got thirty minutes to dress and make it to the pavilion for preparation.

All leap participants from my sub will meet at the pavilion by twelve to be transformed. I pile my soaking hair on top of my head and sprint towards the pavilion.

I immediately recognize some of the other leap testers from my grade as I round the corner to the pavilion. There is already a line forming like a snake winding through the grass.

Dozens of girls wait for their time with one of the two beauticians. I fall in line behind waist length flowing blonde hair belonging to Aria. She's the most stunning girl in our year. She's almost as tall as me but her body's more feminine and full of curves that I just barely have. Aria's smart, probably the top in our class academically. She has a fierce way about her during skills training but I've always out performed her there.

She shifts her weight slightly; her perfect figure sways in a seductive way. My heart constricts with an instant pang of jealousy. I always thought Garrett would end up with someone like her, someone that could match his good looks. I hear a shout from behind me; her raspy voice is nearly a shrill.

"Nessa!" I instantly know who it is from her tones.

She runs to me, sliding to a stop just inches away. She wraps me in her warm arms. All I can hear is her heavy breathing.

"Gwen!"

"How was your training time?" She asks, smiling her devious smile.

"It was good. Helpful." I pause. "It was great having Garrett to train with."

"How *is* Garrett?" She asks.

For years she's insisted that Garrett and I were 'destined for each other.' I used to laugh, but not anymore.

"Good. *Really* good," I say it with as much mischief as my voice can handle. I can't help noticing that Aria's perked up. I've always maintained she had a thing for him and she's confirming my suspicions now. "Actually, technically, *we're* really good."

"Oh my God! Are you serious? I totally called it!" Gwen pushes me backwards.

"Let's not talk about that now. How've you been, how's limbo?" I ask.

Gwen was born in February so she's been shadowing the different jobs in our sector for ten months now.

"Unbearably boring. The shadowing was awful." She rolls her eyes. "Not all of it of course, but most of the jobs were totally miserable." She laughs like she's recalling particulars.

"Did you have any favorites?" I ask.

"Well, naturally I liked the planner position. You know me. It just fit with my personality. Organizing the layout of the homes and businesses and things like that."

I nod, she would be perfect for that position.

"I'm a little jealous you were in limbo. I feel like I'm going into this whole leap cold." I say just before a hand squeezes my shoulder.

"You're next." The man from Central looks perturbed as he speaks.

"Yes sir, sorry." I stare at the ground, walking to the beautician's chair.

My beautician is one of the prettiest men I've ever seen. His brown hair falls in perfect lines just above his eyes. His teeth are bleached white and everything about him is immaculate. His nails are trimmed and shining and I instantly recoil my hands into my lap, embarrassed he'll compare his to mine. His voice is smooth and warm.

"Hello Miss…"

"Miss Hollins. Vanessa Hollins. You can call me Nessa."

"Hello, Nessa. I'm Uri. I'll be transforming you into a more beautiful version of yourself tonight. Are you ready?"

I hesitate, am I ready?

"Yes," I finally answer.

Uri guides me into the silver chair, draping me in a long plastic cloth. He hums to himself as he brushes through my knotted hair. He gets his comb mired in my tangled mane twice.

"May I make a braid Miss Nessa?" He asks and I instantly nod yes.

I'd hoped he'd braid it. For some reason a braid makes me comfortable. Uri expertly twists and threads my strands into a weaved pattern unlike anything I've ever tried. I'm good at styling Emma's hair but that is nothing compared to this. Uri's an artist.

My chair rotates ninety degrees so my back is to the mirror. My eyes travel to meet Uri's. He stands with one arm across his abdomen and the other hand cradling his chin. He's in deep thought as his eyes travel the features of my face. His bottom jaw sways side to side. He's devising his next plan of attack and I sit awkwardly under his scrutinizing eyes.

"Fear not Miss Nessa. I've got a plan for you." Uri snaps his fingers, reaching for a massive pallet of colors. He bends down, grabbing a large brush and begins winding it between several shades. I automatically withdraw as he comes at me with the black bristles. "This won't hurt. I promise."

I relax and hesitantly let him proceed. The brush is soft and actually feels good against my skin. He winds his brush, gathering more colors as he expertly sweeps my face. He changes brushes several times and ends with the small one over my eyelids. My face is tingling from the bristles. Just when I think he's done I see him pumping one last wand in and out of a black tube.

"Look up to the sky and keep looking up." I do as I'm told. The black wand comes dangerously close to my eyeball, I clamp my eyes closed. "Keep looking up please."

I try again. With all the effort I can manage I keep my eyes looking upward. Stroke after uncomfortable stroke brushes my eyelashes. Uri steps back with a beaming smile.

"You are a masterpiece, if I may say so myself." He rotates the chair to reveal the new me. I gasp, I can't believe what he's done. I don't even look like the same person. I launch myself out of the chair and stand so close to the mirror that it fogs from my breath.

My hair is weaved and knotted in the most ornate and intricate way and my face glows in a golden hue that compliments my pink and gold cheeks. My eyes are dark, like smoke charred them and my lips are crimson red.

I never knew I could look so stunning; I'd do anything to have mama here. To have her see me this way.

I turn to Uri, "This is amazing. I can't believe it." I stare at him. "Thank you. Thank you so much."

He nods, directing me to leave his station.

The girls on the other side of the mirror have all been transformed but none of them, not even Aria, looks as beautiful as me. I'm still dancing on cloud nine when I'm snapped back to reality by another shoulder squeeze.

"I'm sorry sir." I feel like a fool.

That's the second time he's had to direct me and he must be thinking I'm challenged. I follow his directions and approach the expansive rack where hundreds of dresses hang, all of them covered in plastic.

One of the Central designers greets me, "I'm Tiffany, I'll be selecting your wardrobe. Stand still while I take some measurements."

Tiffany's slender hands reach around my body as she measures my hips, waist, and breasts. She's quick and serious.

Her fingers punch my measurements into her handheld tablet. Once she presses 'enter' the rack of dresses flies to the left.

Dress after dress passes until at last the rack stops. She pulls three dresses from the metal bar, hanging them outside the dressing room. The back of her head darts side to side as she mentally dresses me in each option.

Her manicured hand reaches to select the middle dress. She throws something into the bag and shoves the hanger into my hands. "No need to try it on here. It will fit and it's the best for your body." I grab my dress and leave the pavilion. In all, preparation took three hours. That leaves an hour to get home and dress before Papa and I take the shuttle to the banquet.

I steal some downward glances at my lace dress as I jog back to the house. The fabric is rich, like something from the past. She selected the darkest green allowed. Much darker than our standard issued greens. I press the fabric between my fingers, swaying them back and forth. I imagine a time when wearing such things was commonplace.

I'm three-quarters of the way home when I feel the first bead of sweat breaking my brow line. I stop in my tracks, dabbing the moisture away. It would be criminal to ruin Uri's work.

I walk the rest of the way home, arriving with just enough time to dress. Emma's hands are flying in all directions as soon as she sees me come through the door, "Oh, Nessa!" She's stunned. I have to admit I was stunned the first time I saw myself in the mirror today too. "You look gorgeous!" She shrieks.

I smile hugging her, "I have to dress, Papa will be home soon." I hang my dress in the bathroom. "I wish you could come tonight." I grin at her. "At least I'll be able to see you on your banquet night. If you think I look gorgeous, that means we'll be speechless for your transformation."

Emma grins wildly, and then suddenly her smile drops. "Don't say things you can't know for sure." Her mood shifts completely. "You're smart Nessa. You could make the leap tonight." She swallows so hard it's like she's trying to gulp an apple whole. "If you leap, you won't come back. You can't ever come back."

"I did fine on my test, but don't worry about me making the leap. I didn't test in the top. Even if I did, I'd find a way to see you. I promise." I squeeze her small body close to my chest. "Can you help me put this confusing thing on?" She releases me, taking a massive inhale before nodding her head yes.

We slide the dress over my head; I practically have to dive into the thing. Emma pulls it down over my hips, tugging at the bottom hem. With each tug the wrinkles smooth out and soon I'm standing in a dress that looks like it's been painted onto me. My chest looks a little bigger and my sides dip in at the middle. This is what Aria must feel like every day I think. Emma's once again in awe.

"Nessa, you look perfect. Absolutely perfect" she says.

Now I wish I'd insisted on trying the dress on at the pavilion. I have no way of seeing the final effect here. Emma helps me slide into the shoes Tiffany threw into the bag. They're nothing like shoes I have ever seen before. They are shiny with bits of lace matching my dress.

The heels are intimidating to say the least. It looks like I'm trying to balance on three-inch stilts. Squeezing my feet into them, I immediately wobble. "I can't do this." I moan as I try walking the length of our house. I sway as my ankles roll like I'm a newborn doe. "I'm just going to wear my sneakers there. I'll change at the banquet."

Emma looks disgusted. I can see why, sneakers don't exactly match my ensemble but if I'm planning on getting there without a broken ankle it's my only option. She helps me into my sneakers. As the second one slides on Papa walks through the door.

"Wow," he says sounding shocked. His eyes lock with mine. He's smiling like an idiot as his eyes travel to my feet. "I shouldn't have expected anything less," he says shaking his head. "Honestly though, you look so much like your mother."

A pit fills my stomach. I've always wanted to be compared to her and today of all days I finally get what I've been waiting for.

"Let me get changed, I'll be quick," he says rushing into his room. His closet clatters as he shuffles around in it. He's out in no time looking handsome in his dress greens. It's time to leave and I stoop to be level with Emma.

"Remember what I said Emma. I will be home later and I promise to be there on your day."

I carry my stilted shoes as Papa and I rush toward the shuttle. Stepping onboard I can't help but stare at the other leap testers. I know most of them by name but we all look so different transformed for the banquet. I can't help but squirm, realizing I'm the only one wearing sneakers.

The shuttle is packed but it's nearly silent. A few of the parents are exchanging niceties but the rest of us are too nervous to talk.

I can't help but fantasize that Garrett and I will be top boy and girl. We'll move to Central and start our lives together in the greatest sector of our nation. We'll get a beautiful home, go to work every day, and come home to eat together. I wonder if they have to eat in a pavilion with all their neighbors. I bet they don't, I bet they get their meals delivered and they can eat as a family every night.

My daydream is in full effect when the shuttle slides to a stop at the banquet hall. Our parents have been here before but it's our first time. The others file out of the shuttle. I purposely exit last. I need extra time to slide into my ankle-breaking shoes. Taking one final breath of air I stumble off the shuttle. Papa threads his arm around mine, steadying me.

"Thanks, papa."

We follow the herd of people walking toward the expansive entrance to the hall. The building is colossal and enclosed by wrought iron gates that are adorned with intricate metal décor. Enormous marble pillars brace the façade. Dozens of torches light both sides of the walkway. The front lawn is symmetrical with a massive oak tree on each side.

We make our way to the entrance and are just about to reach the wooden doors when I feel the electric touch of Garret's hand squeezing mine. I tug Papa toward Garrett. It takes no time for him to put the pieces together.

"I'll wait inside," he says.

I let go of his arm. "I won't be long," I say to Papa over my shoulder.

I turn to Garrett, he's unbelievably sexy tonight. They somehow managed to make him look even better than he already does. His hair is styled with strands falling in perfect sections. His face is clean shaven and looks bright and fresh. All of that is great but what seals the deal is how his body looks in those clothes. He's dressed in charcoal pants and a fitted green button-up shirt. The long sleeves are tailored to hug his powerful body, his muscles press to the fabric.

"Nessa I'm speechless," he says twirling me in a circle. I nudge him, "I'm serious, you look amazing. You always look great, but this is different," he grins.

"You look pretty great yourself."

He inhales as he rolls his eyes towards the back of his head. "I don't know what I'd do without you." He says pulling me toward him.

"Stop it, you'd be just fine," I say falling into his chest.

"I'm serious Nessa, you're all I think about. I wanted to talk to you before tonight." He swallows, "I think you can make the leap, I really do. I'll be lost without you but if you get the chance to leap, you have to take it. With or without me."

"Garrett, stop." I'm furious and dejected at the same time. I grab his chin, cradling his strong jaw in my hands. "I'm not leaping without you, I promise."

He pulls me into his arms and kisses me until my knees weaken, he releases me, "We need to go inside. Meet me at our hill tonight?" He asks.

"Of course."

"I love you Nessa."

I smile back but I'm still unable to say those words. Instead I squeeze his hand as we push the heavy doors open.

Just like the first day of education I stop in my tracks. I've never seen a place as glorious as this. Dozens of chandeliers hang casting a soft and warm hue. There are at least a hundred tables sitting ten at each with blue linens covering them. Grey cloth napkins are placed across the white plates. How fitting, they tied our colors into the décor.

I scan my card and a hologram of the banquet hall appears. There's a blinking red dot over the table I'm assigned to. I wait while Garret gets his assignment; naturally we're at opposite ends of the hall. I smile at him, squeezing his hand just before he releases it.

Without him I feel vulnerable, it's like all eyes are on me. Slowly I descend the stairs. I'll break my neck if I go too fast in these shoes. My ankles wobble and my feet throb as I take step after step toward my table. Papa sees me and rises to save me. He steadies me, guiding me into my seat.

"Nessa? Is that you?" I hear the nasally voice of my classmate.

"Hi Vivian. Yes, it's me." My annoyance is obvious. Of course she knows it's me, she's just being obnoxious.

"Well I would never have guessed! You look gorgeous."

I'm beginning to wonder what I look like every other day of my life. I know Uri worked me over but the way she talks it's like I had a total body transplant. I smile weakly in an attempt to hide my frustration.

"Thanks, you too."

I only have to endure a few minutes of Vivian's back-handed compliments before music blares and the Central banquet master strides onstage. "Ladies and gentlemen, and most importantly, testers... I'd like to welcome you to the ninety-eighth leap banquet!" He pauses, allowing a round of applause. I feel a kick to my stomach, accompanied by a jolt of nerves and excitement. This is the night I've been waiting for. Right here, right now. It is the beginning of the rest of my life.

"As you know, your entire life has been dedicated to the leap test, and tonight your results *and* fate will be revealed. This is without a doubt the culmination, the absolute pinnacle of your lives thus far. Tonight one young man and woman from your sector will make the leap into Central where their opportunities are endless. For the rest of you, your labor roles, housing, and potential mates will be revealed. Tonight truly is a night you will never forget."

My table is near the stage. For those in the back like Garrett, the banquet master is being projected on an enormous screen positioned behind the podium. He's a short man, probably smaller than me. I focus on his brown eyes and black hair shining from the screen. I can even make out his crooked teeth. His voice booms over the speaker system. I can't help but fixate on the small beads of sweat forming along his brow. They're driving me crazy. I wish he'd just wipe them away...

"But before we reveal your results we first must dine!" The parents clap while the rest of us are shocked and totally crushed. I'm not the only one who wanted to get the results out of the way. Almost immediately after his speech a warm body hovers over my shoulders. Staff is serving my first course and filling my water to the brim. Any other night I'd think the food looked divine. The salad wasn't the bland one like at the pavilion; this one has berries, apples, and cheeses over the top. I can only manage three bites.

"Do you mind?" Papa asks pointing at my barely touched greens.

"Be my guest," I answer.

"I remember my banquet. I didn't eat a thing, I was too nervous. I've been waiting all these years to have a second chance. I don't make the same mistake twice, you know." He smiles between forks full of lettuce.

The second course looks less appealing than the first. The server called them escargot, or something like that. Papa forces me to try one but the saltiness makes me gag on the spot. Vivian manages to eat two before her stomach turns on her. Once again, Papa devours both of our servings.

The final course is a stuffed chicken with some sort of cheese in the middle. It's so fragrant and tender; my knife cuts right through without effort. One bite is all I can manage. I don't even make Papa ask before I automatically slide it over to him and listen to him chew through the tender meat.

As soon as the servers clear our plates I realize my mistake. I may never get a meal like this again. I lean back in my chair, folding my arms across my chest. It's a sign of my dissatisfaction and frustration. Scanning around I see that almost all the testers are dejected. Probably reaching the same epiphany I just did seconds ago. We don't have much time to wallow in our self-pity before the banquet master's marching back onstage. His white and black suit shimmers in the candlelight.

"Ladies and Gentleman, I trust you've had a spectacular meal. Let's give a round of applause to your staff this evening." We all clap, keeping it brief. "We're almost to the moment you've all been waiting for, but before we reveal the future, let's take a look at the past."

He's got to be kidding me. I crash my back into the chair sighing in frustration. Everyone within a table's length stares at me. I flash a phony smile returning to my composed self. We are forced to watch a fifteen-minute film of our nation's history.

Explosions and fire open the scene. People from decades ago are burning flags and money as riots flash on screen. We see the construction of our fortified walls and Central patrols from decades ago arming them. They flash to the Outer sector with their fishing and mining communities, and then onto ours with the factory workers and hunters. Finally the screen flashes to Central. I've never seen Central before, not even in pictures and yet here it is in color, right in front of me. Marble structures with intricate gardens and homes bigger than an entire division flash on screen. It turns to images of men and women in laboratory coats standing over microscopes, while others in suits walk into what must be the capital. Central is perfect and beautiful. It's only on screen for a minute but I know it's where I belong. The film powers down and the banquet master begins again.

"Now that we've taken a trip through the past, let's reveal what lies in your future." I sit at full attention, alert and ready to hear. "It's customary to invite the top two girls and boys from your year on stage. The highest ranked from each pair will have the opportunity to make the leap into Central, or, should they choose they can remain here in the Inner thus sending the second place citizen in their place."

The crowd laughs.

"I agree ladies and gentlemen, it's *highly* unlikely." In all the years of the leap, not once has it been passed onto the second place citizen.

"The top two girls from the Inner sector shall be announced first." I'm on the edge of my seat with the escargot sitting heavy in my throat. Papa places his hand on mine; I hadn't realized it was trembling until he steadied it.

The banquet master opens the gold card holding the first name. "Miss Aria Goodall!" I hear her gasp all the way across the hall. I knew she'd be in the top. The crowd claps and some politely cheer as she makes her way toward the stage. I enviously watch as she gracefully weaves between the tables, reaching out and shaking hands as she goes. Tears threaten her eyes.

The banquet master lifts his hand signaling silence. He brings the microphone up to his mouth and I rock in anticipation. "The next candidate is..." His hands dance along the gold envelope as he pulls it open. "Miss Vanessa Hollins!"

My head clouds and I see blackness; I'm too stunned to move. Papa lifts me by my arm. Unlike Aria, I'm stumbling between the tables. I'm sure they're clapping but I honestly have no clue, as I am having an out-of-body experience. Somehow I manage to make it onstage, greeting Aria and the banquet master.

"Now to the gentleman." I look out to Garrett as he pulls open the next card. "Our first candidate is Mr. Garrett Blaine!"

My stomach somersaults. This could happen! We might leap together after all. I play a fabricated reel of us walking hand in hand down the clean streets of Central. I'm sure I've got a dumb expression across my face as Garrett ascends the stairs. He steps directly to me kissing me on stage.

"Well that's something for the books!" The banquet master jokes as the crowd laughs at our amusement.

Garrett grabs my hands before he whispers in my ear, "I love you Nessa." I squeeze his hands and think about saying it too but we get separated. The regulator directs us to stand in our assigned spots as the banquet master clears his throat.

"Our last candidate is…" He pauses, building the suspense. "Mr. Tyler Jackson!" We all look at each other, all of us confused. Who's Tyler Jackson? We never went to education with anyone by that name. From the corner of my eye I see his tall and lean figure coolly approach the stage. He looks even better than he did that night by Grove Street. His fair skin makes his green eyes look sharp. His dark hair falls in short waves that are combed away from his face.

The banquet master continues. "Before we reveal the first and second place positions let's get a better understanding of who our candidates are." Right on cue the screen changes to a video of me as a child. I'm not sure how Central got these shots. Nobody in the Inner owns a camera.

My emotions hit a breaking point as the screen turns to an image of my mother and me swimming in the river. For the first time in over ten years I see her face again. I look out, Papa is crying. I wish I could trade this moment, this chance to leap just to have one more day with her. I'd give it all away. I hardly pay attention to the rest of my film. It's composed of snapshots of me with Papa and Emma. At the end of the video the number 510 appears. It's my lineage score, an average of my parents' leap-test scores.

After my video we're subjected to Aria's. Even as a child she was perfect. At the end, her lineage score flashes 590. I'm pretty sure I'm not going to make it to Central. There's virtually no way I'll make up that deficit. My forehead breaks into a sweat. It's dumb, but I feel sorry for Garrett. I feel bad that I couldn't be good enough to beat Aria. It's really annoying that I feel worse about letting him down than I do for me.

Garrett's video plays next and I fall for him all over again. I see the brown haired boy that befriended me when I had no one else and I get to watch him grow up on screen in front of me. At the end of his video I see his impressive lineage score of 605.

The entire audience falls silent for Tyler's video. It seems he has intrigued everyone. The video flashes to him as a child sitting across his father's lap. One of the first things I notice is the mining equipment scattered throughout the room. As the video progresses it becomes obvious that Tyler's not from the Inner. He's an Outer.

Videos of him fishing as a child and sailing as a young teenager tell the story of a boy who already made the leap at age fifteen from the Outer into our sector. Somehow he managed at seventeen to potentially make the leap into Central. It is unprecedented. The audience gasps when his lineage score flashes. It's 380. He doesn't stand a chance against Garrett. I do the calculations in my head figuring Aria's lineage score beats mine by 80 points and Garrett's beats Tyler's by 225. The videos power down and the banquet-master resumes his duties.

"And now for the results of the application portion of the leap test. Remember, the highest possible score is 1,100." Nobody in the history of the leap has ever tested above an 850. He pauses, building the anticipation. "Aria, please step forward." She does with shaking legs. "You scored a magnificent 800! Congratulations." The crowd goes wild as she collapses to the ground. "Your total is 1,390!" She shakes with joy. "Vanessa, please step forward."

I can hardly move. He looks at me, "Please step forward." I take my step. "You scored..." he hesitates, "An 882! Miss Hollins, you broke the record!" Both Aria and I furiously do the calculations. "That's a total of 1,392." My eyes lock with the banquet master, "You're top girl by two points!"

I nearly collapse and Aria simultaneously turns grey. Garrett and I are going to leap together. Everything we worked for is coming true. Papa claps furiously with tears rolling down his aged cheeks. I've done it; we've done it.

"And for the gentlemen." The crowd goes quiet. "Garrett, please step forward." He strides proudly into the spotlight cast from above. "Added to the 605 points from your lineage score is your application score of 821 for a total of 1,426!" My heart beats furiously. The banquet master signals for the crowd to silence.

"Tyler, please step forward." He does with his chin touching his chest. "To your 380 points from your lineage score you've scored an additional 1,090 points!" Everyone gasps, that beats any record. "It's a total of 1,470. You are top boy!" The audience begins clapping as I stand in shock. Garrett isn't top boy. I've only got seconds to decide my fate. Do I stay here and be with him or do I make the leap. Garrett grabs my shoulders staring into my vacant eyes.

"You have to leap Nessa, you have to." His shaking refocuses me.

"I won't leave you!" I cry, shaking my head.

"You have to; it's the best thing for you." He stares into my vacant eyes as he pleas.

The banquet master interrupts our exchange. He raises the microphone back to his mouth. "As is customary, the right to refuse goes to the women first. Miss Hollins, do you accept the leap?" He jams the microphone into my trembling hands.

I scan the hundreds all nodding yes. I picture myself in white, living in the big homes shown on screen. But then I picture myself alone, no Papa, no Emma and most of all, no Garrett. I raise the microphone to my mouth and pause… Finally I say the word I never imagined I'd say. My gut twists as I say it, "No."

Papa drops to his chair and Garrett runs across the stage for the second time tonight. He grabs me by the shoulders, "Nessa! You *have* to!" He screams but I push him aside.

"No, I don't accept the leap. I refuse!" I shout into the microphone.

The banquet master hesitates, not knowing what to say. He clears his throat and scans the crowd. "Well ladies and gentlemen, tonight is definitely a first for many things. Aria Goodall will be making the leap. Congratulations Aria." Aria looks confused and simultaneously ecstatic as the audience cheers while she is whisked off stage. The banquet master makes his way to Tyler.

"Now to the gentlemen... Mr. Tyler Jackson, do you accept the leap?" The banquet master hands him the microphone as Garrett steps back to me.

"Nessa, why?" He asks.

"You stay, I stay. Remember?" He slides his hand in mine, squeezing it tight.

Tyler raises the microphone, "No. I *don't* accept the leap." The audience goes mad as frantic conversations break out. Garrett's hand drops from mine. The banquet master turns to us.

Garrett screams, "I won't go!" My heart constricts as the regulators step toward us. "I won't go! Not without Nessa!" He shouts.

The banquet master retrieves the microphone from Tyler and marches toward us. Covering his microphone the banquet master steps between us. "You have no choice. You *are* making the leap." He raises the microphone back to his mouth, "How about a round of applause for Miss Aria Goodall and Mr. Garrett Blaine!" The crowd obeys, breaking into a hesitant applause.

I wrap around Garrett's shoulders and cry. This can't be happening. The regulators step closer as tears collect in Garrett's brown eyes.

"I'm sorry, I don't want to leave you," he says as they pull him away.

"I should've gone. I'm so sorry." My voice cracks.

"I'll always love you Nessa." With his last words he is pried from my arms.

"I'll always love you", in my broken state I wrap around one word, always. A word that stands for more than today or tomorrow, it is supposed to be forever, endless, timeless. How can this be endless when he's already being pulled away from me? Endless will be our separation, always will be my pain.

Chapter 20: Garrett

What's happening? I can't process it. Breathe, I have to breathe. I pinch my eyes together and focus. Why am I screaming? Who are these men and why am I being dragged? Focus, breathe.

Finally it hits me, they're regulators and Nessa is gone. I scream again and thrash. I believe I am strong enough to break free. I stumble knocking a regulator off balance.

I'll sprint straight to her and take her away. We'll run away together. She's onstage probably fighting to get back to me.

Another scream comes out of me as a bone cracks. It's an agonizing scream. I fall to the black floor instinctively grabbing my leg. It's probably broken. The second baton falls, cracking my forearm. I scream again, I scream in pain and I scream for her. Crack after crack lands until I black out.

The air is cold and my body thumps as they drag me by my arms. My head rolls limp and loose like my fox did after it died. I'm leaving a trail of blood. It looks strange and unnatural. My head rolls back and I see the regulators white uniforms splashed with my blood.

The thumping stops, they're dragging me across a ramp. Up and up I go until I'm inside the craft. My hands slam against the steel floor.

"Good luck in Central."

I scream as a boot lands against my ribs. Just like that they're gone. The engines hum as the craft lifts off. I slip in and out of consciousness, imagining I'd made it to Nessa. She's what keeps me alive. She is life.

Chapter 21: Nessa

The gasps and whispers fall silent as the spectators watch my body lying on the enormous stage. The spotlight illuminates my broken figure.

Garrett's shouts are growing fainter as the representatives' force him down the hallway that will divide us forever. He's fighting to get back to me but I know it's futile, they will win. They always win.

My body rocks, attempting to self-soothe my broken heart. I always knew this could happen, knew he could be taken from me. I imagined it would be painful but now I see I was distant from the truth. I now comprehend that pain is superficial, this is more than that. This is a torturing bind that's been laid across my soul.

Papa's arms wrap around me, lifting my limp body. The banquet master steps up, "Sir you can't leave, we aren't finished with the banq-"

Papa cuts him off, "This is my daughter, she needs her home and I'll be damned if you or anyone else is going to stop me." I lift my head seeing the banquet master stare coldly into papa's eyes. Papa holds his stare, "Step aside," papa commands and finally the banquet master concedes.

I should be thankful for what papa is doing for me. No one has ever talked to a Central citizen like this without being severely punished.

My body rocks as papa carries me down the stairs. The only audible noise is the grinding of chairs sliding against the cold and polished concrete floor as their occupants attempt to clear our path. The walk seems like an eternity. Papa's arms shake with fatigue.

"I'll walk," I whisper.

He lowers my trembling legs to the floor. I automatically kick off my stilted shoes sending them across the grey floor. Hand in hand we walk out of the hall into the night.

The shuttle ride home is completely empty. Riding in silence I wrap my arms around my chest, stroking my shoulders where Garrett last touched me. I can almost feel the heat from his touch. I wish I could recreate the sensation his electric touch brings but with each passing second I realize I am further from him than ever before. My heart breaks and I sob tearlessly. He's the one person I need to survive; the only one I would sacrifice everything for.

Emotions ebb and flow through me like tides breaking harshly over jagged rocks. I'm fluctuating between pure fury and absolute sadness. I'm furious with myself for not accepting the offer, furious that Central took him away, and furious with Tyler for forcing Garrett to go.

My mind points blame at each source just long enough for the peak of fury to hit before sadness fractures my rage. Papa sits silently beside me with his hands wringing his green jacket.

As the shuttle approaches our stop papa reaches down, cradling me in his arms. He carries me to the front door squeezing my shoulders before entering the house.

"Let me go talk to Emma. I'll be right back," he says leaving me in the winter night.

The wind whips around my silhouette and for once I welcome the cold. It comforts me, like my soul wants to feel the pain and misery. Seconds turn to minutes in the silent night before Papa opens the door.

"Ok Nessa, you can come in."

I've planted myself, not wanting to leave the cold. I want to stay here in the darkness and let my body fall asleep and never wake up.

Emma's small hand reaches around the doorframe pulling it wide. She's standing in her blue nightgown with tears rimming her eyes. She slinks to me wrapping me in her arms.

"Nessa, I'm so sorry," she says. I let her guide me into the house, leading me to our bed. She surrounds me with our blanket and leaves the room.

My head is beginning to ache behind my eyes. I inch myself to the edge of the bed, slowly reaching my hand to find the dried bouquet. I collect the dried flowers I've held for over a decade and my new ones that are still fragrant and delicate. My fingers trace the stems and I imagine watching Garrett break and arrange each one.

I can see his deep eyes staring into mine as a child and then he's morphed into the man I love. Love, why couldn't I bring myself to tell him that? It must be what I feel; it's the only thing that could cut me to my knees like this.

How strong can love be? Is it possible that I'll forever be torn by loving him until my last breath yet simultaneously be crushed by loving someone I must live without? All I have are the moments we've already shared. I can't comprehend that my time with him is over, that I will never see him again. We won't grow old together or spend another summer day by our river.

I replay our moments spent together, and with each time through the images become more and more distant. I'm losing him already.

Eventually sleep conquers my body and I wake in total darkness. It's well before first light but I know it will be impossible for me to fall asleep again. Slowly rising I assess myself. I slept in my banquet dress and my eyes feel glued shut from the black liquid Uri smeared across my lashes. I make my way into the bathroom to prepare a bath. I turn the hot water on full force.

Clouds of steam spiral from the tub and I turn off the faucet and lower myself into the scalding bath. The heat is so intense my body stings like I'm being stuck by pins and needles. The hurt is welcomed; it reminds me I'm alive. I stay rooted to the tub long enough for the curls of steam to long pass and for the water to turn cool, shriveling my skin.

The signs of first light break through the window. Within moments of the first ray I hear the buzz of a Central hovercraft approaching. I launch out of the tub wiping the cold droplets from my shriveled skin. I wonder why they're here.

Maybe they're here to punish papa for the way he talked to the banquet master. If so, they've missed him. He is already at work. Or maybe they are here to punish me for last night, is that possible? Endless speculations bound in my head as I hastily pull my greens on and knot my hair to the nape of my neck. I'm barely exiting the bathroom when the first knock sounds. Even Emma is awakened by the unexpected craft and she stands in our doorframe with her eyes wide and full of fear.

"Go in the room Emma and don't come out unless I ask." She stares vacantly. I grab her slight frame, squeezing her shoulders. The second knock sounds. "Do you understand?" I say urgently. Emma nods, retreating into our room. I exhale, releasing all my tension and walk boldly to the door.

My rage grows as I walk. I want to open the door and put an end to these Central dogs. These wicked people that took him from me but I can't, I don't have any weapons or combat training, it would be useless.

I swing the door open seeing three representatives. Natalie is standing in the lead looking as flawless as she did the day of my leap. Flanking her are two regulators with their eyes and faces shielded by their black helmets.

Natalie beams as she invites herself inside. She walks through the doorway and past me like I'm a shadow.

"Miss Hollins, what a pleasure." She pauses briefly before continuing, "I'm sure this visit comes as a surprise." She looks to me for a response I won't grant. Her abrasive attitude shines through, "I know it must be since it surprised *me* to be sent here on business." She's made her way around our entire sitting room to position herself near the table. "Sit," she directs with her sweeping arm, her eyes narrowing to mine commanding me.

Keeping my eyes defiantly locked with hers, I walk around, taking my seat. "You must understand that what happened last night comes as a shock to everyone. Nobody could've guessed fates would work the way they did Miss Hollins."

She places her hands on my shoulders making my skin crawl. "Word traveled fast, faster than we can see possible. Not just citizens here but citizens in *all* the sectors are talking. You are the first citizen to deny acceptance into a leap and to have that other boy Tyler deny passage too. It's simply unfathomable."

She stares out our window at the neighbor's barren yard. "The leap was designed to give citizens hope, something to work for… a reason to maintain order. Without the leap, people would revert to the barbaric ways of the pre-divide." She drops her hands from my shoulders, walking around to stare at me. "I'm not saying it was your intention to cause such a thing. But that's the path we currently find ourselves on."

I can't follow what Natalie is insinuating. It sounds like I've unintentionally made our society doubt itself. My mind tries piecing together what it means as my hands fist.

"If the citizens believe there's more to their purpose than making the leap, that's when an outbreak begins. By denying the leap you two made them start to doubt the worth of it." My eyes meet hers. "We need to remind them that the leap is the *only* thing that matters. The leap and all the preparation and order surrounding it *are* a necessary means to prevent absolute chaos."

Finally, I prepare myself to address her, "So why are you here? What am I supposed to do?"

She flashes her evil grin, "You do speak? I was beginning to worry."

I fold my arms across my chest, "*Why* are you here?" I demand.

"Miss Hollins, I'm here so we can discuss how we are going to snuff this ember you and that boy Tyler lit. We must extinguish this before it turns into wildfire. Central decided we won't punish your family for your actions. That wouldn't be fair." Natalie strikes a chord immediately.

"Why *would* you punish them? They didn't do anything wrong. I didn't do anything wrong either. It was my right to refuse."

She sneers at me. "You really think it was your right to refuse?" Her head sways side to side, "Miss Hollins, I'm afraid you weren't listening. Our nation was constructed on the premise that the leap is the ultimate mission in life; you and that boy temporarily diffused that belief. Without it, order cannot be maintained. Now as I was saying..." She trails off, placing her fists squarely on the table in front of me. "Your family won't be punished for your actions last night. You however, *will* have consequences. Central's decided the best action will be to separate you from the other citizens."

She takes her hands off our wooden table. "In order for the citizens to rekindle their love for the leap they must believe you and Mr. Jackson refused because you'd been offered something favorable, a once-in-a-lifetime opportunity from Central."

A wicked grin pulls at the corners of her mouth. "Luckily, Central created a scenario that'll convince the nation that you two made your decision out of patriotism. You'll *want* to accept our offer... unless you want us to exile Emma to the foreigners."

I push to my feet crashing my chair to the floor. "Emma? You can't send her there! She didn't do anything wrong!" I tremble with rage.

"Calm down Miss Hollins. Nobody *wants* to send her there. That's why we're certain you will cooperate." She walks around me, tipping my chair upright and forcing me onto it. "As I was saying, you'll go on the announcement confirming the story. We'll tell the citizens that just prior to the banquet you were told of the 'scout' position we planned to offer to the second place testers."

"Scout? I've never heard of that."

"It's a position Central created last night to cover the damage you and Mr. Jackson caused. The citizens will be told that your job requires you to live free from the others. We'll tell them that you and Mr. Jackson will be spies, protecting us from the foreigners."

Her steps sound hollow against the floor. "Of course it's all a lie. You'll live in the wild and provide for yourself. Nothing but the clothes on your back will be given to you. You must *never* have contact with another citizen or else Emma will find herself imprisoned by the foreigners."

My hands shake with rage. My world is caving in around me. I thought the pillars of my life were crushed last night but now I realize there were still beams to be struck. Garrett is gone and soon I'll be without my family.

"How can you expect me to survive alone?"

She grins at my question, "Oh no Miss Hollins, you won't be alone. You and Mr. Jackson will face this fate together." My heart stops. I'd rather die than be forced to live next to him.

"I'll kill him."

"Then kill him or let the elements kill you. Either way it's no matter to me. You will be at the announcement tomorrow to convince this nation of your excitement to be offered the scout position. You will make them believe you refused the leap for this opportunity and then you will disappear. Do I make myself clear?"

The rage has reached my eyes, they're burning with a passion. "Crystal clear," I choke.

"In that case, I will see you tomorrow." She places a bag on the table as she turns to leave, "You'll wear this, we insist."

The door creaks closed behind her as I reach for the package. Inside is my uniform, a green bodysuit with a gold zipper splitting the center. I pull out the heavy black boots that lace-up the front. My costume to play the part of 'scout.' I'll do it for Emma, but I will get my revenge.

Chapter 22: Nessa

I grab the package and storm from the house just as the hovercraft lifts towards the sky. I spend what remains of my last day at our river. The water seems to flow slower and the trees look smaller than ever before. Twice I think I hear Garrett approaching from the brush behind me. My heart jolts with excitement only to endure it crumbling with disappointment when I turn finding the woods empty. The winds are cold but I fight them and stay. I haven't broken down today, not like yesterday. Yesterday I was weak. I let my soul feel the sharp edges of reality. Not today, I've had to numb myself the best I can. Today Central wins, and I lose what's left of my life.

I slip home well past dark. I watch papa in his restless sleep as he tosses and turns, whispering my mother's name. Maybe that will be me. Forever belonging to one person, a person that's no longer part of this world. Mama was the love of his life. All these years later I wonder if he only feels the loss as he dreams or if his heart aches for her during the daytime as well. Has he found a way to calm the torturing binds?

I leave papa and turn my attention to Emma, she sleeps peacefully with the tiny rising and falling of her chest nearly eclipsed by our heavy blanket. Who's going to take care of her when I'm gone? She's too delicate, too soft to be without me. Will she think I abandoned her? Of course she will. She has to believe I wanted to leave; it's the only way to keep her safe. She will slide into bed tomorrow night and for the first time ever her heart will know loss. She will feel the pain and binds that I've always tried to shield her from.

This is my last night to see them. Central announced that a mandatory meeting of all citizens would be held at noon tomorrow. Each sector was instructed to meet in their pavilions where they will watch Tyler and I accept our role on the projectors. Emma and papa will be standing among the other citizens and be fed a lie that I must make them believe.

First light has just broken when I hear Emma rising from our bed, pattering down the narrow hall. She rubs the sleep from her eyes. "Nessa, did you hear about the meeting today?"

"Yeah, I heard."

"We should all go together, don't you think?"

My voice falters for a moment but I regain my composure. "You two go without me. You'll see me there, I promise."

Emma *has* to believe this is something I want if I'm going to protect her. Papa joins us with a grunt.

"I was just telling Emma that you two should go without me, I'll come on my own." Papa's treaded lightly since the banquet, he wouldn't dare question me now.

"Suit yourself," he says as I push myself from my chair.

"I have a few errands to run before noon," I say letting my eyes take a final sweep around our small home.

Years of life flash before me. I try absorbing all the love and warmth this place holds. I'm being robbed of so many things today but I can't let them see that. I hold onto one of the paper creations Garrett made for me. I took it from my dresser last night and turned it over again and again in my hands. It felt so flimsy, so small in my palm but somehow it gave me strength and courage. It gives me something to hold onto. I reach the door and at the last moment I stop. I'd planned on leaving without a goodbye but I'm not strong enough.

"Emma, you be good." She looks at me intently as I turn to papa. "Papa, thank you for making me strong." I turn, pulling our creaking door wide as I exit. My heart breaks as the door closes behind me. Tears threaten my eyes as I round the corner but I refuse to let them fall. I stride boldly to our hillside to retrieve my uniform from the branches where I left it yesterday.

I undress, tossing my green uniform aside. I no longer need that uniform, it's a part of the old me. I stand in the chilled air a moment before pulling the new uniform over my pale and shaking skin. It fits tightly, sealing the cold from my body. I fasten my boots and twist my hair into a braided knot.

I must have read the note affixed to the package a hundred times since Natalie left it with me yesterday. It's burnt into my mind. I take one last inhale and look at our river as I picture Garrett bathing in the waters only to see him fade away.

My boots feel heavy on my legs and my breath's hot against my lips as I walk to the shuttle. I board, riding alone toward the banquet hall. When the shuttle arrives I don't stumble like I did nights ago, now I stride to the front door with my head held high. I won't let them see me broken.

I reach the wooden doors surrounded by the towering marble pillars. I tear them open. The room is hollow and barren, with the exception of Natalie, Tyler and a regulator. I can't tell which of them makes my blood boil more. I hate Natalie with fierceness only Tyler can compete with. I want to run on stage and attack them both. The only thing stopping me is knowing Emma would be exiled to the foreigners if I do. Natalie steps to me, flashing her cold smile.

"Miss Hollins it's a pleasure to see you. I trust you know what is expected of you?" My eyes glance to the projection screen that amplified the banquet master's beady eyes nights ago. This time I see my face reflected with raging eyes.

"I'm fully aware," I snarl at Natalie. Tyler's voice startles me, stirring an ardent revulsion.

"Try to look excited," he says looking at me. I immediately turn away. "Neither of us wants this, but we don't have a say. I'm sure they threatened you like they did me." He glances down at his feet, letting the pain reach his eyes. "We have to snuff our anger, make the nation believe. Tryin' isn't good enough either. We *have* to convince 'em all."

I want to lunge at his throat but he's right. The animosity in my eyes will give away our charade. His eyes travel back to mine.

"Whatever they're using against you, picture it safe. You can do that. You just gotta make 'em believe." I see Emma smiling on our bed as I braid her hair. My eyes soften just as the clock strikes twelve.

Natalie interrupts, "Stand near me at the podium and remember what is at stake here." We fall in line beside her. The spotlight powers on and the cameras buzz to life. Natalie clears her throat and the show begins.

"Ladies and gentleman, it's been years since an announcement such as this has been made. I can assure you Central would not have brought you together if it weren't for reasons of utmost significance." She smiles, "Three years ago we came together on a day much like today, standing in the very places you stand now. Each of you learned that the foreigners had managed to find a weakness in our walls and successfully laid an attack to the Inner sector. Lives were lost that day." She skillfully pauses, letting the listeners absorb her message.

"I'm here on behalf of Central, not to break news of horrors such as those, but to bring word that new measures are about to be put in place that will ensure the foreigners *never* have the chance to breech our walls again. *Never* rob another citizen of breath!" She pauses and I imagine cheers rising from the pavilions nationwide.

"Since that attack, Central has been devising a new line of defense to thwart future attempts. Central is proud to announce the first line of defense will be held by the highest ranking citizens in the Inner sector! Let me introduce you to your new protectors," she waves and Tyler and I to step into view. The cameras scan to us, we're frozen on stage.

"Miss Vanessa Hollins and Mr. Tyler Jackson! They proved themselves worthy of making the leap, however deferred their placement to pursue the role of scout." Natalie pauses. I envision the hordes of people muttering in the pavilions, trying to understand what she's saying.

"Two nights ago the top contestants were told that the second place boy and girl would take the distinguished and most important new role of scout. It was for this reason that these two brave and honorable citizens stayed. They made the ultimate sacrifice to forgo a life in Central in pursuit of providing protection for all the Inner citizens." We nod our heads in agreement, just like the note told us to.

"They'll serve as an elite task force like shadows in the night. They won't live among you; instead they'll patrol the walls, providing valuable information about the strengths and weaknesses of the Inner *and* those of the rebel foreigners. They're prepared to sacrifice *everything* so we'll continue to be safe!"

Tyler grabs my hand and I instinctually try wrenching it free. He holds strong and raises our arms in a triumphant pose. His smile isn't like the one I saw that night by Grove Street. It's forced but still convincing. He squeezes my hand, reminding me to follow suit. I force the best smile I can manage. The humming of the cameras cease and the spotlight dulls, the show is over. Natalie steps from the stage, leaving us standing with our arms raised.

"Let's hope that was enough for both of your sakes."

I retract my hand from his warm grasp. I'm about to ask what's next when the hum of a hovercraft breaks my thoughts. I exit the stage running to the sound. I don't know why I'm running, why I'm in a hurry to begin my death sentence. As soon as I fling the doors open the wind from the craft nearly knocks me off my feet. Tyler steadies me and I instantly recoil. I glare at him.

"Don't touch me."

"Sorry, I was just tryin' to help."

"That's the thing; I don't want your help. The sooner you get that the better. Got it?"

"Yeah. Got it." He looks wounded. For a minute I almost feel bad for him but then I think of Garrett being dragged off stage. I hear him yelling my name as Central took him from me. My hate's re-kindled.

The wind from the craft calms as it maintains its position fifteen-feet off the ground. Blades of grass bend from the wind pressure. The base of the silver craft expels a steep ramp that glides to the ground. Without hesitation I square my shoulders and enter. I want to look back for one final glance at the place I call home but my pride won't let me. I climb aboard with my eyes fixed forward. I hold my head straight and steady.

I've never been on a hovercraft before. As I seat myself across from Tyler I'm suddenly jolted upward. My head hits the bar above me, bursting my vision with patches of light. I recognize he didn't jolt when the craft took off. My eyes narrow and I see he's fastened a belt around his waist. My hands sweep my sides finding the straps, I secure them around my stomach.

I'm not sure how long we've been flying; it's hard to tell time without a window to watch the sun. All I know is my mind has been wandering as I picture Emma and papa sitting together tonight, alone. We didn't have a proper goodbye. I can't help wishing I could go back and hug them more, kiss them more, and tell them how much I love them. Looking back I see all the wasted moments in my life. Moments with them and Garrett.

Suddenly my stomach's sent into a cartwheel as the craft abruptly drops before it holds steady. Sadness is instantly replaced by fear. I appreciate that this is it, I'm about to exit into territory that is completely foreign to me, with no food or shelter and wearing only the clothes on my back.

My fingers fumble with the buckle; it reminds me of my leap test. The way my fingers danced across the cuff right before Natalie rescued me. My mind is brought back to the present as the hovercraft opens its floor, lowering the ramp. I push from my seat, determined to exit the craft before Tyler. I don't want him thinking I'm scared or need anything from him.

The first thing I notice is how dark it is outside. It's the blackest black I've ever seen. I stride down the ramp, my foot sinks into calf deep mud. I want to curse but I know that's what Central wants. They want to see me struggling one last time before they leave me to die. I bite my tongue and lift my leg from the sinking mud. It makes a sucking noise as it breaks the surface. Tyler shouts as he hits the mud.

"Shit! Can you believe this?"

"Yes I can, and I can handle it. If you can't, that's your problem." I'm annoyed and it's obvious. "Listen, I'm going to live out here alone. I don't want you around so just go your own way."

"Vanessa, you can't be serious? It's too dangerous out here alone. We can look after each other. We don't have to be friends, but we can keep each other alive." He sounds almost desperate.

I keep pulling myself through the mud toward the tree line. "I'd rather take my chances and die alone than be with you."

He groans, exasperated. "What'd I ever do to you besides save your ass that night with the Borgs. Remember?" I freeze, I'd hoped he wouldn't recognize me.

"So what? You saved me from a stupid mark. Who cares about marks *now*? Look where we are! I wouldn't be here if it wasn't for you. I was supposed to be with him. You ruined that, you ruined my life." He doesn't say anything for several minutes, and then finally he talks.

"I did what I had to. One day you'll get it."

"Whatever, Tyler. I'm going to those trees and I expect once I'm there I'll never see your face again." He gets the message because he finally stops talking and breaks his trail in the opposite direction.

The only sounds are my heavy breathing and the sucking noise of my boots sinking into mud. My body's trembling from exhaustion. Sweat pours across my forehead. By the time I break the trail to the tree line my body feels weak and ragged. My muscles knot and burn as I scramble on my hands and knees, clawing my fingers into the mud-ridden grass.

I reach the first trees, they're weak and snap under my pull but I keep trying to grasp at their weak silhouettes. I need them to wrench myself the last few feet onto solid ground. I break the first three saplings in half but on the fourth I finally have hold, wrenching myself out of the mud onto the hardened ground.

I need a moment to rest, a few minutes to regain my strength. My breath steadies and my burning thighs turn to a dull ache. I'll move in a minute...

Chapter 23: Nessa

I awake dazed and utterly confused. The first thing I'm able to focus on is the aching pain radiating throughout my entire body. I prop myself onto my forearms, listening to the loud rapping noise of a bird. I sit listening, it becomes clear, I'm at the edge of the Inner, exiled and alone. Alone, the word is hollow, yet holds so much weight.

I can't dwell on that now, I need to find water. There's got to be some around here; the mud didn't come from nowhere. Turning around, I see the mud pit from last night glazed with frost. My fury ignites, Central did it on purpose, they probably spent an entire day melting the ground so it would be thick mud for our arrival. Just another reason I'll get my revenge one day.

My legs shake as I break my way through the thick masses of trees. The smallest rustling in the bushes makes me jump. My confidence and courage have left me. The woods near my home used to be a welcome retreat. I suppose knowing home was just a short walk away gave me security and strength that I don't have here. The midday sun is just breaking through the clouds when I see a small winding stream that will be my water source.

I drop to my knees, scooping handfuls of water, sipping it slowly. It's cold and earthy but I drink. Sitting back on my heels I see a rolling hill that looks down over the stream. It'll suffice as my home base, it's got high grounds to protect me from flooding plus I can keep watch for any incoming foreigners.

My boots seal out the water as I walk through the stream toward the hill. My stomach knots in hunger but I keep climbing toward the peak. The hill is somewhat steep, barren the first half before it becomes closed off by towering trees. I make my way around the hill, finally finding what I was looking for, saplings bordered by strong trees to support a shelter.

I rest my hand on one of the giant oaks; I can't believe this will be home. It's not right. My home was supposed to be with Garrett, supposed to be with family and friends. Home is a place where food is served in a pavilion, where there's a live oak tree by the water and Garrett waiting for me. I have to move forward, I have to survive here until I get revenge.

I stalk out the closest animal trails, fastening snares like the one I'd shown Emma just last week. I'll have to come back tonight to check them. I make my way back to the river, praying they'll work. Along the way, my eyes dart wildly searching for rocks I can use to clear my hilltop. I collect a handful of them and spend my afternoon sharpening the stones to hardened blades.

I start cutting down the smaller saplings nestled among the towering trees. I work from sunrise to sunset, cutting through the brown bark of the small trees littering the landscape. Cutting, clearing, and re-sharpening my stones, over and over I repeat the process.

I dedicate my first week to clearing my space. By the time it's freed of tangling brush my hands are raw and my skin is scraped off. The first days are unbearably exhausting. I hardly remember to eat and what I do is barely enough to keep me alive. The occasional rabbit or squirrel my snare catches is hardly the diet I'm accustomed to.

I wonder what papa and Emma are doing back home. With each sunset I'm relieved knowing they are home in time for curfew. It's the only time of day that I'm certain where they are. Each night as the sun slopes down I picture them in our house and I pretend I'm there with them too. The nights stretch for an eternity. I lay on my back looking into the darkened skies. I see past the blackness to the stars and a part of me relaxes. It's familiar; I know the stars and what they mean. Education taught me about the stars, moon cycles and farming. I hate Central but I do appreciate what they taught me. Without them I'd be dead. I wouldn't have the shelter I've made, the food I've caught, or the fire to cook it in.

Every night I am thankful that Emma and papa are safe. I carry them inside my mind, in bins made for happy and protected thoughts. I focus on the good and pure always before I pull open the ugly box of hate. I open my mouth and say the only words that bring me comfort, "Natalie, Tyler, and Central, I will get my revenge." It's my nightly promise I make, the one thing that keeps my body warm in the cold.

Chapter 24: Ty

I got her name at the banquet. I was crawling in my skin; I couldn't wait to say it out loud. It was obvious she was with Garrett but what did that matter? I knew I was meant for her. That didn't make it any easier watching her crumble to the floor and reach for him. I was jealous and embarrassed, she loved him not me. I should have expected it; it's not like she knew what I'd given up to be with her.

Turns out she's more than a little complicated, she's downright impossible. On the hover over here I wanted to make her understand *why*, but I couldn't find my tongue. How would I even explain myself? What would I say, "Hey Vanessa, sorry to ruin your life but I saw the future and I know we love each other?" Ridiculous to even think about it, so I let her keep on hating me.

Luckily the two years I'd spent looking for her prepped me for sleep deprivation. Since Central exiled us to the wilds I've spent almost every hour fishing or trapping for myself and searching for a way out.

I saw her on fire and if I'm gonna save her she'll need a healer. Every morning after I eat I head toward the wall, looking for an exit. It took a week to find the closest border of the massive concrete wall. Now that I've found it I run the length looking for a fracture in the enormous structure. I finally accept that I'm gonna have to dig my way to the other side. I scout the concrete until I find ground easy enough to break. I wonder if anyone from the Inner has ever made it to this wall. Probably not, it's too far from civilization.

I lift my head, glancing up the wall that borders the lands between my two homes. It cuts a divide between the Inner where I'm standing and the Outer, the sector I was born in. I collect my rocks for digging and start the process of tunneling to the Outer.

Hour after hour I dig like a dog, dirt flying to the sides. I'd learned how to make strong tunnels in the Outer. It was a skill we needed as miners. The brown dirt mounds at my sides and by the end of the fourth day I'm waist deep. The wall keeps plunging into the ground, with each inch I think I must almost be there.

My body aches and my hands are raw from digging. It's the end of my seventh day and my body is slowing down. My hands hardly move but I've got to keep going. Somewhere dozens of miles away Nessa's by her river and she's a day closer to dying. I drive my rock into the hard ground, finally meeting the end, I found bottom. With renewed energy I pull inch after inch of rock and dirt from the concrete barrier.

Night falls and I've dug a full three inches closer to the Outer. I fall asleep inside my hollowed hole, too whipped to find cover. I wake up aching and dazed before I'm able to focus. The sun's just rising as I make my way to the watering hole I found. Unfastening my pants I lower into the cool water waiting for breakfast. The fish scatter as soon as I sink in but I hold still, my man-made spear in hand. Eventually forgetting the danger, the fish return. They swim past me wildly. I pick my target and release, spearing the fish right through the gut. I devour my breakfast and am back to work, making my way to the wall again.

I count my days in inches exposed, not hours. After three weeks I'm through the wall. I lie on my belly and pull my way along my tunnel. For a blink I get hung up. My uniform snags on one of the jagged pieces I left hanging down. I roll and kick, I'm afraid I'll be stuck for good. At last the fabric rips and I pull myself into the Outer sector. Seventeen inches of wall and twenty-one days of work separate Vanessa and me now. I'm back in the sector I was born in. The same sector my family is in now. I never thought I'd be this close to them again. Part of me wants to go to them and stay but I can't. I have to move forward to save Vanessa.

I push toward the next border, staying undercover and using the stars to navigate. My body is weak but I keep moving. The rains are steady and my uniform is soaked day in and out. I forgot how tall the mountains were here in the Outer. It only took two years for my memories to fade. They look even bigger now. They're intimidating as I scale their rocky ledges. I push up and down the mountain range heading toward the final wall, the one that separates the Outer from the foreigners. I press on through the woods and rocky cliffs until at last I see the wall. It pushes into the sky, cutting across the trees between us.

I trudge through thick mud toward the wall that stands in the distance. I can hear a raging river moving through the woods even before I see its rapids breaking the rocks. I pass up and down the river, hoping for a safe route that isn't there. White peaks beat the rocks as the water swells and thrashes. I don't have a choice, I've got to cross now or risk losing Vanessa.

I sway on the shoreline trying to build my courage before I make my first move. I can't tell if my head is buzzing or if it's the noise of breaking water that fills my ears. I take a breath before leaping onto the first glassy rock. Time slows as I take in my surroundings. I see my feet stretching out as white peaks of water dance at my toes. I pull my leg around aiming for the glassy rock. My knees rebound as I land, teetering I try catching my balance.

My foot slips and drops into the raging waters. I lean to my side trying to pry it free. It lifts and I center myself on the boulder, preparing for my next leap. I crouch and launch to my next rock. My toes graze the backside before I slip landing on my stomach. The wind's knocked right outta me. The water pulls at me like it's a dark pit with a thousand mauling hands reaching out for me.

Hands that grab and tug and twist as they try drawing me under. My arms tremble as the fibers tear; I fight, pulling myself onto the brown rock. Finally I lift myself into a crouched position as I pick my last target, one more leap and I'll be across.

Without thinking my knees bend and I leap forward. On this jump there's no slowing of time, no processing or adjusting, it's all too fast. Water drives into the back of my throat and I'm gasping for air before I realize my foot missed its mark. I bob up and down like a broken branch barreling downstream. The rapids pull me under and I snap and crack like a branch would as I'm tossed into hardened rocks. Again and again I crack and with each hit water tries to fill my throat. It's a watery fist that slams straight down to the pit of my gut, it tries filling me, sinking me if it can. I choke and gasp and even try screaming but the watery fist drives harder.

Again I bob as water surrounds me. It pulls and lifts me then pulls me under again. It's too fast to process plus the waters too murky to see through. I used to be such a strong swimmer. How did I get into this mess? I cut my arms through the water, I've gotta get to the top. Another rock slams against me and for a second I forget where I am. More water drives into my mouth reminding me to keep trying. I wrench myself to the surface as the sun blinds me, then I'm taken back under. I'm running out of breath. With each slam I'm losing a little more.

I resurface again gasping for air as the current pulls me farther down river. I turn just in time to see a fallen tree spread across the river. I'm barreling towards it, rebounding from rock to rock. It's my last shot at survival.

I'm pulled under again. The fallen tree is just above me. I shoot my arm through the top as a branch hits my hand. I close my grasp but I'm too late. I bob one last time. There's just one more branch I might be able to reach. Thrusting my arm into the air I feel the slick bark. I close my grip, grasping to the last branch hanging from the tree.

Fighting against the rapids I pull myself onto the rotting tree. I lie across it, spitting up water. After an hour I make my way back upstream across from where I'd started. I move forward, making my way to the final wall.

Chapter 25: Nessa

Two moon cycles have passed, its mid-March now. My green bodysuit hangs off my bony body like a snake shedding its skin, I've lost so much weight. I can't imagine I'll be able to survive another month at this rate.

If this is going to be my home then I need to forage, and plant. I need a plan. My first month I was so consumed with making my shelter, collecting water, and scouting animal paths that I completely neglected the fact that my life was unsustainable. It wasn't until the end of the first moon cycle that I felt secure enough to slow down. Once I did, it became obvious that I might never get up again.

Every day between the first and second cycle was filled with absolute darkness and feelings of complete loss. I spent my days hugging my knees to my chest watching sheet after sheet of pounding rain beat relentlessly against the ground.

For hours I would vacantly stare at one puddle watching the dropping moisture rebounding as it broke the surface. My uniform was soaked twenty-four hours a day. The arctic wet would've sent me into shock only months ago. Instead I laid in it, numbed to it. Numb to the world around me. It wasn't long ago that I'd hoped for that numbness, hoped for anything that would replace the longing pains that stabbed my heart. I remember laying there numb and wishing I'd feel anything else. I had to move and live, I just needed to figure out how again.

A full two weeks passed with a relentless barrage of rain. In my head I thought Central had orchestrated the whole thing. I thought I'd never see the sun again. Then one day it stopped, like someone had left a faucet running and suddenly realized it. There were no more drops assaulting puddles and no excuses to be depressed. Once the sun broke free from the wall of clouds I made a conscious effort to live. I'd had my time to be sad, my time to starve, lay, cry, and be weak. That time was over. I'm Vanessa Hollins, I tested highest in my year. I'm smart and strong and I can prevail. I've done it before, after mama died. I can do it again. It's the only thing I can do, I must live and grow and move forward. Move toward revenge and a life after revenge.

So here I am in mid-March, peeling the sagging uniform off my hollow frame. I drape it across one of the giant boulders along the stream. My naked body hums as the sunlight touches my white skin. My mind wanders as my uniform dries.

My stomach churns in hunger as I dress and walk to my snares. The first one comes up empty. Crashing through the trails I come to the remains of my second snare, it's been destroyed. It isn't the first time this has happened; probably a deer or a bear stumbled across it. I almost don't want to check my final snare; I'm scared I'll fall back into depression if I come up empty.

My stomach growls but I push forward. A pit of emptiness hits my gut three hundred feet from my snare. Once I cross these next bushes I'll see if I've had any luck. My stomach twists in fearful anticipation. I break through the tall green shrubs. I stop in my tracks, my stomach unknots. The white rabbit dangles with its head twisted.

I reset my snare and walk back to the hill starving. I separate the skin from the rabbit. Cooking the meat I spin it just above the flames. The tough flesh is exactly what I need. I eat like a savage, tearing the meat from the tiny bones as I pick it clean. It's time to start foraging.

I pass all my snares and continue walking; I'm about an hour out when I find myself in a sort of clearing. The sunlight passes through the trees. It casts shadowing pillars onto the field reminding me of the pillars separating the lines at the pavilion. A longing pain stabs deep in my stomach, extending into my soul. I force myself to look at the shadows, seeing them for what they are, not what they remind me of.

I control the pain and move further into the field. I walk directly over shoots of wild carrots, they sprout through the soil. I drop to my knees, letting them sink into the soft and soaking ground. My fingers greedily dig into the mud. If I'm careful I can ration the field until July.

I'm satisfied with my first day's forage. After mentally congratulating myself for getting out of the shelter I decide I've earned an early retirement. It'd be somewhat wasted to take the exact route back, I know what I'll see…an endless expanse of trees, their canopies of branches stretching towards the sun as if greeting a friend for the first time in years. And of course there was the mud and snags of thorns I'd have to beat through too. Another route is in order. I circumvent my initial path approaching my shelter from the north.

My heart beats steadily as I pound my way through the thick forest. I hadn't imagined terrain much thicker than the trail I thrashed to get to the wild carrots but I was wrong. I progress at a crawl. I catch my breath, stopping to look side to side as the heavy foliage overtakes me. I can hardly see where I came from let alone where I'm going. I let myself recover five minutes before pushing forward. I know I'm a short distance from my shelter, I can hear the water rounding the bend leading to the base of my camp.

I break through a tangle of thorns and right in front of me are berry bushes, red and edible. I've been here for months and somehow I'm just finding these divine saviors. I pick up my legs and barrel full force through the thicket, stumbling and recovering once before I'm on them.

They're not quite ripe but that doesn't matter, the thought of berries and carrots sends me into a sort of jig, similar to Emma's when she discovered her snare worked that day in the woods a lifetime ago.

I pack myself full of berries, stopping once I feel like I'm about to pop. I've found another project, another preoccupation to keep my mind from slipping into the depths of depression. I walk to the shelter, passing out across my makeshift cot.

I wake-up with the sun breaking the horizon, my stomach still full from yesterday's gorge. I stand up stretching side to side before I make my way to the berries to start the tedious process of transplanting them. I want fields of them so I don't have to fight through thick and thorny masses to get to them.

Chapter 26: Ty

It's nuts that two months have gone by. It all feels like a blink ago. I keep trying to push my near drowning out of my head but somehow it stays there. I try putting my attention on Vanessa instead.

In my sight I'd seen a field of raspberries and I know she'll be planting 'em right about now. There's still time to get supplies but I need to hurry. I trudge toward the final wall. It climbs straight into the sky, throwing its threatening shadow over me as I dig. My healing blisters re-open but I keep working.

It blows my mind that I've come so far and I'm just about there. This is the last wall I have to cross. I dig inch by inch, deeper and deeper until at last the hard packed clay gives way to the other side. Two weeks closer to Vanessa's death but I'm finally free. I belly crawl through my passage. I break ground into the foreigner's territory. Shit, of course there's an open field I've gotta cross. I tear from the wall as fast as I can. No time for thinking, I just act. I crash through the field. Man I hope there aren't any regulators patrolling. I sweat like mad but I'm halfway there. I'm closing in and about dying wondering what they'll do if they catch me. Who am I kidding? They'll kill me for sure. At last I make it to the woods.

I never thought I'd be this happy to see trees. I move south through the brush. Hours pass before I hit a road. It's in the middle of nowhere, no hovers or homes, just me and a shoddy road. I turn left and pick my way along its cracked and buckling shoulder. The sun starts setting just as I crest a hill. Right at the peak I see the tops of massive buildings, tall enough to practically touch the sky. I've never seen buildings like this. We were told the foreigners lived in sheds in the wild. No water, heat, or order. Just chaos. Clearly a lie.

Spread in front of me is a city with lights blasting into the sky. The sounds of engines and life plug up the air. I make my way toward the center. There's no other way to get the supplies.

I get closer and closer until I'm finally absorbed by the shadows of the buildings. There are no walls stopping passage into the city. I step back onto the paved road, walking to the first street light. I stop underneath the giant pole taking in my surroundings. A group of people stand across the street circling around each other. They don't pay attention to me. I turn trying to get my bearings. There's a bright orange flyer on the pole across from me.

'*Bring Freedom to the Citizens of the Divide. Help end their suffering.*' Below the writing is an emblem I've never seen before. It has a giant red 'x' striking through it.

Two tabs are left at the bottom so I pull one off, shoving the address in my pocket. I'm totally outta place with my soiled clothes but people pass me without minding. If they knew I was a citizen of the divide I wonder if they'd kill me on the spot. That's what we've always been told.

I roam; half the time dazed the other half in awe. Music blares from tiny pavilions, some citizens called 'em restaurants. People dance and parade in the streets way past curfew. I nearly get run over by a dozen different hovers that barrel through the streets. Around and around I go until I randomly stumble across a faded map of the city. It's plastered across a wall with its edges fraying. I trace my finger along the roads until I find my location. I fish for the crumpled address, pulling it from my pocket. I find it on the map. Daylight's breaking when I finally find the home on 133 Jackson Ave. That doesn't matter though because I've finally made it.

Chapter 27: Garrett

Central's white uniform pressed against the casts looked ridiculous. I twist my ankle and wrist side to side. The freedom feels good. It's been eight weeks since the breaks. Eight weeks to heal my broken bones but I doubt centuries would be enough time to fix my heart. Stupid we're made with such a vital thing that's so soft and vulnerable.

Not a day has gone by that I haven't thought about Nessa. The hurt cuts just as deep now as it did two months ago. I teeter down the stairs, my ankle's unsteady. The other citizens pass me, none of them noticing me. I take my favorite route back to the compound. I torture myself daily on my walks. I walk the roads and paths that remind me of her. I pass the trees and flowers that I know she would have loved.

The massive buildings tower above me, their shadows are imposing and grand. Detail after detail is strewn across each building. Central is magnificent.

The regulators that gave me the beating were suspended for their use of 'unnecessary force.' I suppose in a way that made me feel a little better, at least they'd been punished. That helped me start to accept this place as home.

The marble steps to my unit are much easier without the crutches. I climb them toward my third floor apartment. I get to the door and hold my forearm to the scanner. Most citizens have their implants in their right arm. Mine was in a cast when they implanted it so I've got mine in the left. The alarm clears and my door slides open. I step inside shedding my white jacket.

I slump onto my sofa assessing myself. Both my forearm and leg are atrophied compared to the other side. They look strange and shrunken. I wiggle my fingers and grab the paper from my coffee table. I've wanted to make one of these since they immobilized my hand. I know it's just another form of torture but somehow I think it will help.

I start folding the paper, shaping it like a fox. I know I'll never see her again, never give it to her, but it makes me feel closer to her.

Chapter 28: Nessa

The peak of July's dry season has carried in an arid and suffocating blanket of heat making my body feel like it's hanging on every inch of my skin, right down to the insides of my throat. I wake this morning like I have almost every morning for a month now, soaked in my own perspiration and sucking on dehydrated air. My mouth's nearly as dry as my streambed.

I swing my legs off my makeshift cot, pattering barefooted down the worn trail leading to my dying stream. The blades of grass have stopped attempting to grow along my beaten-down trail, leaving me with a dirt path littered with stones.

I've been clearing the rocks. My motivation is the wound on my left forefoot that's finally healing after stepping on a particularly jagged rock about a month ago. As I continue my trek towards the stream I pull at some of the ripened raspberries that have come into season. I transplanted the bushes months ago and now my rows of berries gleam red and delicious. I toss a handful in my mouth letting the burst of sweetness fill my tongue.

The berries and dandelions I cultivated have been a savior. Game has been sparse in the unforgiving heat. The watering holes have dried up and without them food was forced to travel elsewhere. I continue toward the water with the sun glistening across the top nearly blinding me. I squint momentarily. When my vision recovers I see a man lying on his back, arms cradling his head. My heart stops as acorn-colored eyes turn to look at me. My stomach somersaults as I run. My legs peddle downhill cutting through the dandelions.

"Garret!" I shout.

He rises and turns to me. His eyes bear deep into mine, he opens his arms as I bound toward him. He tenses as I leap into his open arms. I feel pain as I've registered I have fallen.

Dandelions press into my head. A small trickle of blood dances across my forehead. Grass, dandelions and blood are all I lay on. Not Garrett. I lift myself to my hands and knees, squeezing my eyes so tight that a gush of blood falls. It coats the green blades below. How could I be so stupid to think he would be here? He can't leave Central. Even if he could, he'd never find me. It's been a long time since I let myself be weak but right now I do. I relive the heartache of losing him. I want to cry but my body is too weak and dehydrated to let any moisture escape.

I sit on the blood-coated grass for the better half of the morning. By this time the sun has crawled into the endless blue sky and scorches my parched and ragged skin. I slink my way to the bony remains of my stream sipping straight from it. I move toward my cot as the sun begins to set. As it does the unrelenting heat collides with a burst of cold air that sprints in from the north.

I've felt nights like this before, the makings of a perfect storm. Many summer nights I have stay up watching the long tenuous bolts of light dance across the skyline. They'd reach their jagged fingers toward earth. Emma was terrified of storms. I wonder who has been comforting her now that I'm gone.

I boil a handful of dandelions for dinner. None of my snares were tripped today. The idea of food is unappealing anyway. I force myself to finish my stew. I close my eyes, awaiting sleep. The cold northern winds push hard as the epicenter of the warring temperatures hover above me.

An ear-splitting crack suddenly awakens me. My heart bounds against my ribs as I reorient myself. This is my first storm in the wild. There is something terrifying about being exposed like this. The wind crashes against my shelter as the assortment of supplies I've collected sway wildly in the assault. I should secure them but I'm temporarily paralyzed. Another crack wails and the sky's lit like midday, I see a large timber across the river tip toward the earth.

Darkness falls again and I hear the crash of the tree as it meets the ground. Of course I knew lightning could be dangerous, I just never feared it before. Never really thought it would have the chance to hurt me. Now I see its power. Another whip of thunder cracks, and my entire hilltop quakes. The bolt strikes down in the middle of my field. The thirsty land's no match for the fiery energy. Within seconds the field is ablaze.

Bright orange walls of fire extend over the field, consuming everything in its path. The gusting winds carry embers of light scattering them all around me. I leap to my feet sprinting to the closest fire. I stomp out the wall that formed along my dandelion field.

Intense heat attaches to my back and dances along my spine. There's a wall of orange against my shelter. My home and everything in it is about to be destroyed. I run uphill, choking from the assault. Smoke creeps its way into every crevice of my lungs. My eyes water and burn and my throat and chest constrict.

I should leave and run away but I can't, I have to fight for my home. I stumble to my shelter grabbing armfuls of dirt, desperately throwing them onto the encroaching wall. I'm fighting a losing battle but I don't care. I fling armful after armful of dirt but the wall continues growing.

I can't win, I have to surrender, and I accept that now. I backpedal past my shelter as another wall of heat scorches me. I'm surrounded. Smoke and heat blanket me and I can't see past the thick barrier of grey ash. My throat constricts and I hear a sick wheezing from my chest. My legs buckle and I collapse. I gasp for air like a fish out of water. I close my eyes with the heat and smoke closing in around me. I see Emma smiling on our bed and then papa smiles looking straight into my eyes before he hugs me. This must be death and I can't fight it.

Chapter 29: Ty

I've dragged myself this far, I don't even let myself think about turning back. I need supplies for Vanessa. The black door is solid and strong so I make my fist tight and bang on the wood. A deep voice startles me.

"Be right there," he says. There's a sliding noise coming from behind the door and I figure it must have something to do with the hole facing my head. I step to the side worried it could be used for a weapon.

"Who are you?" The man barks in a gravely tone.

"Sir?"

"Who are you?" He repeats.

"Sorry. Name's Ty, I got your address from the flyer."

"Did you not see it said every Tuesday night, 6:00?"

"I'm sorry but I sorta need help now. Can you open up?"

"I'm not opening without a damn good reason." He's clearly irritated.

"I'm a citizen of the divide. I'm from the Inner sector, I need help." I cringe as I open my mouth, waiting for foreigners to pounce and demolish me. Right as I finish my sentence there's a string of beeps and the door pulls open. He's a tall man, well built and strong. If I had to guess I'd say he was probably thirty, maybe older. He has dark skin and eyes and a look of suspicion when he sees me.

"This way," he says, gesturing me off his front stoop. "I'm Jon by the way."

I follow him into his enormous loft where cream and black leather couches and chairs break up the open room. His panoramic television is on. He even has a kitchen all to himself. I can't believe foreigners live like this. I feel awkward and outta place in his unspoiled home and I fidget clumsily with my growing beard.

"You can sit." His hand points to an oversized leather stool next to the counter. I sit looking into his kitchen.

I must have interrupted his breakfast, he's got pans and bowls scattered along the black marble countertop. I watch him alternating between beating eggs and stirring thick batter. He reaches into his refrigerator pulling out extra eggs and milk, adding another portion to each bowl. It would probably be polite to object but my stomach's knotted in a tight and spinning ball from starvation.

I keep twirling my hands through my beard while I try stifling the noises coming from my gut. I can't help watching the food the entire time, right up till he slides it onto my plate.

"Pace yourself, you don't look like you've eaten a decent meal in a while." He says as he pushes the plate of eggs and pancakes in front of me. "You'll get sick if you eat too fast."

"Uh huh, thanks." I say as I take my second bite of eggs. They're perfect, mouthwatering and delicious. I eat like a wild animal and realize the knot in my stomach is releasing. As the knot fades I can't help but feel a little sting for Vanessa. She's not lucky like me; she's still in the wild probably dealing with that constant ache of hunger that you never really get rid of.

"Let's get down to business," Jon snaps. "What are you doing here?"

I swallow my last bite of eggs before I talk. "I'm sorta lost... I don't really know where to start." I trail off, "Central told us the foreigners," his eyebrows raise as he smirks. I swallow, "Sorry, that's what we've been taught to call you." He relaxes letting me continue. "Anyway, we've been told you're murderers and thieves living in filth. It was supposed to be chaos out here. And then I show up and you have cities, homes... lives. Actually, your lives seem better than ours." I pause, "Does that mean all those years we were lied to? I don't get it." He waits, probably hoping I'll piece the puzzle together for myself.

"You don't get it?" He asks. I sit dumb as he stares at me. "It's all about control with Central. It always has been and always will be." Swallowing he continues, "There was the crash of the dollar years ago and more crime than before, but there *wasn't* civil war *yet*. It wasn't until the government tried to take our freedoms that the war started. It was a divide of sorts." He stares past me, "Half the nation conceded to blindly follow the government and the other half, my half, stood and fought. We weren't willing to give up our freedoms." I sit, absorbing his words.

He starts again, "You're kept corralled and indefensible. Living under their rules unnatural to human existence while we're out here, *free*." He looks at me as he says the last word. "I'm free to come and go, to travel or not. I can do whatever I want. Central's too proud to ever admit their way was wrong. They've built walls around you so you'll never find out just how bad you've got it. For years sympathizers all over the country have been collecting intel and raising forces to liberate your people."

"What did you just say?" I ask.

He looks at me sort of confused. "Which part?" He asks.

I can't hide my tone. "The part about savin' us."

"There are groups all over the country whose singular charge is to take down the walls of Central."

"And what about the other foreigners? The ones that want us dead?" I ask. He looks confused.

"There aren't any 'foreigners' trying to kill you. What are you talking about?" He asks exasperated.

"That's why we have patrols surroundin' our walls, to keep the foreigners out. You attacked us three years ago; you killed dozens of people with a military hover." He barely pauses before laying it out.

"Ty, I'm sorry you believe that. It's hard to tell you this but that wasn't us. It was Central." I squirm in my chair. A part of me doesn't believe it, but a bigger part of me does. "We have a treaty and we follow it. No attacks have been made in decades. Our only efforts are at liberating you," he pauses, "I swear."

I'm standing before I even realize I wanted to. I'm nauseated and dizzy. "I need to use your bathroom," I say watching Jon point toward the narrow hall.

"Second door on the right."

I'm up and turning so fast that I nearly knock over the small black table sitting neatly against the wall. A warm burn lifts from my gut. I make it to the toilet just in time to lose my breakfast.

"You shouldn't have eaten so fast," Jon shouts as he clatters in the kitchen.

True, but that's not why I'm sick. I'm sick because I'm the only person that knows the truth about Central. I want to believe Jon's wrong but deep down I know he's not. Central exiled Nessa and I to die together. They lied to us about the foreigners. I know they are bad, Jon just happened to be the one to confirm it.

Somewhere over those walls my family is going through their routines like sheep being led to slaughter. Vanessa's a day closer to dying for a society and government that puts so much stock into its own power that it actually attacks its own people to keep them in fear.

I flush the toilet and rinse my mouth with the fresh water that empties from his silver faucet. I lift my eyes to the gold-framed mirror and automatically do a double take. My cheeks have sunken in looking like chiseled rock. My eyes sit too deep and my hair is matted in layers of filth. I almost do not recognize myself.

Sinking my hands under the water I watch the trail of dirt slide down the glass basin. Layer after layer melts away, it seems never ending. I turn the faucet off and make my way back to the living room.

"Tell me Ty, if you thought we were murderous barbarians then why'd you leave?" He asks from the kitchen.

"I didn't have another choice. I was born in the Outer. Do you know about our sectors?"

"I know about them. It's revolting the way they treat you."

"Well I was a part of the Outer. I managed to make the leap and move to the Inner when I was fifteen." I look to Jon.

"Go on, I know about your leap." He says, so I continue.

"I met a girl from the Inner and we fell in love." It's a bit of a lie but I'm too proud to admit it's a one-sided love affair. "We both got offered the leap but at the banquet we refused to take it." He looks puzzled. "We would've been separated if we took it and we wouldn't go without each other." Now I'm really fabricating the story. "We were punished for refusin'. They exiled us to separate parts of the Inner. But they hid it from the other citizens. They paraded us in front of cameras and forced everyone to watch as Central declared us 'scouts.' They said we'd turned down the leap in exchange for a once-in-a-lifetime chance to protect the Inner." I pause letting my stomach cramp, reminding me its empty again. "I haven't seen her since we were exiled but I know she's in danger. If I don't get back to her with medical supplies she'll die."

"You know this how?" He asks. This definitely isn't a conversation I wanted to have but I can't really avoid it.

"I can see the future." I pause, waiting for him to laugh but he keeps his composure. "I've been seeing the future since I was a kid." Still no laughter or questions. "In my sight I saw her die in a fire. I know it's comin' in the next month or so. I have to get back to save her." Jon bites his lower lip raising his eyebrows in a sort of suspenseful look.

"You're telling me you're a Prem."

"A what?"

"Fine, I guess I'm telling you...You *are* a Prem" he says. I gawk at him.

"What the heck is a Prem?"

"I shouldn't be surprised your government hasn't warned you about this." He lifts the sleeve of my torn uniform exposing my immunization scar. I jerk my arm back to my side. "I bet they told you that scar was from your childhood immunizations," he says as I nod. "It wasn't medication Ty, it was conciliate serum. Central injects it into all newborns to placate them. Since you were infants they've been controlling you."

"What do you mean?"

"It's used to soften your responses, keep the citizens mollified. Free thinking and unruly citizens could mean trouble for Central. They could start questioning things, things Central doesn't want to answer."

"And what's a Prem?"

"Nothing's perfect, not even the serum. In a fraction of the citizens the serum alters them on a genetic level. The side effect gives them premonitions. Or as you call it, 'sight.' Researchers document those outliers as Prems for short."

"So I'm some genetic mix-up?"

"You could look at it that way. You *are* special, I'll say that. Most Prems don't last long in your position. Their free-thinking personality usually gets them murdered well before they reach maturity."

"Murdered?"

"Prems are a threat. The conciliate serum doesn't work on you plus you can predict the future. Two threats Central can't ignore. They look for people like you and try to eradicate the threat."

"How do you know this?"

"My people are the good guys, no secrets or mind control. We've known about conciliate serum for a long time. We've even developed a cure." My head hums with information. "So here's the thing Ty, I'm not really sure how to handle this," I can tell this isn't going to be good, "our government has a treaty with yours and if we catch anyone who escaped from the divide we're obligated to surrender them back. According to our government you don't have asylum here."

"Are you gonna surrender me?" I ask.

"Well here's the thing, being that I'm one of the ringleaders of the largest sympathizer network, I don't think it would be right for me to surrender you back to the organization we oppose." Jon refills his cup, "Instead I think I can use you. In fact you might be just what we've been looking for."

"What do you mean?"

"We've never had access to someone from the inside that *wants* to get back in." I'm starting to see where he's going with this. "I think if your people were given the opportunity to live free with us they'd take it. If those walls were to fall and someone led them to us they'd take arms against Central. If they knew what you know now we could end the divide."

"And how would I do that?" I ask with his eyes cutting into mine.

"We need Central's defenses incapacitated; we need the walls to come down." He swallows his juice, "I have reliable information that makes me believe we have located the two areas where Central maintains control over the missiles. If we destroy those two areas Central would be defenseless. They won't have weapons to combat our crafts. You and your lover could lead the citizens to freedom."

"Why would anyone follow us?"

"Don't you see Ty? You two are perfect. You said it yourself that Central broadcasted your faces across the televisions nationwide. You're probably still being celebrated to this day. Central is probably using their cover story to boost morale. There are probably posters of you two all over and fabricated press releases reporting on the incredible work you two are doing. The citizens already love you and would recognize you. If they heard

Central was a sham from you two they might believe it. You could lead them to freedom."

"You'll help me save Nessa then?" I ask.

Jon sets down his glass, "I guess so."

Chapter 30: Ty

I found Jon on Sunday and the first two nights I felt like an intruder as I bumped into things randomly. Jon set me up on his black leather sofa and I felt guilty when I heard him tiptoeing around his own loft before leaving for work Monday. Sure the accommodations are temporary but I still feel awkward accepting his invitation to stay.

Jon left for work early yesterday. He'd shown me how to work the microwave and television, both were foreign to me. He left clear instructions that I wasn't allowed to leave his loft for *any* reason. Just cause the foreigners weren't homicidal thieves didn't mean I was outta harm's way.

It's Tuesday morning now and there's a thud in my gut. My nerves are acting up for tonight's meeting. Tonight he'll reveal me to the other sympathizers and he'll share his plan to rescue Vanessa. I've been anxious and fidgeting since I woke up. I've been pacing Jon's dark wood floors till my feet ache. I sit for a blink before I'm back pacing. By noon I've flipped through every magazine at least once.

I manage to sit for thirty minutes as I stare out his bay window at the hordes of people bustling along the streets. They wear all sorts of mismatched and colorful clothes. Some carry shopping bags while others push strollers. So many of 'em with their freedom probably taken for granted. At last five o'clock hits and I hear the chain of beeps sounding Jon's arrival.

"Any problems today?" He asks.

"Nope, none."

"Good. The group should be arriving soon. Remember what we talked about last night. Give them time and let me do the talking," he reminds me as I nod my head.

Within twenty minutes the members start showing up. I sit uncomfortably in the cream chair catching bits of Jon's conversations with them. One by one the group filters in and again and again I see their probing eyes settle on me. Jon hardly raises his voice over the hordes of quiet murmurs.

"Okay everyone let's take a seat and get started." Everyone follows and sits, filling up every chair except the one next to me. "I may as well address the elephant in the room," he says with his voice raising a touch. The members shift awkwardly in their seats. "This is Ty Jackson. He is going to be joining us and quite possibly will be the primary force behind executing what we've been planning for so many years." I don't need to look around to tell eyes are burning into me. "Ty miraculously came to us a couple days ago, he escaped from the divide."

He grabs the hook fixed to the scroll in the front of the room. With one quick tug he unravels an oversized representation of the image I'd seen on the flyer two nights ago.

"Ty came from the Outer." He traces his hands in a big circle around the outermost ring. "It's unclear which of the four regions he came from but it's safe to say it was probably in quadrant three." He points to the lower right quarter. Finally it starts clicking that this isn't a random symbol, it's a map of my nation. I had no clue till now that there were four Outer and Inner sectors.

I gawk at the map of my nation, a place I'd lived my whole life and clearly never understood. For my benefit Jon points out that Central sits in the middle, as far away from the foreigners as possible. Moving circularly around Central are the four Inner sectors, each divided by a massive wall. Just past the Inner sectors are the Outer's four sectors, again divided by concrete walls.

Jon's probably right, that lower sector's most likely where I'm from. It has the ocean on one side and a range of mountains on the other where my people mine. Directly south is the city I'm in now.

"Ty made the leap at fifteen and was most likely transferred here." He drifts his finger toward the Inner sector just above. "He's a Prem so it helped him make the leap. It also brought him to a young woman named Vanessa. She's from this area too." Jon pauses, "Ty and Vanessa were both offered the leap to Central but refused." The members mumble, sounding like bees swarming a comb. "I know what you're thinking but it's the truth. It doesn't matter *why* they refused, all that matters is they did and Central punished them. They were exiled to die in the wilds," he says. A man sitting in the middle of the room speaks up.

"Their citizens wouldn't be ok with that. They may be sheep but even *they* would have done something. They would have tried to stop Central."

"Thank you Dave, you're right. Central didn't want to risk losing face among their people. They concocted a story that Vanessa and Ty had been offered a new and prestigious job opportunity. A…" He looks at me.

"Scout," I say.

"Yes, a scout. They were told they'd be an elite team that would spy on us and provide intel to keep their people safe. Central made like they were martyrs when in reality they were serving a death sentence." Some of the members start shaking their heads side to side. "Ty escaped and he's pressed for time to get back to Vanessa. He knows she'll die soon unless we help. He tunneled his way out of the divide undetected and we *are* going to help him." Jon stops, letting his people absorb that this isn't open for debate.

"Once they're both back we'll use them to carry out *our* mission. Once their people see their esteemed Central deceived them, that they left their martyrs for dead, they'll join our cause." Heads start nodding in unison, his plans coming together. "The fewer people that know about the details of the mission, the better. We haven't crossed the walls in decades and if our plot is exposed we'll *all* suffer the consequences. That being said, I need Jake and Kara to stay. The rest of you are dismissed."

The members must understand the risks or respect Jon enough not to gripe. He's a good leader. He stands at his door embracing each member and thanking them by name as they leave. He has a way of making people feel important and cared for without compromising his status as leader. The room empties and he turns to Kara and Jake.

"Sorry to spring this on you two, but-"

"Don't even Jon. After all you've done for us, it's nothing." Kara cuts him off.

I look over to Kara and it hits me that she's attractive. She's older, probably in her early thirties, but there is something mature in the way she carries herself. Her brown hair spirals in tight coils just below her square shoulders.

"Just tell us what you need and we'll do it." She smiles and Jake nods agreeing.

Jon holds up his index finger instructing us to wait. He withdraws to one of his rooms. We hear the sound of boxes being shoved and pulled followed by squeaking wheels coming down the hall. He crosses the threshold of the sitting room with the projector screen coming first. After minutes of watching him attach cords in and out of his tablet the map of my past nation flashes on screen.

"According to my talks with Ty, Vanessa is somewhere in this region." He traces a red circle around the area we think she's in. "We've got one month to get the three hundred miles of land between us and her secured from detection." I'm confused, but Kara and Jake sit focused. "I've activated our contact in Mourse and they can provide two thousand beacons. Our source in Gorham will cover the remaining ones." He'd told me not to talk, but I want to know details.

"Beacons?" I ask.

Jake talks for the first time all night, "They obscure Central's hovercraft detection devices." I stare at him. "It takes a massive amount of energy to block out a hovercraft's signals, so their range sucks. You put them within five hundred feet of each other and voila, you've got an undetectable path." He grins.

"You're takin' a craft into Central?" I ask in shock.

"God no," Jon says. I'm immediately relieved. A craft over the walls would be suicidal.

"We're going to take the craft to Vanessa," Jon says. That isn't much better. Jon looks at me, "Your job will be to secure the beacons starting ten miles outside the wall all the way to her location. The slightest mistake will result in Central detecting our craft, meaning certain death to our pilot and Vanessa."

Jake speaks up. "So what do you need from us?"

"You two will be manning the craft."

Jake looks at me. "Don't mess up boy, you hear me?" He smiles, clasping my shoulder. He's taking it in stride like it's all fun and games but this isn't a joke. This is life or death.

"Kara, you're the best emergency physician I've ever met, you'll need to tend to Vanessa. You can anticipate fire and smoke related injuries," Jon says and Kara nods. "And Jake, you're the best damn pilot our city has. Ty will set the beacons and when he's ready for the rescue he'll activate his tracker. It'll be programmed to the beacons so you'll have a clear route from home base to their location." Jake smirks. I can tell he's one of those adrenaline junkies.

I clear my throat, "How do I do these beacon things? What if I mess up?"

Jon sits down, "You've got a lot of land to cover so you need to start tomorrow. You *will* succeed, there's no other option."

Chapter 31: Ty

Jon shakes me awake. "Ty. Ty," he whispers.

"Yeah?" I yawn. It's still dark outside and it feels like it's been only a couple of hours since I crawled onto the couch.

"We have to get you to the rendezvous point. Mark will be waiting."

I stumble to the bathroom. The steaming shower blasts me awake. I scour my body with Jon's sweet-smelling soaps. It might be months before my next shower. I bend forward with the hot spray hitting my back. Jon's got breakfast wrapped in foil before I've even toweled off.

"We need to leave now, daylight's breaking and we *must* limit your exposure. You never know who could be looking for you," he says and I nod grabbing my breakfast.

He escorts me outta the loft leading me to the underground. We pass two other people awake at this hour, a couple jogging along the park bordering Jon's loft. Cutting through the park we take the stairs to the underground shuttle. Jon is all business. His focus travels to me, making me uneasy.

'Crosstown D approaching the platform' the overhead system announces.

Jon gives me a nod letting me know this is ours. The shuttle pulls to a halt and the doors lift upward revealing a half empty shuttle. I tug the blue backpack Jon gave me over my shoulders and step onto the shuttle. My eyes are set forward. I sense Jon trying to relax but his fidgeting gives him away.

'Mercury Center' the overhead announcement booms as Jon nudges me. The shuttle pulls to a stop and we file out, pressing between the now-crowded vessel. I follow Jon from a distance just like he instructed last night. I think he's paranoid but I keep moving forward telling myself we're dealing with important matters and I should respect Jon's choices. He takes the stairs two at a time as we climb the rounding flights exiting into an open landscape.

The outline of the city's skyline lies behind us. Orange waves of the rising sun push between the buildings. Jon walks straight for a small grey hover at the end of the street. I hear it beep then hum to life as we get in range. Following his lead I climb into the craft. Once the doors are sealed he relaxes.

"We're safe in here; I have it swept every day."

"Swept?" I ask.

"You're not the only person from beyond the divide that cares about our organization. For years Central's been trying to infiltrate our unit. Nail us for any sort of treason possible. If they caught wind that I'm aiding you, let alone what we plan on doing, there'd be hell to pay." His unease sort of makes sense now. He shifts the hover forward.

"All the precautions, the paranoia, it will be worth it in the end, once your people are freed."

"Why do you care what happens to us?" I ask. I don't mean to sound rude but I do.

Jon turns, "Why does any man do what he does? For love." I keep my mouth shut and wait for him to clarify but he doesn't.

He pulls the hover from its street-side spot. My gut is instantly tossed into my throat. He's a reckless driver, flooring it on the straight aways and taking corners half tipped. By the time we reach the open stretch the sun has risen and the mist that fell last night is drying against the green grass. Trees fly by as we rocket forward. Without warning he careens the hover to the right throwing me against the door. We fire forward across the open land, grass and plants spiral as the hover skims over their tops. Jon shouts over the hum of the hover.

"We can't take the main roads the whole way. Mark's meeting us out here."

He presses the lever into full throttle and we hurtle forward, weaving treacherously close to trees. My stomach flip-flops with every adjustment of the hover. I watch the gauge rise dangerously high as he throttles the hover faster and faster.

"Are we almost there?" I ask desperately. He smiles jerkin' the throttle down. I'm slammed forward as he hits the emergency brake. We cut our way in a massive circle skidding to a stop inches from an enormous oak.

I'm a little pissed and questioning his sanity but then I'm laughing too, mostly because he's laughing. We carry on for several blinks before he stops.

"Listen Ty, you have to live, you have to test yourself. Make sure you have what it takes to make major moves. We're about to make some *major* moves here."

He releases the hatch and fresh air gusts between the open doors. I jump outta the hover as Jon whistles a complicated yellow marlow call. We immediately hear one answered back from the distance.

"This way," he says, taking me into the woods.

Occasionally Jon and Mark whistle to each other as a sort of honing system. Step after step we beat our way through the brush until we finally break the trees. There's a gigantic hover that looks like it was dropped straight outta the sky. The trees shield it perfectly. There's hardly any room between the hover and the pines.

Standing atop the massive black hover is an outsized man with graying hair. He's obviously much older than Jon but he looks just as imposing. His whole body is crammed and sorta awkwardly restricted in his plaid shirt and blue jeans.

"Who do we have here!" He shouts as he leaps six feet off the back of the hover, landing gingerly on the ground.

"Mark! You old fool!" Jon barks as they hug each other.

"I must be a fool, agreeing to stick my neck out for you."

"This is a good plan. It's the beginning of the end my man, I promise." Jon says, clasping his hands around Marks shoulders. Jon points to me, "This is Ty." I step forward and Mark throws his hand out.

"Ty, nice to meet you," Mark says.

"Same," I answer as he releases me. Mark smiles, his teeth are white and straight.

"Jon hasn't told me much about you but I trust him, if he says jump, I jump."

Jon interrupts, "Well, now that the introductions are done I'll see myself out of here."

"Wait, you're not stayin'?" I ask. Jon never told me the exact plans but I thought he'd stay longer.

"You two go it alone from here." He says nodding his head. He turns beating his way through the pines.

"Well Ty, let's get started. Catch." Mark tosses me a military duffle bag. It almost knocks me off my feet. It slams into my chest noisily as its contents collide.

"What's in here?" I ask.

"Beacons and supplies. We're ten miles from the wall. We're going to start laying the beacons. You'll learn by doing, it's the best way to get the skill down." Mark starts walking my way. "I'll cover the first eight miles with you. After that you're on your own."

I lower the bag to the ground and Mark stoops over pulling it open. I see hundreds of small black orbs with a single circular glass window that splits their round design. I pick one up; it fits nicely in my palm.

"This thing can block a hover detector?" I ask.

"Don't let the size fool you. Hundreds of scientists dedicated their lives to creating this thing. They have enough energy to hide this craft," he points to the black monstrosity behind us. "Problem is they're only good for five hundred feet. This craft here's nearly six hundred feet long."

I admire the scale of the hover. The black vessel has two enormous broad wings protruding from the side. At the base I can spot six reverse flows facing the ground. Most hovers I've seen Central use only have four.

Mark grabs a beacon. "So here's how it's going to work. You'll be wearing this," he hands me a small grey box. "Every time you lay a beacon you sync it to this," he taps the grey box to the beacon, its glass screen lets off three blue flashes. "Three blues means it's connected. No flash means no go." I nod my head. "Once it's secured and synched," he says, driving a stake through the ground and placing the beacon inside its basket. "Once those two things are done you just walk forward until that thing beeps." He points to my grey box as he hauls off with half the supplies.

After five hundred feet the grey box beeps and I look down seeing the gauge flashing 'five hundred.' We beat the path through the woods walking, securing, synching, and repeat.

Occasionally we come to ground that's too solid to break. Mark shows me how to secure the beacons to the trunks of trees or bury them under nearby creek beds. We're averaging just over thirty minutes a mile which isn't bad considering the weight we're carrying and the fact we have to stop so often. By one o'clock we're at mile eight.

Sweat drips off Mark's forehead. In fact his entire body is saturated. "Well Ty, this is where I leave you." He takes a huge swig from his canteen. "There are enough beacons to get you another eight miles. That'll put you six miles inside the wall." He turns my grey box on its side pointing to the two white buttons. "The craft can only come after sundown; it could be spotted during the day. Once you get to the end of your beacons wait until nightfall and hold these buttons down for five seconds." He takes another swig of water. "It'll alert us you're ready for more. Jake will be standing by every night waiting. He'll make the drop at your location and go back."

"He's gonna be riskin' his neck daily? That's nuts." I say.

"He knows the risks. We all do. Trust me, we've all got our reasons for doing this."

"If you say so." I can't imagine what his reason is; I guess it's not my problem. Mark clasps my shoulder shoving his half of the supplies into my arms.

"Good luck."

Chapter 32: Ty

It would be quiet if it wasn't for the bags that clang together. The extra weight of Mark's supplies slows me down. It takes forty minutes to cover the swampy lands between miles eight and nine. No doubt this job sucks but I gotta stay focused on the end result. If I pull this off I'll save her. Everything I've done for the last three years has revolved around this. Now that I'm finally here I gotta suck it up and do it.

It's almost two o'clock and the wall should be coming soon. I keep walking forward till outta nowhere I see the top of the massive wall climbing above the tree line. The disgusting yellowing concrete towers like an oppressive symbol corralling my people in.

I scan the top of the wall with the worn binoculars Mark left. Shit, a Borg. I make out his black boots, sleek helmet, and his gun cradled in his arms. He's pacing waiting for someone like me.

Screw it I think as I stow the binoculars and keep walking. I pick my way to the point where I can't risk securing any more beacons. My fingers wrestle with the worn strap until I free the binoculars again to confirm his position.

I lower the binoculars to ground level. I spot the disturbed ground I tunneled out from. It's hard to believe it was only a week ago I escaped. It feels like a lifetime ago that I broke free and found Jon.

Luckily the Borg's haven't found the disturbance yet. According to Jon the wall is constantly undergoing perimeter checks. His best guess is that they'll re-check this area in another few days.

The binoculars hang from the strap around my neck as I thud down against a rounded boulder. The minutes grind by painfully slow. My stomach knots and growls until I pull out a protein bar from the side pocket of the duffle bag. Jon packed them for me. The texture reminds me of hay and mud mixed together.

Apparently I only need three a day to survive. At least I'll have more time to secure the beacons since I won't have to hunt or fish. Jon figured I needed to cover sixteen miles a day, putting me at roughly twelve-hour days. Each night I have to activate the box signaling Jake to come make the next drop.

Numbness spreads from my back to my feet. I've been sitting here for four hours waiting for the Borg to leave. I have to make my move now. Jake needs me two miles inside the wall before he can make the drop. That means an hour of my work will be done in the dark tonight.

Thousands of needles jab my stiff legs as I stand. I shake 'em out and sling the duffle bags over my shoulders. It's pretty impossible to be unassuming with two military bags and a backpack but I shrink down as low as possible and run forward.

I step onto the open field as my heart squeezes. The wheat grass sways in the breeze. I wish it was much taller. Instead it leaves my torso exposed; my most vital areas open to the Borg. I imagine him returning to his post, I can almost see my blood spraying across the wheat field. I've got to push on though. I sprint forward ten steps before my grey box beeps. I drop my bags. My sweaty hands fumble with the stake. I don't even look to see if the Borg is back, if he is I'm dead no matter what. I slam the stake with my hammer. It bangs as it drives into the ground and I cringe. I can hardly get a hold of the beacon my hands are so wet. I rub the sweat onto my pants. Shakily, I line the ball into position on the stake. My hands tremor as I place the grey box next to the orb. I wait for it to sync, time seems frozen. I wait for one of two things, either the blue flash or a Borg's flying bullet. At last the screen blinks blue.

Scooping up my bags I sprint forward, my heart beats fast. Two more times my grey box beeps reminding me to secure more beacons. Two times I'm a sitting duck waiting to be exterminated. I shake as I line the third orb to the box and wait. Again it flashes blue and I'm off with only one hundred feet between me and the wall. I grab my bags and sprint for the tunnel. My bags slam against each other. I'm closing in. Just five steps and I'll be there. The Borg's booming voice echoes from above.

"Hey Albert, any problems today?" The one asks.

"No, quiet day. I just finished patrolling the tenth parallel, it looked good there."

I lunge forward squeezing myself against the concrete wall. I roll my head skyward. If I stay right here I'm hidden. Three steps out and they'll see me. My stomach knots as the protein bar tries to make its way out. I hold my breath trying to steady myself against the wall. An hour passes, my arms feel the strain more than anything. The bags are tearing at every fiber inside my body as they try pulling me downwards. It takes everything inside me to keep the bags up. Any movement will trigger the patrols to look down. My arms tremble as sweat rolls down my face.

"Well Albert, I guess you should get out of here. Craft should be here any minute."

"Right. I'll see you tomorrow."

This might be my only chance. I sidestep toward my tunnel. The beacons sway against each other, clanking with each step. I glue myself to the wall and continue sideways. I lower the first bag toward the entrance. My arm still burns without its weight. I stand directly over the loose dirt, I sink as it gives way under my weight. I lower the other bags to the open side and crouch. I push the loose dirt to the sides. After thirty minutes of digging I re-expose the bottom of the wall. I creep into the tunnel. It's a brutally slow process of reopening the tunnel to accommodate my baggage. I work for hours with the Borg pacing a nearby wall.

Its pitch black outside once I've finally finished. I drag the bags through the tunnel, coming across inside the wall. The dark is so thick there could be a Borg two feet in front of me and I'd have no clue.

I take the better part of an hour masking my tunnel before I lift the bags back to my shoulders. I move forward into the black, I still have two miles to cover tonight.

The job seems impossible in this darkness. I pick my way through the woods using the stars and Mark's compass to guide me. These two miles would have taken under two hours in daylight but now it takes me four.

I secure the last beacon, it flashes blue. I sink to the ground with the grey box fisted in my palm. I hold the white buttons down just like Mark showed me. Across the wall Jake's sitting there waiting for my signal.

I unwrap another protein bar. I'm through the second bite when I hear the crashing and breaking of branches overhead. I follow the noise until I find the dropping box, it's probably five-feet by five-feet in size.

It lands on its side with a small parachute skipping in the gust. I pry it open as beacons and stakes pour outta it. I transfer half of them into the duffle bags before I fall asleep on top of the box.

Chapter 33: Ty

It's hard to believe I've been out here sixteen days. I've been getting up at first light to haul brutally heavy bags through the thick forest, mud and rivers. At last the end's here. Jake made the final drop last night and when I pried the crate open Jon had left me a note.

'Only the strong and good will persevere and save not just himself, but all humanity. We will be waiting for you on the other side.'

I guess he meant it as a sort of compliment. Thinking about being back on the other side with Vanessa keeps my spirits up even in the cruel heat that is carpeting everything for two weeks now. The air is heavy but I pick my way through the woods, crossing dry creek beds.

Daylights winding down when I come to the dried bed that Vanessa and I crossed our first night here. It feels like a generation ago that I watched her drag her way across the mud. I say a silent prayer. I pray she's still at the hillside like I'd seen in my sight years ago.

As I finish my prayer, a gust of wind picks up my shirt and I shiver. I realize a storm is coming and I must hurry. I grab the bags and start running toward her hillside. Every five hundred feet the grey box beeps reminding me of my job. I've gotten fast at securing the beacons but it feels like it's taking too long. The sky darkens as rolling thunder bangs in the distance. I cover the ground sprinting. Even with hauling the bags and securing the beacons, I'm at a ten-minute-mile pace.

The threatening storm pushes me faster through the woods. I break through the trees and I'm a half-mile away from her when the first bolt strikes. It reaches from the sky like a hand with fingers open wide. It was close to her, for all I know it was on top of her. The tree the bolt struck lets out a dying groan as it crashes to the ground.

My box beeps and I stop, sweat pours outta me. I secure the beacon and run, pushing myself forward. Two minutes and I'll be there. Another loud crack vibrates as a bolt touches down. I'm in the middle of securing another beacon when the lashing wind carries smoke to me.

This is it I realize grabbing my bags before I take off. I hurdle rotting logs and tear through sticker bushes that grab at my flesh. More beeping and more smoke. My heart tells me to run but I know I gotta secure the beacons. I drive the stake into the ground and sync the orb. I leave the grey box and backpack next to the last stake. Clouds of smoke roll through the darkening skies. I break the trees bordering her thirsty stream.

A wall of fuming heat hits me head on. Her hill's almost totally ablaze. My eyes sting and burn as I scan for her but I can't find her. I'm too late, the hill's on fire. Her shelter's getting swallowed by flames as I sit helpless at the base of the hill.

Then I hear her cough. I sprint toward her, there's a wall of fire surrounding her. I can't tell how wide it is. Without thinking I drop my last bag and shield my face. I run straight into the flames. My skin sears and heat burns into me. I take three steps through the wall of flames before I break free.

Vanessa's on her side, bits of her are charred. I lift her lifeless body as smoke and flames frame us. I do the best I can to guard her as I sprint back through the wall. The wind spins smoke around my face disorienting me. I can't make my way through the blinding fog. The gusts calm for a blink and the smoke clears.

I leap the wall with flames burning what little clothes I've got left. I beat out the flames scorching into Vanessa then throw myself to the ground. I roll side to side. I can't tell if she's alive, she's lying so still.

I sprint to the last beacon and grab my grey box. The tips of my fingers are raw from the heat but I jam them into the white buttons and hold. It's raw pain for five seconds.

I crawl to her body and drag her past the beacon. Opening her mouth I breathe into her. I hardly have any air in my lungs but I'd give it all to her. It's because of me she's here. Her chest rises and falls. I push on her chest just like Kara showed me.

Drops of blood fall from my arms onto her shoulders as I compress. I repeat the cycle ten times. At last a light shines above me and the wind of the hover drives downward.

Jake lowers the basket from the base of the hover. It drops painfully slow. I carry Vanessa onto it, throwing myself on top of her. He lifts us into the hover. My body shakes wildly and Vanessa still hasn't moved. My breath is quick and shallow as we're boosted up. Everything becomes a haze as I black out.

Chapter 34: Nessa

It's the first time in two weeks I've seen him open his eyes. "Are you okay?" I ask. We've been next to each other fighting for our lives. He's finally opened his eyes, his bandaged hands flinch as he arouses.

He lets out a low guttural growl. I imagine it's difficult for him to talk. Kara has us both pumped full of morphine and other 'cocktails' as she calls them, but even still, it doesn't totally numb the pain. Somehow Tyler has stayed in a state of unconsciousness for two weeks, even during the scrubbing.

I'm sure that's not the medical term but it's what I've started calling it. Kara and Jon submerge us in pools of sterile water to irrigate and re-open our burns. All the morphine in the world couldn't numb that pain yet somehow Tyler stayed unconscious throughout it. Kara told me his body is in shock. The severity of his burns were much greater than mine.

I don't remember much about the fire. From what I've pieced together it was Tyler who saved me. He nearly died, actually he still might. Maybe I should feel indebted to him but to me this makes us even. He's one less person I need to take revenge on but that doesn't make us friends.

"Vanessa?" He whispers.

"It's me, I'm here." The hate that used to course through my veins has calmed. How could I hate someone who nearly sacrificed himself for me? His mouth draws into a smile followed by an immediate wince. The abrasions tug at the corners of his mouth.

"Where are we?" He asks.

"You tell me. Jon says you're one of the masterminds behind this whole thing."

"Huh." He half laughs. "Nope, no mastermind, just a foolish boy."

"He told me." I pause waiting for a response that doesn't come. "He told me how you tunneled your way out. That you found him here. Told me about the beacons and the craft."

"Yeah." He stops himself.

"I asked him why you'd do that for me." I stare at him. He's quiet and statue-like in the bed next to me. He keeps his eyes directed straight for the ceiling.

"What'd he say?" He finally asks.

"He told me to ask you."

His green eyes stare unfalteringly straight ahead.

"So, why? Why *did* you do all that? And how'd you even know?" I ask just as Kara's gentle knock sounds from the white door at the foot of Tyler's bed. "Come in" I say. Really I want to tell her to go away. I've waited weeks to hear his reason and I was about to get my answer.

"Oh Ty, it's good to see you awake!" She hustles straight to his side with her curly hair bouncing as she goes. "Are you in much pain? I can help with that if you need it."

"I'm alright."

"Well it's time for your debridement, we have the whirlpool ready." She flashes a halfhearted smile, trying to convince him it won't be so bad. "I'll get the wheelchair." She turns to leave but pauses, "Listen Ty, it's your first time being awake for this and it's not pleasant. Do you want me to give you something to knock you out?"

"Nah, I don't wanna go back to sleep. Let's just do this."

Jon comes in pushing the wheelchair. They lift him out of bed together. The bandages do the best they can to conceal the horrible charred skin but even still the blood seeps through exposing the extent of his injuries. I shudder involuntarily.

He looks at me again, "See ya soon," he says as they wheel him out.

I lay in bed with my head racing as unanswered questions rattle inside. Why, I wanted to know why. I need order and reasons for just about everything in my life and this seems so out of reason and order. It makes me uncomfortable. There's no sense behind why he saved me, how he knew. So many things still unanswered. I daydream for at least a half hour before I finally hear his screams. It takes Kara thirty minutes to unwrap our burned skin before we're finally submerged in the agitating pool. My stomach knots and turns as I listen to him screaming in agony. Screams of pain he wouldn't have to endure if it wasn't for me.

Chapter 35: Nessa

Since that day I haven't had a chance to talk with him. That night Kara and Jon flew us to a private treatment center for skin grafts. Tyler's surgery was the night after mine. That was six weeks ago. After days of agonizing boredom and countless hours staring up at stark white lights the doctors finally say we can go home. Not that we have a home but I'm guessing they mean to Jon's.

I can't imagine the expense Jon's paying to cover our treatments and keep the doctors quiet about us. It must be a lot, not that I really grasp what that means since I've never actually seen money.

I recognize Kara's voice. "Hey Vanessa we're about to transport you back so I'll be sedating you for the trip. It's safer that way."

"Is Ty coming too?" I ask. I started calling him Ty. It's a habit I picked up from Jon and Kara.

"Of course." She says sinking the needle into the IV. Unlike the medication at the leap, this cocktail takes immediate effect. My eyes flutter closed.

I wake gasping as my throat tries to suck in the air I need to survive. Ty's hand covers mine, "It's ok Nessa, I'm here"

"What? Where am I?" I'm frantic.

"You had a bad dream. You're safe now. We're at Jon's, remember?" I stop to think and then it comes back. I'm not in the woods with the fire surrounding me, I'm safe. I withdraw my hand from under his.

"Sorry," he says noticing my retraction.

We've been back at Jon's for two weeks now and I've been trying to avoid these interactions with Ty but they seem to happen nightly. Some nights I wake in a cold sweat, other times my screaming wakes us both. Either way he comforts me, always by my side reminding me I'm safe.

"Remember before goin' off to surgery? You'd asked me why I saved you," he says. The room's pitch black and only a muted streetlight casts its subtle rays into the corner of the room, but I know he sees my eyes on him now. "I was gonna tell you, I just didn't know how. Actually I still don't know how."

"Try," I coax.

He inhales, holding the air in his lungs before he begins. "I guess you know but I'm gonna say it anyway, I'm from the Outer." I sit immobile and patient. He continues, "I was pretty happy with my life before all this. I had family and friends. I did things I loved. I went swimmin', fishin', and sailin'... all sorts of stuff we didn't have when I came to the Inner. I was blissed in the Outer. I didn't wanna leave, I wasn't like you; I never wanted to get to Central. I just wanted to stay where I was."

"So what changed?"

"You can't laugh, alright?" I nod as he continues. "I can see the future. Not like the whole future, just parts and it happens randomly. I can't control it either. I had a vision with you in it when I was fourteen. It's stupid but I sorta fell for you. It was blurry but I saw us meet that night by the house and I saw us on stage at the banquet, and then I saw you die in the fire." His eyes search mine but I sit in a trance. "From that day on I promised myself I'd find you and save you. It's stupid and you probably don't believe me but it's the-"

"Stop," I say cutting him off.

I can't believe I'm about to tell him this but for the first time ever I don't feel alone. For years I've carried this with me, certain that I was the only one with the affliction. Scared that the truth could ruin me.

"I believe you, I have visions too. I get them like you, I don't think you're crazy." We lay in the darkness absorbing the revelation that we're not alone.

He breaks the silence, "It's not our fault ya know? We're not freaks. Central did it to us. Jon told me."

"Excuse me?"

"Our shots from when we were kids weren't immunizations. They were supposed to tone down our personalities and make us obey like Central wanted."

"So everyone has visions?"

"Jon says a real small number of people have a reaction to the serum. That's where the visions come from. We're called Prems, short for premonitions." He answers as I turn to my back.

"I call mine my 'visions'. I named it when I was a kid. I always supposed I was a freak," I say.

"Nope, just a side effect from Central's attempts at mind control. Central doesn't like people like us. If they find out we're Prems they'll kill us."

"Kill us? That's extreme."

"Extreme measures taken by a pretty extreme place don't ya think? You gotta let go of those ideas that Central is good. They're bad, they're the enemy."

He's right, they are the enemy. Sometimes I forget they're the ones that exiled me to the wild; they're the ones that took me away from my family. I've spent the better half of a year blaming Ty for that but I should've blamed Central.

"Why do you think you had a vision about me?"

He pauses, "I dunno. I've been askin' myself that a lot lately. When I had it, it felt like we were in love, like I'd known you forever. I saw you die and I knew I had to stop it. Now I sit around wonderin' why I saw you that day. If I never came to the Inner then you woulda been in Central with Garrett and happy and I woulda been in the Outer livin' my life."

"Ignorance isn't always bliss Ty."

"I suppose but you wouldn't have known you were ignorant. You woulda just thought Central was perfect, the foreigners were bad, and your life was great. I came along and mucked it all up."

I lay wondering if my life would've been perfect. Superficially it would've appeared that way. I would've had so many opportunities but at the same time I wouldn't have felt complete. Maybe one day Central would've found out I was a Prem. They'd eradicate me or maybe exile me to the wilds like they did. I never could've told Garrett about my visions, he wouldn't have understood. Knowing the truth might be better than living a lie.

"I wish things had happened differently but I am glad I know the truth." I say turning on my side to face him, "Do you think you could do me a favor?"

"Sure," he answers immediately.

"Stop asking yourself *why* you had your vision. You had it and you acted the only way you knew how. As far as I'm concerned we're even. I'll piece my life together from here. At least I have a better understanding of what I'm up against."

"What *we're* up against. I wanna get back at 'em too."

"Fine, what we're up against." There's a long pause before I break the silence again, "What was it like in the Outer?"

"It's a whole other world over there. Pretty much everything we had was handed down to us from the Inner. The white clean shuttles I rode on in the Inner don't exist in the Outer. We've got the old busted trols, ya know, the trollies you had decades ago." He snickers, probably thinking of them. "Everything had a sorta dingy film settled on it. From the buildings right down to our skin. Lookin' back I don't know how I didn't go ballistic, guess I just didn't know any different. Our jobs were harder too. Minin' and fishin' were the most common and that's some serious work."

"What about education, and the subs?"

"I suppose that was different too, all except everyone was obsessed with makin' the leap."

"Everyone except you," I add.

"Yeah, everyone but me. Our skills and education were different than the Inner, so I guess that's somethin' to think on. You all focused on jobs and skills you need for the Inner. We didn't learn any of those skills."

"So you had to learn all new skills when you made the leap?"

"Yup. I had two years to cover all the stuff you learned in your career."

"How's that possible?" I ask in awe.

"You're forgettin' I'm a genius." He jokes. "Naw, it wasn't too hard. I knew I'd have an advantage, being a Prem and all. I didn't know that was the name for it but I knew it helped me on my first leap."

"You think we tested in the top because we're Prems?"

"I don't think it hurt us if that's what you're askin'. Anyway, things were just different in the Outer. Smaller homes, harder work, older things. It really was a step up comin' to the Inner."

I lay wondering if Garrett noticed the same differences moving to Central. I wonder what sort of hand-me-downs we'd been given from Central. I imagine my former life being drastically different than Garrett's is now. I close my eyes and let my imagination carry me away.

Chapter 36: Nessa

I must've fallen asleep because the smell of Jon's cooking drifts through the hall rousing me awake. Ty's already awake, and helping Jon in the kitchen. I feel a little self-conscious knowing at some point he was in our room seeing me sleep. My hair is a mess and my leg is flung over the edge of my tiny bed.

I roll out of bed to do my morning stretches prescribed by the doctors. I stretch daily to prevent my skin from healing incorrectly.

"Nessa, breakfast!" Jon shouts as I'm finishing my neck stretch. It pulls from my ear to my shoulder like a searing hot blade driven through my skin. I throw on one of the soft white robes Jon gave me and patter my way to the kitchen.

"Pancakes, strawberries, and sausage," Ty says as he heaps the last links of sausage onto a plate.

I flop onto the chair pouring my juice. I stare in wonder at Jon's oversized and pristine loft. I don't think I'll ever get used to homes like this, I never even dreamed something so nice could exist. The sound of the plate on the rich dark table refocuses me. I flash a smile to Ty as he sits next to me. Jon sits across from us; it's the same routine as always. I'm halfway through my stack of pancakes when Jon clears his throat.

"Kara tells me you're both healing well and are strong enough to travel." I stop my fork midway through the fluffed cake. He continues, "Nessa, we helped Ty rescue you. We had a mutual agreement that we would help him rescue you and in return you two would help us." Ty shifts in his seat.

"What?" I ask.

"Listen, we were talking about it this morning and you didn't agree to anything, so I won't hold you to the arrangement we made. I will say it's going to be almost impossible and very dangerous for Ty if you decide not to help."

"I'll do it." I don't know why but I don't hesitate. I suppose it's a million reasons all rolled into one. This is my chance to get revenge on Central for separating me from Garrett, for threatening Emma, for taking me from my family and nearly killing me.

"In that case we have a debriefing tonight. It'll be just the three of us, seven o'clock." Jon scrapes his plate into the trash before heading out the door for work, leaving Ty and I staring at our half eaten breakfasts. Ty tries to break the awkward silence.

"Jon ever show ya how to play cards?"

"No, what's that?" I've never heard of such a thing.

Ty pushes from the table and grabs a stack of rectangular cards. He begins the tedious process of teaching me the number and suit system. Just as my head feels like it's about to explode he deals out five cards.

"Poker." He smiles.

"Poker?" I ask

"Yup, five card draw." He grins.

The afternoon rolls by as we play game after game of poker. We laugh hysterically at each other as we try bluffing each other out of the caramel candies Jon had in his glass candy bowl. Ty's a patient teacher, especially since I figure the game out at a painfully slow rate. After my second hour I start gaining momentum and actually think I'm getting the hang of it.

"Ty, I shouldn't tell you this since it's to my advantage but it's just not fair to keep this from you."

"What?" He asks.

"You're a *terrible* liar. How do you think I've won six straight hands? Every time you try and bluff you bite your bottom lip. It's a dead giveaway your cards are crap."

"What! No I don't." He says biting his bottom lip involuntarily.

"You're doing it now!" I laugh pointing at his mouth. He throws his cards to the table tossing his arms dramatically overhead. His scars are healing; they're hardly noticeable now. His perfectly straight smile no longer hurts like it did that first day.

"Well I quit. You're a cheater and I'm a terrible liar." He groans as I drive my shoulder into his, knocking him to the side. He repositions himself, "What do ya wanna do now? Jon won't be back for another hour or so."

"You could tell me what we'll be doing on our mission."

"I honestly don't know, Jon hasn't told me much. He showed me a map of our nation and some basics about where we might be goin'."

"A map?"

"Yea, hold on," he says. Standing to stretch he tilts his body to the side. A hint of his stomach's exposed and I see the bottom of his abs. I jerk my eyes away hoping I don't blush.

He walks down the hall. I listen to his steps as they stop by Jon's home office, he clatters around in there. There's a loud thump as something falls against the polished floor.

"You alright in there?" I shout.

"Yup, got it," he yells over the squeaking wheels of a giant projector. "I'm not really sure how to do this, but I sorta watched Jon a couple times so give me a few blinks." Ty plays around with the screen hooking it into the tablet Jon left on the coffee table. "Ta da!" He exclaims as the image flashes on the projector. My heart drops straight into my stomach.

"What is that?" I demand. I can't control my voice.

"That?" He jerks his thumb to the screen, "It's the symbol Central uses. The three circles represent our nation." He points, "Central's here, the Inner's here, and notice there's four of 'em. Friggin liars." He traces his finger along the loop. "And then there's the Outer sectors. Jon said the symbol's part of our nation's flag."

"You're telling me that's a Central symbol? Nothing to do with the foreigners?"

"It's Central's seal or something."

I drop to the couch feeling sick. My head begins replaying my vision from years ago. I'd seen that symbol before, I'd seen it plastered along the base of the craft that bombed our sector. But it couldn't have been a Central craft...

"What's the matter?" Ty shifts towards me as he asks.

"In one of my visions I saw the attack that happened almost four years ago. I saw the craft come and bomb all those innocent people. I saw this symbol painted on it." Ty walks over lowering himself next to me.

"I didn't want to believe it either but Jon told me the foreigners haven't launched any attacks in decades. The attacks are comin' from Central, not the foreigners."

I shake my head, not wanting to believe it. Ty draws me into his chest with his solid arms. I don't fight it, I let him hold me. He runs his hand across my back like I used to do for Emma.

"I'm sorry Nessa. We're from a terrible place."

My anger rises, "It makes me sick. I want to end this, not just for me or Emma but for all of them." He drops his green eyes down to meet mine.

"We will end this, I promise. We'll do it together." I hadn't realized how mesmerizing his eyes are. "I'm sorry this happened to us." I tilt my head to meet his as he sighs. "I never wanted you to get hurt. If I could go back and change everything, part'a me would."

It feels like he's kicked me in the gut. "Yeah," I respond. Of course a part of me wishes that's how things happened too. My life would've seemed complete, but a lie. The core of the person Central wanted me to be was a lie.

"It's better this way," I say. "I'd rather know the truth. I'd rather stand up and fight for my sister and all the citizens who are forced to live a lie. You told me you'd stop asking yourself *why* you saw me in your vision and I need you to stop."

Just then the door beeps as Jon lets himself through the front. He follows his usual routine as he hangs his jacket and lays his leather messenger bag neatly on the bench.

"Hello?" He calls from the entranceway.

Ty kisses the top of my head just before he stands. My stomach jolts as I pat down my frazzled hair trying to find a distraction from the warmth.

"In here," Ty shouts.

Jon smiles striding toward the projector. "Oh wow, you got the projector up all ready? You are eager!" He swiftly punches in the code to his tablet to open a large-scale version of the map Ty had projected.

"So here's the story." We take our seats as Jon wastes no time diving into the plan. "Intel verified that you two are in fact somewhat of celebrities in the sectors. I'm not sure how Central contained your story but they apparently spent a lot of time and effort to make everyone believe you're scouts." I shake my head. I'm not surprised they'd do such a thing. "So here's the deal, you two have been made like saints. You made the ultimate sacrifice for your nation and they're using that to keep the people content. Heck I've even been told there *are* posters of you two in every pavilion."

"That's just ridiculous. They can't keep that lie going forever." I sneer.

"Well they've fabricated much worse." Jon sounds unfazed. "Apparently they're constantly giving citizens updates, false accounts about the foreigners you've stopped and the threats you've uncovered." I look to Ty, he's half smiling. It's like part of him enjoys being a hero even if it's all bogus. "The good news is your faces are recognizable and you're loved and trusted. We're going to use that against Central."

"How?" I ask impatiently.

"We're going to make a video of you two out here, in the 'foreign' land. You'll tell them what they did to you. Tell them how you were banished to die alone in the wilds. You'll tell them how you narrowly escaped and were freed with the help of the foreigners. You'll tell them Central's a lie; their lives are a lie and it's time to be free." I can't help but laugh.

"And how do we get this video into Central?"

"We have some very talented people on our side. We're able to access the digital mainframe and override Central's telecast. We can turn their videos off and run ours in its place. Our guy can hold it for three minutes before Central will cut us off." I shake my head in disbelief. "The video will be played at the banquets. We'll feed it straight into the halls and pavilions where the citizens will be watching. As soon as the video's done the bombs will go off."

"Bombs? Did you say bombs?"

"Yes, we need to take out the control centers they use to arm their crafts and missiles for attack." Jon directs his laser pointer at the map. "There are two control centers in the Inner sector you both came from. It's in the testing facility. Your job will be to find the rooms, set the bombs, and detonate them."

"Simple as that huh?" Ty taunts.

"No, it's not. You have to get yourselves back to the pick-up point in one piece."

"So where's this control center?" I ask, my mind races to think where it could be.

"Our source tells us there are two rooms off the main testing site. Between these two rooms they control the weapons and defenses of the four Outer sectors."

My mind flies as I see myself following Natalie down the hall on my leap test nearly nine months ago. I hear her shoes clanging as we traveled the tunnel and then I see it flash in my head…left at the first fork followed by my nervous counting of steps. One hundred and two until I saw that door. What was it labeled? I strain my mind and then it's there, OS1-2 and OS3-4. OS, Outer Sector.

"I know where the rooms are!" I shout. Jon and Ty both stare, puzzled and disbelieving. "I saw them when I was at the test center for my leap test. I remember exactly where they are. I can get us there."

"You did? I mean, you remember?" Jon can't hide the shock even though it's obvious he's trying.

"I can take us there."

"That's just half the battle. We have our team ready to construct the false identities you'll need to access the facility. There will be patrols but you have to keep your heads and stay calm. Once inside you'll build the bombs from pieces you carry in secretly. You meet Hank tomorrow; he'll be teaching you the necessities to ensure the plan goes without fault." Ty and I simultaneously take a massive inhale as we try absorbing it all.

"I'm not doing this unless you get my father and sister out first. I need their safety guaranteed." Jon rings his hands together before rubbing the back of his neck.

"I was waiting for this part."

"I'm serious. No one wants to get back at Central as much as me, but I refuse to do it unless Emma and my Papa are safe and under our protection." Jon nods his head.

"Deal, I'll have Mark make the pick up right after the bombs go off. He can't get in any sooner without the craft getting shot down."

"Fine," I agree.

"Tomorrow you have your lesson with Hank. Thursday we film the video and a week from Friday you leave. Jake will use the beacon path Ty laid to drop you back where we recovered you. You have less than three months to get yourselves ready for this. I wish you could stay here but it isn't safe. If anyone found out I was harboring you two I'd be arrested and you'd be sent to Central and executed."

Ty and I both look to each other, "We understand."

Chapter 37: Nessa

Ty throws out his hand to the burly middle-aged man standing alone behind the sterile stainless steel table, "You must be Hank." Hank politely extends his hand but I can tell he doesn't like the contact.

Hank looks ex-military. He stands too straight, too tall, and too strong to be anything but military. "I'm Nessa." I don't try shaking his hand. I don't want to make him uncomfortable. Hank's deep voice cuts the tension.

"Today we're going to cover the basics you two will need to execute your mission safely and more importantly, effectively. You're going to be put in the field with all the components you need to execute the mission. What you'll learn today is how to assemble, secure, and detonate the device."

The insides of my palms begin sweating as the intensity of the conversation escalates. I try inconspicuously wiping my hands against the white jeans Kara loaned me but Ty catches me out of the corner of his eye. He glances down and smiles, quickly squeezing my hand trying to reassure me.

"This is the charge." Hank lifts a large black box holding it between the two of us. "It's what gives the device the capability and force needed to detonate. This…" he lifts four long cylindrical tubes capped at each end. "This is where the explosive materials are contained. Don't mess with these. You understand?" We both nod. "Basically what needs to happen is this component needs to join with this," Hank holds both pieces up. "Once you're at your target location you'll secure the bomb to the generator." Hank slides a pixilated photo of a large machine with dozens of buttons and knobs.

"Where exactly are we supposed to attach it?" I ask.

"We'll get to that part. First off, you each target one room. Inside each room there's one generator that controls the missile and defense weapons surrounding the perimeters of the Outer and Inner sectors." Hank pauses letting us memorize the photo. "Once you're in position, you secure the bomb to the base of the generator," he points to the center of the device in the picture. "Use this material as the adhesive."

Hank demonstrates by pressing the malleable substance against the silver cylinders and presses them against the steel table. He tries lifting the device, effectively convincing us of its strength by letting us pull in vain trying to release the bomb.

"Now that it's secure, you sync the bomb." He pulls out a watch and holds it to the device. "Program it for 2000 hours." He can tell I'm confused. "That's 8:00 p.m.," he says clarifying. I nod. "The watch will start counting down thirty minutes before detonation. At exactly 2000 the bombs will detonate." I look to Ty and swallow. Hank claps his hands and we both jolt. "Let's get to practicing," he directs.

We spend three hours learning how to handle the devices, assemble them, and mock detonate the bombs. This is the most important and dangerous part of our mission and the pressure is physically and mentally exhausting.

"You okay Nessa?" Ty asks. We've just finished our last lesson and my eyes burn from the steady state of anxiety I've been under.

"I'm fine. Just a little overwhelmed, I guess."

"It's okay, me too. We'll be fine. Jon wouldn't ask us to do it if he wasn't sure we could." Ty smiles and for a second I believe him. Hank comes back from making a call.

"Okay you two. I've just notified Jon that you've completed your training. If you have any questions, now's the time to ask." Ty and I both glance at each other then back to Hank.

"No sir. Nessa and I are ready."

Jon arrives and I sit numbly in the back of the craft, drifting in and out of consciousness. Their conversations sound distant and muted. Eventually I close my eyes and fall asleep. I wake gasping for air and disoriented. Ty's already at my side.

"Nessa, it's okay. We're at Jon's, we're safe." I crash back against my pillow exhaling.

"How'd I get in bed?"

"You passed out in the hover. I hauled you inside and put you to bed. You must've been exhausted."

"You did?"

"No big deal, you're light. Don't get me wrong, you're a bit heavier now that you're eating but I'm a pretty strong guy." He laughs as I glare at him. "We're only a few hours away from our video shoot. We're gonna be superstars ya know."

"Ty, do you think this will work?"

"I dunno, I wanna believe it will. We owe it to ourselves and the people we left behind to try."

"Who did you leave behind?" I realize I don't know that much about him.

"My family and of course my friends. I have good parents, two younger brothers, aunts, uncles, cousins, the works." I can tell it's painful to talk about them.

"What's going to happen to them after all this?"

"I dunno. I hope they get out before Central gets to them."

"Can't we get them first? Like they're doing for my family?"

Ty pauses, "I asked Jon but we don't have the hovers or the time to get them in the Outer. We could only spare one for a rescue mission and it makes sense to get yours, we'll be in that sector already."

"I'm sorry," I say meaning it. I can tell he's hurt even though he tries to hide it.

"It's okay Nessa, don't worry about it. Let's get some sleep, big day tomorrow." He glides back to bed leaving me awake and wondering about him.

I want to ask him so many questions but I don't dare ask. I want to know why he is still here, why he won't give up on me. I want to know about his visions, know if he wishes he didn't have them too. I wonder if he's scared like I am. Scared that we may fail, scared that this life wasn't destined for us. So many questions but instead I let him sleep.

Chapter 38: Nessa

Jon knocks on our door, the sound startles me awake. "Time to get ready," he announces from the hallway where his steps retreat back to the kitchen. Ty yawns and stretches.

"You can shower first," he groans. I toss my pillow hitting him square in the face.

"What the frig was that for?" He asks with his voice cracking.

"Don't pretend to be doing me any favors! You just want to stay in bed longer." He rolls to face the wall nestling into his pillow. He's such a tease I think as I make my way into the bathroom. The hot shower invigorates me. I take my time enjoying this moment.

Ty shouts as he bangs the door, "Almost done in there?"

I turn the water down toweling myself off before I shove past him in the hall. I walk into our room and my stomach drops. Neatly folded and sitting on my bed is my Central scout uniform. Jon walks in behind me.

"We had a replica made," he says. I nod. "You'll be wearing this under it." He hands me a red bodysuit, it's a deep fire color that's unlike anything our nation wears. "Once you've exposed Central for their atrocities you'll remove their issued uniform and be wearing this underneath. It'll symbolize a new chapter for you *and* your people."

Jon turns and walks away. I slip into my uniform and stare at myself in the mirror. The green suit paired with the high black boots brings back so many horrible memories. I envision them wrapped in the package Natalie placed on our table. The table I used to sit at with Emma. The table in the home I'll never see again. The uniform that hung from my withered and ragged body, the same uniform that charred and burned into my skin. Finally I break. Ty walks in from his shower as I'm slumped in bed crying. I try hiding myself under the covers as he rushes over taking me in his arms.

"What's the matter?" He asks frantically. I pull down the sheet revealing the uniform and he understands immediately. "I'll go say something. That's bullshit. They can't make you wear that. Don't they get what that uniform means to us?"

"Ty it's okay. It's part of what we have to do. It just feels so wrong you know? It brings back so much hurt."

"I know Nessa. Trust me, I probably know better than anyone."

I dry my eyes, "How'd we come to this?"

"What do ya mean?"

"How did we get *here*? How are we supposed to take on Central?"

"One day at a time I suppose. We'll do it as a team. I got us into this mess and I'll get us out too. I dunno why I saw you in my vision and felt the things I did but you're right, I did what I had to do."

"You think we can do it?"

"I think if anyone can it's us. We're different, we're fighters. They couldn't snuff it outta us with the serum. I think we were born for this." He wipes the tears from my eyes, "We can talk about it later. Let's get ready to go. Okay?" I nod leaving the room.

After an unusually quiet breakfast Jon takes us to a private filming studio on the south side of the city. "Floor fifteen, room 202, code is 1022." Apparently Jon isn't coming inside. He does his best to keep a low profile. I call him paranoid but Ty's told me it's for good reason.

My boots feel awkwardly heavy as I climb the stone steps leading into the brick structure. We ride to the fifteenth floor in awkward silence. The floors pass painfully slow and just as I'm about to force a conversation, the ping of the elevator sounds and the doors slide open.

We follow the signs and key in the code to room 202. I don't know what I'd expected the room to look like but this is nothing like I'd imagined. I thought there would be cameras, lights, people, and scenery; instead there's a simple green screen, a few stationary lights and one guy behind a camera.

"You must be Nessa," he takes my hand. "And Ty," he shakes Ty's hand and begins talking a million miles an hour. "I'm Paul and this," he throws his arms overhead and spins, "Is my studio! Jon's told me all about you and what you're doing and it's fabulous. My job is to make you believable, make the people trust you, *and* convince them that this is what they *need*. It's so exciting, isn't it?" Paul spins again, "Come this way, my assistant Dora will be getting some makeup on you."

Paul ushers us behind the green screen to a small station where a round lady with vibrant makeup stands at the ready. Dora shoves me into her chair and in no time begins working on me like Uri did that day months ago.

I'm terrified she'll put that electric blue on my lids like hers but I'm pleasantly surprised when she turns my chair and I see my subtle enhancements. She's kept me natural, just cleaned me up and made me look finished. Ty's transformation is even faster than mine and before I know it we're standing in front of the green screen.

"Hold each other's hands and raise them over head like you did for Central's telecast." Paul shouts out directions to us and Ty and I robotically abide. "Now it's time for your lines, ready, set, action!" The camera flashes on and I freeze. Ty speaks first breaking the silence.

"One year ago tomorrow Central told you we'd denied the leap to take the position of scouts. You've been told we're protected by Central as scouts and that we keep you safe. That was a lie." It's my turn and Paul drifts the camera to me, I swallow and go.

"The scout position was a lie, a cover Central created to keep you in order. We were punished for not accepting the leap. Central threatened our families if we didn't comply. They banished us to the wilds without food, water, or protection. They sent us to die alone." It's Ty's turn again.

"But we didn't die, we survived. The foreigners rescued us. They took us in, sheltered us, fed us, and rehabilitated us back from death's door. They are *not* our enemies. They do not wish us harm. Central has lied to us all. The foreigners are not the threat, Central is." I inhale as the camera drifts back to me.

"Join us." I say my lines as I unzip my green uniform exposing the fiery red underneath. "Break the lies and binds of Central and come with us to freedom. Tonight the walls come down, tonight you can start the first day of the rest of your lives." The camera powers down and Paul claps!

"Bravo! You two are naturals, truly!"

I turn to Ty automatically hugging him. The stress melts away as the hot lights turn off and we're left in the dark. I wonder if I should pull away. He wraps his arms around me, surrounding me. There's no tension, no hesitation from him. He reacts the way I need him to. I can't pull away, I need his arms and comfort right now. I've found peace with our past, and hope in the future. Hope that we'll get revenge together and hope that one day my life will feel normal.

"I'll get this video straight into editing and ready to go before the reveal on banquet night." Paul yells as he and Dora make their way to the back. Ty and I wait in silence for Jon to arrive and take us home. He pulls his craft to a halt in front of the stone steps. Our steps echo as we run toward the craft. Ty hoists me into the craft, his strong arms guide me to my seat. Jon takes off before Ty's even shut his door.

"You two are going to have to go undercover in order to infiltrate the testing facilities. I have some people at the house waiting for you. They're going to transform you and make new identities to back-up your story."

We both look at each other in clear concern. This is the first mention that we'll be transformed to look like other people.

"Don't worry, it's all temporary." Jon adds and we ease somewhat, but I can't help wondering what they'll do to me.

Jon ushers us into his loft. "Nessa and Ty, this is Zane and Marissa." Both are vaguely familiar from one of Jon's liberation society meetings.

Marissa bounds forward, "Hello again! I'm Marissa. I'll be doing the transformation part."

Marissa isn't unattractive by any means; she's a cute girl, probably in her mid-twenties. Her blonde hair sits below her shoulders and falls in rolling waves. Her face is plain except for her stunning green eyes. They sort of pull my eyes to them.

"Nessa, let's start with you." Marissa says and I look to Ty as she whisks me away into another room. "Ok, sit right here for me." She directs me into a portable salon chair she moved in just for the occasion. "We have to change your hair and definitely those eyes."

"What?"

"Yeah, those are the two easiest things to change and they'll make the biggest difference in hiding you."

"What are you going to do?"

"Don't worry." She must hear the fear in my voice. "I'm just going to cut some off. Not much," she adds after I shoot her a death stare. "We're going to have to change the color too. I say we go for auburn red. Your chestnut brown will pick up the color nicely. It should stay for the next few months."

"And my eyes?"

"Don't worry about that. I'm going to show you how to use colored contacts." I stare in utter stupidity. "They are lenses you place in your eyes to change their color. You just have to put them in on the day of the mission."

Marissa gets to work by covering my hair in a foul-smelling substance that tingles as it sits, working its way into my scalp. I sit still, irrationally fearful that the dye on my head is a ticking bomb that will blast if I make the slightest movement. My neck aches as I hold myself stiff. I think about the day I sat in Uri's chair as he prepared me for the banquet. I chastise myself for being so naïve back then. How did I believe in something that was all a lie? Just when I think I can't take the smell any longer the timer rings and she ushers me into the bathroom to rinse.

I open my eyes seeing bright red dye spiraling around the base of the tub as it slides down the drain. I really hope my hair doesn't turn out that bright. She towel dries my hair before guiding me back into her makeshift beauty station.

Her scissors snap furiously as inch after inch of my hair falls to the floor around me. For some reason my heart begins bounding dangerously fast and sweat begins forming on my palms. I try focusing on my breathing to steady me. When that doesn't work I think about Ty. My heart slows as I pretend he's here with me telling me I'm safe, just like he does with my nightmares. Finally I've got a grip. At this point Marissa's already running a dryer through my hair.

"Ok, let me put these in for you." She's holding a small round container where the contacts float. She dons a pair of gloves and pries my eyes open as she places one in. I instinctively flinch and try to retract but she holds me steady. It reminds me of the shackles I wore during my leap test.

"And now the other." She repeats with the other eye, at least I'm prepared this time. I blink a few times to clear my vision and then I see myself. Actually, I see what looks like a stranger's head atop my former body. My hair is a rich auburn red that no longer falls near my waist. It sits just below my shoulder blades but still curls at the ends. Green eyes just like my mother's and Emma's replace my blue eyes. The resemblance is so overwhelming. I sit for a minute fighting the tears. Is it normal to try so hard to contain your emotions that it actually starts to hurt? I don't want to cry but as soon as I look back at the mirror I see Mama and Emma staring back at me. Finally I cry.

"I'm sorry, you hate it." Marissa sounds defeated.

"No, no. I love it." I hug her and sit back in my chair. Marissa helps me practice putting in the contact lenses and once I have the hang of it my transformation is complete. I let the tears dry before I make my way back into the kitchen with my contacts still in.

Ty and Jon are in a heated discussion, as I cross the threshold into the living room they both stop. Jon's eyes are huge and Ty's jaw literally drops.

"Nessa." He manages to say.

"Yes?" I ask sounding more flirtatious than I meant to.

"You were good-lookin' before but now…Wow." My cheeks turn crimson at Ty's assessment.

"Well it's your turn. Marissa's waiting for you."

Ty gets up and on his way by he stops in front of me, kissing me innocently on the cheek. I'm mortified but at the same time the butterflies shifting in my stomach ease my embarrassment. I make my way over to Zane.

"Nessa, I'm Zane." I shake his hand. "I'm making your new identification. You'll only need to use this once, for the entrance into the testing facilities. It'll be activated and cleared to take you on the shuttle systems should you need it, but like I said, the plan is to just gain access to the center."

Zane snaps a headshot of me and then takes a mold of my fingerprints. He types furiously on his tablet. "I'm erasing the old you. These prints are no longer tied to Vanessa Hollins, they're linked to Lindsay Barnal now."

"Who?"

"She's a fictitious character we've made for you to assume. She was born in Central and tested highly into a university for tactical engineering. You have the credentials and now the access to enter the testing site."

"So the old me is gone? No record?"

"No more Vanessa Hollins." The small machine plugged into Zane's computer spits out an ID card. I see the new me with auburn hair and deep green-gold eyes.

"Lindsay Barnal." I say the name out loud. Part of me is relieved to start new while the other mourns the abrupt end of my prior self.

How am I supposed to feel? How would anyone feel if they found out they could be erased with a few clicks on a tablet? I was worth more than that; Vanessa Hollins shouldn't be able to be replaced so easily. I wonder if I'll go unnoticed, if with enough time that name will hold no weight, no draws or emotional binds to anyone.

Ty's transformation didn't take quite as long. She lightened and shortened his hair. His contacts cover his deep green eyes turning them brown. He looks handsome both ways but I prefer the old Ty. There's something about his green eyes that make me feel like I'm falling weightlessly into them. Like they're windows to his soul that only I can see into.

"Well, here goes nothing," Ty says as he smiles taking a seat next to Zane. The process of erasing Ty begins and before I know it Zane hands him his card. "So I'm Eric Barnal?" Ty asks.

"Wait, did you say Barnal?" I glare from across the room.

Zane answers, "Yes, you two are Mr. and Mrs. Barnal, happily married." Our eyes meet, we both look like we've been hit in the gut. First they take our identities and then they marry us.

Jon interrupts, "Okay Zane, I think it's time we let these two get some rest. They have a long day ahead of them tomorrow." Jon's right, tomorrow we start our weeklong intensive combat course.

Chapter 39: Nessa

I pull on the black and purple elastic pants Kara left for me. The fabric stretches with my movement. It's supposed to give my limbs the freedom they need for today's training.

"Ya ready for this?" Ty asks as he strides into the room.

"I guess. What do you think we're learning?"

"No clue but I'm pretty pumped. I hope it's something cool." He pulls his sweats from the hanger and flings them to the bed. I pull my hair into a knot, some red still stains my scalp from yesterday's dye. Ty's voice interrupts my efforts at taming my hair.

"Don't turn around," he says.

"Huh?" I turn around. He's standing in his black briefs. I hadn't imagined he'd look so strong. I take far too long to turn away.

"Or you could turn around and stare." He shakes his head grinning at me.

"I'm sorry! I didn't mean to." My cheeks flame.

"No problem Nessa. It was a warning for your own safety. I didn't want you gettin' one look at me and fallin' head over heels in love." He digs his elbow into my ribs as he walks past me, pulling his sweatshirt over his head.

"Hey you two, crafts leaving in five!" Jon yells from the sitting room.

Ty and I make our way to the craft, I ride in an anxious state wondering what's in store for us. Ty and Jon sing to the music playing over the radio, it's funny how fast Ty's picked up the songs. He's got a memory for this sort of thing.

Jon slows down outside an abandoned brick building. The roll-up garage door in the front has half the glass panes shattered out of it. "Here's your stop," he says.

Ty and I look at each other, he's smiling and I'm terrified. We pick our way across the cracked and uneven lot toward the busted door. Jon pulls away before we've even made it inside. Ty opens the door and my stomach jolts. Sitting in front of us is a ring with ropes on all sides. An echoing voice interrupts my mind.

"Welcome to the hole." I turn to see a salt-and-pepper haired man approach from behind one of the hanging bags. "I'm Clint," he says shaking Ty's hand. "We've got one week to 'show you the ropes' as they call it." The man smiles grabbing the elastic cords surrounding the ring. "Half the day is combat training, other half will be spent shooting."

"Shooting?" I ask.

"Guns, shooting guns," he answers. That's what I was afraid of. Ty beams like a child. I do my best to appear unfazed but adrenaline and nerves course through me. Clint pulls the ropes open directing us to step through.

I'm just about to swing my leg over when Ty grabs my hand, "It's okay Nessa, don't be nervous. We'll do this together." I acknowledge him with a half-smile as I try figuring out what my giveaway was. I was doing my best to look calm.

Clint interrupts my thoughts, "This is the hole. Let's hope you never need hand-to-hand combat skills but if you do, you better be prepared." He moves into the corner. "Line up!" He shouts. Ty and I jolt. "Line up!" He shouts again. We scramble toward the middle of the hole. "Face each other," he demands. We turn. I can tell Clint means business. "Now fight!" We both stop and stare dumbly ahead.

"Excuse me?" Ty asks.

"I said fight."

"No, I heard ya, you just must be kiddin'. I'm not fightin' her." Clint marches towards Ty, his strong shoulders are square and imposing. I flinch waiting for him to hit Ty. At the last second Clint turns hitting me across the face. I drop to the mat with blood spitting from my nose.

Ty reacts winding up to hit Clint square in the jaw. Clint dodges the blow and drives his fist straight into Ty's gut. The wind is taken from Ty but he stumbles forward toward Clint, wrapping him in his arms. Ty's black sweatshirt is a blur as he lifts Clint off the ground landing on top of him. I crawl myself toward the corner trying to staunch the pouring blood. Ty lines up for a blow but is suddenly tossed to the side as Clint rolls him over, pinning him down.

I push to my feet, blood still falling to the mat. I've got to help Ty. This guy will kill him, he's crazy. Clint lines up to hit Ty as I throw my weight behind my kick. My foot sounds like thunder as it hits the side of Clint's head, throwing him off Ty. Before I know it, Ty is back on his feet ready to fight. Clint stands, pleased as he brushes the blood that drips from the corner of his mouth.

"Good. Get mad, get pissed! This is *war*!" he yells pounding his chest. "Drawing your first blood is the hardest. Once you've drawn it, once yours has fallen, there's nothing left to fear." He smirks, blood still dripping from his mouth. "Let's review what you did wrong," he sneers.

"Never hesitate. If I say fight, you fight. When you're out there you won't have the luxury of stopping. It's do or die." He paces around the hole as he talks. "Fight!" He screams, but we don't.

Clint walks forward lining up to hit me again, this time I dodge it swinging my fist into his ribs, he stands up laughing. "Can't hit like that, it's too weak. No power behind it." He grabs my hand closing it into a tight ball. He guides my arm through the motion once before he reaches for my hips, "Your force comes from here," he squeezes my hips. "Not here," he says swatting my hand away.

Repetition after repetition Ty and I practice our punches, leading with the hips and blasting through our arms. Half the morning is gone and Clint has taken us through punching, blocking, and now we're onto tossing.

"Wrap her up in your arms," Clint directs. Ty reaches his arms around my thighs squeezing as he lifts me up and over, tossing me to my back. I slam down, the wind is knocked out of me again. Somewhere inside a fire has been lit. With each crash onto the mat I no longer cower, I rage. Over and over Ty flings me down and at last I can't take it anymore. I fall to my back and this time I react, kicking my leg into his gut. I throw Ty over my head and watch him sail to his back. He slams down as the wind gets knocked out of him. Ty pushes onto his hands and knees coughing.

"What the frig Nessa?"

"No, don't question her," Clint snaps. "That's what you want. That's what you *need.* You're gonna need a partner that won't hesitate, someone with that rage and courage." I walk to Ty, my body aches. I reach my hand down to help him up. His green eyes piece mine as he ignores my help.

"Fight!" Clint screams.

Ty comes at me ready to wrap me in his arms. I drop to my knees and thread my arms through his legs lifting upwards. I drive him backwards until he falls. Something inside him ignites and he barrel rolls on top of me, I drive my arm forward ready to block his punch but Clint interrupts, "Stop!"

Ty lowers his arms. Both of us are gasping for air. "That's enough combat for today. It's time for shooting."

Just like that it's over and my coursing adrenaline settles. Ty reaches down, his strong hand ready to help me. Seconds ago we were at each other's throats and now here we are, ready to take hands. He helps me off the mat, steadying me as I stretch my sides. Clint leads us away from the pit over a concrete ramp. His body sways, cat like and frightening. Off to the side he grabs ear muffs from a table, handing us each a pair. The guns sit in a line across the second wooden table. My stomach tosses, I think of the regulators pointing them at me, like they did that night I snuck out of the house to meet Garrett.

"These are the bullets." Clint rolls the brass shells between his fingers. "You load them into this," he picks up the magazine. Ty and I mirror what he does. It takes us twice the time to load them as it does Clint. "Do it again" Clint demands.

Ty and I load and unload the bullets, with each pass we get a little faster. My fingers move quicker and my technique gets sharper.

"Never point this," Clint points to the barrel, "at anyone or anything unless you plan on shooting them." He slams the magazine into the gun, Ty and I copy him. Clint takes us into an empty room where three alleys sprawl in front of us, targets hanging at the ends. "You pull this back," Clint directs dragging the slide backwards and releases it. "Now you're live and ready to shoot."

Ty and I pull our slides back but we're both clumsy with it. "Again!" Clint barks. Over and over we repeat it until we're efficient. "Now aim," Clint staggers his stance pushing his arms forward as he looks down the sights. I notice him exhale as he shoots, the gun thunders even through our ear protection. The target sways; he's landed a perfect head-shot.

Ty lines up to take his first shot. The gun jerks and the bullet drives into the concrete floor.

"Again!" Clint snaps. Ty tries again, this time the bullet barely strikes the target. Clint walks behind him and pulls the gun from his hands.

"Let the gun surprise you when it fires. Don't be afraid of the shot. Every time you pull back on that trigger you want it to surprise you. The idea's to pull the trigger without moving the sights." Clint wraps his finger around the trigger pulling it back, landing another kill shot. "This time pull the trigger back as slowly as possible and embrace the sound." He hands the gun back to Ty.

Ty lines his feet up and mirrors Clint. He draws the trigger back slowly, hitting the target in the gut.

"Again!" Clint yells.

Over and over Ty repeats. Clint hangs back, coming forward from time to time to adjust Ty's technique. Finally Ty's gotten pretty accurate, his bullet holes group close together at least.

"You're up," Clint stares at me. I move toward the range with my stomach flip-flopping.

"Good luck." Ty smiles stepping aside.

I've learned a lot from watching Ty. I copy his movements by opening my feet up wide. I pitch myself forward slightly and narrow my eyes down the sights. Exhaling I draw the trigger back. I'm immediately jolted by the sound and power. The gun jerks upward sending my bullet off course.

"Again!" Clint screams. I squeeze the trigger, this time better prepared for the force as I fire. The bullet flies through the air hitting the shoulder of the target. "Again!" Clint demands.

Over and over I shoot until I've finally gotten my gun sighted in. I aim and fire until the bullet holes bunch up around each other.

"That's enough." Clint strides over to me. I shoot my last round and set the gun on the table. "First day's over. Time for you to get home." Ty and I instantly look relieved, we must've been tensed all day because our shoulders instinctively relax. "Jon's not coming to get you. You'll run home."

"What?" I ask.

"It's four miles. You can make it. Consider it part of your training. I want you running here and back every day."

"What if we get caught?" I'm in shock.

"Who's going to recognize you? You've already been transformed." Clint sneers as he walks back toward the hole.

Ty and I run home. The cool air constricts my breath. My sides split as I pound my way towards Jon's loft. Ty's faster than me and it's obvious he's slowing his pace to stay next to me. I should tell him to go on but right now I want his company.

Chapter 40: Nessa

"Nessa time to get up, Clint's gonna kill us if we're late." Ty says nudging my shoulders. I turn to my side feeling my ribs instantly protest. I pull at the hem of my tank exposing my bruised ribcage. "Ouch. That looks pretty grisly. I got some nasty ones too." Ty grins drawing up his pant leg. The entire side of his calf is black and blue, marks I left during yesterday's training.

I turn to my back lowering my shirt. "I feel like death."

"Dead or not I don't think Clint cares. We gotta head out soon, he's already gonna annihilate us today since it's our last session."

The thought of training ending today is the only thing that motivates me out of bed. My body aches from the past six days of relentless drills. Clint took the second and third days to teach us grappling and engaging multiple targets. Ty was a better grappler than me but I beat him at shooting. The last three days Clint has virtually been killing us by setting us up in two- versus-one combat scenarios. Yesterday we learned how to disarm our attacker and turn the weapon against them. Intense doesn't come close to describing the level of training we've had. I roll out of bed letting my ribs scream as I push into standing.

Ty pulls my sweats from the closet and tosses them to me. "Catch," he warns. I reach my arms out snatching the pants midair. My shirt drops to the floor. I crouch to gather it but my beaten ribs catch me and I wince in pain.

"I got it." Ty scoops the shirt off the floor reaching under my arm he hoists me up.

"Thanks." I smile weakly.

"Let's get outta here." He says before moving into the hallway to give me privacy.

I change and join him, grabbing my lunch on the way out. It's still dark as we round the first corner towards the hole. We run, my legs reach forward trying to keep pace with his. My breath finally steadies a mile out from the hole. My body warms and the tension eases in my ribs. We run together until we make it to the broken-down building. Ty pushes the door open. The hole is in absolute darkness.

"Clint?" Ty shouts.

We circle around the hole haphazardly knocking into debris as we go. My ears pick up breathing, it's shallow and steady. I make my way to Ty squeezing his forearm. Our eyes can't adjust to the darkness, it's simply too black. I lead him across the room toward the breathing. I tap his ears signaling him to listen. He follows my cues picking up on the sound. He directs me to approach from the right. We separate. Ty closes in from the left. Ty makes his way around when I hear the sudden exhale of air as someone drives a punch in Ty's direction. Ty's arm deflects the punch just like we've been taught.

I hurtle forward toward the fight. I focus my concentration and make my way into the brawl. Ty gets taken down and just as the attacker pounces on top of him I lunge forward, kicking him square in the face.

Ty launches to his feet and wraps his arms around the assailant, pinning his arms behind him. I step forward ready to attack. My stomach heaves as the man drives his foot straight into my gut. He vaults Ty over his back. We both recover just as we hear the gun slide into firing position.

The first morning rays begin casting a dull glow into the hole, shining a light on the pistol pointed at Ty. Without thinking Ty reacts, hitting the man above his elbow, disarming him. Ty points the gun at the man just as I feel my body wrapped in powerful arms pinning me down.

"Drop it," Clint demands. Ty turns seeing me held down. Clint's gun's pressed to my temple. Ty drops his gun and Clint releases me. "What did you do wrong?" Clint barks. We both hesitate. Clint cocks the weapon pointing it back at me. "Answer me!"

"We didn't identify all the threats." My voice resonates as I stare down the barrel of the gun. Clint lowers the weapon as the second assailant pulls off his night vision goggles.

"This is Liam. He's one of my men, a graduate." Ty and I nod at our attacker, both of us ashamed we were overpowered.

The rest of our day is spent reviewing everything we've learned this past week. At days end my body trembles with exhaustion. I sit on one of the red benches gulping water from my green jug. Clint walks towards me.

"This is the end of the line," he barks. I stand, half waiting for him to punch me. He reaches forward awkwardly patting me on the back. "You did fine. It's vital you two practice while you're in the wild. *Never* let your guard down. Not even for a minute."

"Okay, got it." I half smile as I begin gathering my things.

Ty bends forward packing his bags, "Nessa, I'm gonna head back on my own. I gotta do something first."

"Sounds good." I hoist my bag over my shoulder and look back at the dingy hole, somehow I know I'll miss the blood, sweat, and tears we shed here.

I push through the door into the cold night. The dull streetlights hardly illuminate my path. I pump forward, pushing through the first mile with ease. I take the right turn onto Vance Ave when I hear a call from behind me.

It's an unfamiliar voice but it's human I know. I keep running forward moving out of the light into the half-a-block stretch of darkness. A call sounds again, this time in front of me. It's close and my instincts tell me to prepare. I sprint forward.

I hear a man approaching from my left before I see him. I drop my bag, it will only slow me down. He looks barely older than me. His dark eyes dig into me as he runs straight at me. He leans forward ready to tackle me. I dance to the side shoving him forward toward the pavement.

"You little bitch." He gets up, coming back at me. I ready myself for his attack.

He slams into me, his hands shove my shoulders in reverse. I let him drive me against the wall before I prop my foot against his gut and kick him backwards. He stumbles briefly, just enough for me to tie-up his legs and lift him off the ground. I hear his head crack as it slams into the pavement. My hand winds up as I throw my fist straight for his nose. I hear the bones crack.

Today's lesson resonates as my body picks-up another assailant from my right. I stand ready for the next attack. This man's bigger than the first, stronger too. He runs towards me and I remember his face. I've seen him before, sitting on the stoop to the brownstone building just up the street. He was watching me run with Ty. His eyes pierced me, my heart skipped uncomfortably hard in my chest. It must have been my intuition. I must have sensed the bad inside him.

He hits me across the face, my vision bursts like a bright light's blasting directly into my eyes. His second shot is straight to my gut, I double over and roll missing his third strike.

I push to my feet, kicking him square in the sternum. He staggers forward but recovers before I get my next hit off. The dark-eyed boy rolls to his side with blood dripping against the pavement.

"Let's teach this bitch a lesson," he snarls as the two surround me.

My first attacker launches at me and I do my best to fight him off. I get one hit in before the second attacker pins me down dragging me into an alley. I try screaming but the first kicks me in my bruised ribs taking my breath away. They take turns savagely kicking my ribs, I do my best to block their blows.

The first's breathless voice brings me back to the present, "Where's your boyfriend? We've been watching you all week. Running past us, teasing us." He grins. "You thinkin' what I am Drew?"

"What's that?" The other asks.

I open my eyes as the first smiles and undoes the belt of his jeans. I try pushing to my feet but the second attacker pins me down, forcing my jaw closed. The first one wrestles with my pants trying to tug them off my waist. I squirm and buck trying to fight them off. His belt clangs as he rips the top of my pants.

Their hands are rough and heavy. I want them off of me, I want to break each finger in two. My pants rip and I imagine this is all a dream. I imagine that any second now I'll wake up and Ty will be here telling me I'm safe. My eyes burst with light as I'm hit across the head, I don't know what they used but it was hard and effective. It feels like my brain's being slammed inside my skull, over and over it slams. It's pavement, that's what they're hitting me with. How didn't I figure that out sooner? Blood rolls down my face and across my eyes. I wish it was their blood. I need it to be theirs not mine.

My stomach wads and spins as they roll me on my back. Out of nowhere I hear a loud crack. The jangling belt falls silent as my attacker crashes to the side, blood gushes from his head. I focus my eyes and make out the bloodied rock that cracked his head open. Just as my eyes adjust I feel the second attacker pried off me. Ty drags him by his grey sweatshirt pulling him away from me.

"Get up!" Ty shouts. The man sits for a moment before he jumps to his feet ready to fight.

His grey sweatshirt is a blur as he barrels toward Ty. Ty meets him head-on. Both their bodies slam together as they wrestle. They dance in a circle, arms tied together. Ty throws his hip into the man tossing him like a ragdoll onto his back. The man frees a hand and swings to punch Ty but he isn't fast enough. Ty blocks the punch as he pins the attacker's arms to his side. I hear the man's bones cracking as Ty slams him over and over in the face. By now the man is unconscious, maybe even dead, but Ty props him up punching him ruthlessly.

"Ty," I whisper but he doesn't hear. "Ty!" I shout, my ribs jab with pain as I yell.

He drops the man, blood covering his fists. I let him hoist me into his arms. These are the arms and hands that I need to feel. The only ones that I can trust out here. His jaws clenched as he bites down hard. I know what he's thinking because I'm thinking it too. We should have killed them. He carries me back to the loft cradling me in his arms like papa did the night of the banquet. I feel his heart pound the entire way. He carries me past the kitchen, artfully avoiding Jon along the way. He lowers me into the bed and turns to leave without saying a word. I hear him run a bath as I lay in shock. Ty comes back into the room.

"I'm gonna help ya up, okay?" I nod as he scoops me up, carrying me to the bathroom. "Bath's for you. You should take one, it'll make ya feel a little better." I nod again. "I'll be right outside the door. I won't leave."

I nod as he steps out. I peel the torn pants off and assess the damage. My bruises are already more prominent than earlier. I lower myself into the bath and soak, instead of crying I think about what I did wrong. That's what Clint would have wanted and it's the only way I'll get stronger.

Chapter 41: Ty

I don't know what I would've done if I'd been two blinks later. Those two animals coulda killed her. I keep replaying it over and over in my mind. Seeing her on the ground like that made me ballistic. Like something snapped inside me and all I saw was red.

I've known for a while that I've got a special connection to Nessa. Every night before her dream terrors hit I know it's coming, even before she wakes. I can sense the building anxiety inside her. It reaches out to me, waking me. I've been trying to find a way to tell her but the right time just hasn't found us. I talked to Kara about it a couple weeks ago. She said she'd read that Prems can be hyper-sensitive to other Prems.

Basically I've tapped into Nessa's emotions and I can't find a way to turn it off. Thankfully it's really only the extremes that I feel. I pick-up her fear, excitement, and sometimes rage. The in-between times I'm free from her emotions.

Right now I can't tell exactly what she's feeling, I know there's some rage, I can feel that for sure, but there's something else in there too. I prop my back to the door, the blood covering my hands has dried into a rusted red color. I reach into my pocket and feel the box wrapping around the necklace. Somehow it managed to stay in my pocket though all the crazy.

Jon has been letting me do odd jobs around the loft to save up money. I saw an advertisement a while back selling a silver locket. I liked the idea of a necklace that could hold someone's pictures or memories. It seals em up tight, keeping em safe. We don't have jewelry in our nation so it's pretty safe to assume Nessa doesn't have one yet. It's nothing special but I figure she deserves something nice from me. It's because of me she's in this mess. The night we got our new identities I had Zane hack into Centrals records to get her parents and sisters name. I was picking up the locket from the engraver tonight when I felt her terror.

I grabbed it and ran outta the building towards where I felt her. That's how I found her tonight. If it wasn't for being a Prem I wouldn't have been there to save her. I rest my head against the door just as the tub starts draining.

Chapter 42: Nessa

I towel off, my skin's been sheared from my calf, probably from when they dragged me into the alley. I wrap the damp white towel around me and step into the hall. Ty's propped against the door.

"Hey," I say as I step past him.

"Hey. I'm gonna shower. You'll be alright?"

"I'm fine. Thanks for saving me tonight."

He smiles, "Don't mention it. We're partners now, we get each other's backs."

I walk into our room closing the door behind me as he runs the shower. He laid my pajamas on the bed for me. I crawl into them and lower myself into bed. My head touches down and I hear a crackling sound from under my pillow. I'm confused, like maybe the attackers dislodged something in my ear that's making the rustling sound. I sit up fishing my hand underneath my pillow, hoping to find the source. My fingers wrap around a box. I pull it out, the blue paper has two smears of dried blood that frame the bright yellow bow.

I clumsily untie the ribbon letting it drop to my lap. I've never opened a present before and I try saving the paper as I carefully unwrap it. Ty steps through the door with his towel around his waist. I set the blue paper aside and open the box.

"What is it?" I stare at the silver object in my hand.

"It's a necklace. A locket to be exact." He sits down next to me taking the locket from my hand.

"I've seen people wearing these on the streets. How's it work?" I ask. He grins opening the oval charm. I gasp, "Don, Emma, and Emilia…" I say them as I trace my finger across their names.

"I had Zane get their names for me. As long as you've got this, you've got a piece of them with you forever."

"Ty I don't know what to say?" He stands drawing his towel around his hips.

"Thanks is usually standard." He smirks grabbing his clothes from the closet. He turns to leave but stops at the door. "Nessa, there's somethin' I've been meaning to tell ya." I look up, the locket still in my palm. "I didn't just get lucky and come across you tonight." He pauses.

"Did you have another vision?"

He turns to face me, "No. It's somethin' different... I can sense your feelings." My face screws-up in confusion. "I know, it sounds crazy even to me. It started durin' your night terrors. At first I thought it was a coincidence but then I realized I could actually *feel* you gettin' scared. That's why I was always by your side in less than a blink."

"That sounds crazy."

"Yeah, I know. I talked to Kara about it. She said Prems can do that. We can sorta attach ourselves to another Prem and tap into their emotions."

I don't really know how to feel about this. I keep my eyes locked with his as I squeeze the necklace tight.

"So you *feel* what I feel?"

"Not all the time. Just the extremes. I tried makin' it stop but I can't. Kara says it just happens to some people. I'm sorry."

"And the necklace?"

"What do you mean?" He looks confused. "Nessa the necklace was a gift. It had nothing to do with me feelin' anything for you other than sorry for puttin' you in the situation you're in. It's a gift."

"Thanks," I say as I release my grip slightly.

He turns towards the door grabbing the frame with his hand. "There's a cure ya know." He wheels back to face me. "They've got a cure out here to counter the conciliate serum. It might cure us from being Prems." My eyes meet his, I'd never thought of curing my visions before. I didn't imagine it was possible. "I'll take it if you want." He hesitates. "I'll never have another vision with you again and I'll stop feelin' your emotions. It's the best thing I can come up with."

I freeze as the possibilities prattle in my head. I'm mad that someone's able to meddle in my brain and feel my emotions but at the same time it gives me some comfort. If it wasn't for that I could've been killed tonight.

"It's okay. We've just found out we're Prems. We're starting to learn what that means, let's not break that yet." I answer.

"Deal." He smirks as he turns to leave the room. I clasp the locket around my neck and fall into a dreamless sleep.

Chapter 43: Nessa

Jon knocks on our door waking us well before first light. "Time to get up you two. Bags are packed and Jake's waiting." He fidgets with his watch as he opens and closes the door three times before he shakes his head walking away.

"Why's he acting so weird?" I ask Ty. I've never seen him like this.

"Don't mind him. He gets this way before a big mission. He'll be alright."

I roll out of bed pulling on the long elastic outfit Kara gave me. It's insulated but light-weight. The next few months leading up to January are going to be brutally cold. Thankfully Jon and Kara packed provisions to take us through until the mission.

"Morning, Jon." I yawn as I greet him.

"Morning Lindsay," he answers. It takes me far too long to catch onto what the heck he's talking about.

"Lindsay. Right..."

"I suggest you and Eric start using those names. Read your file; get to know your new identities. You never know, it could save your life."

"Don't worry, we'll do it. Right, Lindsay?" Ty's hands are on my shoulders. "She can be a bit ornery but that's why I married her." He playfully squeezes my shoulders and walks away.

"Joke all you want but I'm serious. This could mean life and death for you two and the freedom of your people."

All joking aside I get it. I just don't like admitting the importance and responsibility I've gotten myself into. Jon escorts us out of the house taking us through the underground shuttle system. We exit to street level climbing inside his craft.

"Buckle up," Ty says.

Just as my buckle clicks in place my body's plastered against the seat as Jon flings down the accelerator. He drives like a maniac on the open roads and before I know it we're interlacing in and out of trees and rocks.

My heart's hammering and my knuckles are clutched white. Ty and Jon look relaxed in the front. Guys can be so dumb. Just as fast as we took off we slam to a skidding halt. The craft idles a foot above the ground and my stomach churns, threatening to expel breakfast. Ty opens the door and I robotically give him my hand.

"You okay?" He asks sinking me to the ground.

"What was that?"

"I told ya he gets weird before missions."

"Well you could have warned me a little more thoroughly."
I shake my head as we take off behind Jon walking through the
thick woods. Out of nowhere there's Jake standing beneath the
most monstrous black craft I've ever seen. "Holy," I gasp. Ty
turns to me.

"You don't remember it?"

"Should I?"

Jake interrupts, "It's only the craft that saved you."

"This is? I don't remember anything about it."

Jake grins, "Yeah, she's a beauty isn't she? No time to fool
around though, daylight's almost here and we've got to get across
the walls before patrols spot us."

I turn to give Jon a hug and thank him for all he's done.
Words can't express the gratitude I feel or the debt I owe him.

"Where'd he go?"

Ty looks unfazed. "Jon? He's like that. Doesn't like goodbyes
I guess. Did the same thing to me when I went after you." I'm
speechless and wounded. Jake waves from the ramp leading into
the craft.

"Come on you two."

We haul the oversized duffle bags to our shoulders trudging
up the ramp into the belly of the massive craft. I can see what
remains of our rescue months ago. There's a hospital bed in the
corner with medical machines and oxygen tanks stacked to the
side. I can only imagine the chaos it was here.

The craft flies smoothly through the night, touching down to our charred hillside just as first light breaks. Jake powers off the craft helping us unload our supplies.

Since Ty and I have never set up a tent, Jake takes the morning teaching us how to build and secure the tents Jon packed for us. It's a fortress by the time it's done, a real camouflaged castle.

The first room holds all our meals and cooking supplies, they lay tidily along the left side. Straight ahead are the beacons and radios we'll need to communicate with the team on the other side of the wall. To the right is a large metal chest with the words 'caution explosives' written across the sides. It's our bomb materials.

The tent is tall enough for me to stand straight up in but Ty has to duck or else the top of his head scrapes the roof. He's tall, almost six-three. I commandeer the room to the left, setting it up as my own. I have my own cot, a stack of clothes, and a sealed container carrying my contacts, Central uniform, and my new ID badge. Ty's room is in the opposite corner of the tent. He seems so far away now. I'm used to having him next to me, close enough to hear him breathing.

By the time everything is unpacked and we are settled, the sun has gone down and Jake's safe to leave.

"Well you two… God speed." He says smiling as he leaps up the ramp in three steps. As the craft lifts off it hits me how quiet it is out here.

"Well wife, what should we do with our time?" I glare at him. Joking or not, I'm not happy that Zane felt the need to marry us. I storm my way to the tent with Ty on my heels. "It was a joke, alright?" I nod. Ty's hand wraps around my arm. "I swiped something from Jon's place before we left." He flashes a devious smile as he pulls the deck of cards from his jacket pocket.

I could use a distraction, "Alright. You deal," I say. Ty deals hand after hand. An hour into our game I start complaining, "It's not fun without the candies, there's no incentive now."

"I can think of an incentive." He smiles.

"What?"

"Our clothes." He smirks again. "I believe I've heard it called strip poker."

I flush, "You aren't serious!"

"It's nothing I've never seen before." He smiles. I'm stunned that I'm jealous. He hasn't seen me naked before so who's he talking about?

"Fine." I chime as he starts picking up the cards.

"It was a joke."

"No I want to. Unlike you I haven't seen everything before. Let's play so I can laugh when you stand naked in front of me."

"That sounds like a whole lotta awful." He pauses as I stare at him coldly. "I'll take my chances, I guess," he says as he hesitantly deals the cards.

I lose the first hand and peel a shoe off. Ty loses the next two and sits shoeless. I hit a bit of a losing streak and am down to no shoes, socks or shirt. I've still got my bra, pants and underwear covering me. Determined not to lose I buckle down and before I know it Ty's sitting across me in his black underwear, which are tight to his strong legs. I have to win the next hand; I'm down to my bra and underwear too.

"Let's just call it a night. No need to embarrass either of us." He says with a sort of urgency in his voice.

"No. We go *all* the way."

"Your call." His face scrunches.

"Show me your hand." I smile, I have a full house. I fan it out before him. No way will he beat me. He sluggishly puts down his straight flush.

"What!" I shout as he frowns. I freeze momentarily and then begin fidgeting with my bra from the back.

"Whoa, whoa! Let's just call it a night." He turns his eyes away as he talks.

"Huh?"

"I don't need to see you naked. It was just a game." He scoops up the cards and his pile of clothes taking them toward his room. It feels like I've been slapped in the face. What's so wrong with seeing me naked?

"Wait a minute!" I shout. He turns to face me, he's totally confused. "What's so wrong with me?" I demand. He laughs so I push him backwards.

"What the frig?"

"Seriously, what's so wrong with me? You don't want me anymore? What happened to you 'loving me, and wanting to save me?' Now that you've done that you're over it?" He looks shocked as he tries collecting my swinging arms.

"Nessa calm down. It's not like that at all." I keep twisting my arms. He's hugging me trying to restrain me. "I've loved you since the start but I respect you, too. I don't wanna take advantage of you."

There's that word again, love. How am I supposed to react to that? I could let myself react naturally, the way my heart tells me to. I could let my heart hammer against my chest and tell me to believe him. Maybe I could let myself drift away in the moment and hope for more moments like this. Or I could turn away, hide my heart and continue shielding it. That's what any sane person would do, isn't it? But then my pounding heart slams hard, knocking on my chest begging me to yield. I want to yield. Not just to stop the hammering inside but because I know he might be the only one to ever make me feel this way again. Without thinking I reach up pulling his lips to mine. His hands hesitate then furiously run down my neck and shoulders. He pulls me into his kiss.

I was wrong, my heart only hammers harder. My pounding chest soars as we stagger backwards over his pile of clothes, dropping onto his cot. I straddle him kissing him, my breath quickens with every touch. My fingers fumble with the clasp of my bra as he grazes his way down my long neck. My bra releases freeing my chest, I throw my bra to the side. He makes his way towards my exposed chest. My heart beats faster and harder as the sensations take me to the verge of shattering.

My body shivers as my skin rises on edge and I feel his solid arms lift me up, turning me on my back beneath him. My breathing is fast and shallow while his is calm and even, his confidence is exciting and so controlled. His hand plunges downward and my breathing stops as I arch my back twisting and turning.

I'll never be able to look at his hands the same. He works his fingers as his mouth finds its way upwards until he's at my chest again. In no time the sensation begins building and it's like I'm about to crack open, and then it happens. Amazing blissful sensations peak and I scream and moan in response. Ty relaxes his tense body and positions himself behind me.

"What did you do?" I ask breathlessly.

"Just one of the things I've wanted to do for a long time." He kisses my cheek holding me in his arms. His body's pressed to mine but he doesn't push me for anything more. "Let's go to sleep." He sighs as he kisses the back of my head, "I love you."

My heart hammers with the word. I can't bring myself to say it back. I feel something for him too but it's still too soon. I close my eyes hoping the guilt will go away. I keep telling myself I'm not doing anything wrong. I would have been with Garrett if Central hadn't taken him away. I can't spend my whole life alone anyway. I squeeze my locket and let Ty drape his arm around my waist. Ty's deep breaths rise and fall from behind me.

With each breath I struggle to let myself be at peace. I wonder if Garrett is sleeping somewhere, breathing in the same rhythm as Ty. I wonder if his breath would have felt warm across the back of my neck too. Impossible questions, ones without answers. Answerless questions, the types that I should banish from my mind but never have the power to overcome them. Isn't it awful that this is the way it works? The things that we can never wrap our minds around become the very seeds that consume our thoughts.

Chapter 44: Nessa

It seems like it was just yesterday that Jake dropped us off at our hillside. It's hard to believe two and a half months have passed already. Ty and I moved our cots into my room after that first night. We've spent every night together since. Today's our last day on the hill. It's time to start making our way to the testing facility.

"Lindsay you wanna help put this stuff in my hair?" Ty asks. The roots of his dark hair are peeking through.

"Yeah, let's do this." I rub the dye through his strands. We sit along the embankment waiting for the twenty minutes to pass before we rinse.

"Tell me about your family," he asks for the hundredth time. He told me all about his family a long time ago but I've done my best not to talk about mine.

"You really want to know?" He nods his head. "Okay, let's see…" I trail off, trying to grasp my thoughts before I start. "My sister was born when I was five. My first vision happened a week earlier. My body stung from head to toe and woke me up." I turn and see Ty focused on me. "I wanted so badly to move and free myself from my bed, my clothes, even my own skin but I was held hostage. I was paralyzed. The stinging turned to a steady buzzing and suddenly I was watching scattered images flash inside my mind. My head buzzed and blurred with snapshots of my mother lying with glazed green eyes and skin so white it was virtually transparent. After what seemed like an eternity the images stopped and my body was released. I'd soiled my grey gown and cried, I remember I lay all night in my soiled gown too afraid to move." I look to him as he reaches for my hand.

"I was afraid I might wake my father who even then was already exhausted to the point he looked broken from the inside. But worse than waking him, was the thought of waking my mother. I couldn't bear to see her after what I'd just seen. Two months earlier the healer had told her she needed bed rest. Her belly had swollen so much those last few months and the more it swelled the less dancing light I saw radiating from her green and gold eyes. Since the day the healer had come she hadn't taken me to the river bordering our house for my swim lessons." I laugh remembering those lessons.

"A week after my vision I walked into our three-room home to find my father frantically pacing back and forth with his hands fisted and pulling at his graying hair. Tears streaked his pale face. I'd never seen him cry and I remember thinking it looked strange. In that moment he must've been too overcome with emotion to conceal his tears or wipe them from his face. Maybe he needed to feel them cool against his skin to know this was all really happening. The creaking of the door snapped him back to reality and he shot his wet eyes straight at mine." I pause, wiping the corners of my eyes.

"He shouted to me to get the healer as fast as I could. I knew he was shouting but his voice sounded muffled and distant. I stood in our doorway unable to move. I knew what he needed but leaving was impossible. I was only five but I knew what was happening." I wipe my eyes again as tears begin filling the corners. "He shouted again, interrupting my mental lapse. Before I bolted out the door I managed one final glance over my shoulder. I saw my mother drenched in her own sweat. Her skin was no longer tanned and glowing, it was sickly pale and wet like she'd been plunged in an icy bath. I ran out of the house and down the walkway."

Ty holds his steady stare as I continue, "My mother's entire body shook so hard I could hear the bed quaking from the dirt walkway. As I rounded the first street corner I heard one final cry breaking her lips followed by a high-pitched scream from my newborn sister. I turned right with my naked feet slapping the dirt. I felt my sides split with pain. My chest pounded hard as my body fought to force air out as fast as I could take it in. I ran and I ran. I flew past the collectors' station and took my final turn. I didn't see the rock until it was too late and before I knew what was happening I was propelling through the air. I hit the ground with such force and momentum that I skimmed across the paved streets of the sub-one neighborhood. My knees felt like someone was holding a torch to them and searing them with black tar."

I pull up my pant leg, "That's where this scar came from." I drop the fabric and continue, "I collected myself on all fours and let my cheeks feel the tears rolling from my eyes. In the middle of my weakness I felt a hand on my back. I lifted my head and pressed my eyes together and standing above me was a small boy with golden hair and deep brown eyes like acorns." I turn to Ty and I can tell he knows the boy was Garrett. "His first words were asking to help me. I told him I needed a healer and where to find our house. Without hesitation he was off. I brought myself to my feet. I couldn't bear waiting on the black tar for the healer and I didn't want to be so far from mama. I dashed toward my house with my mind numbed. I forgot my heaving heart and splitting sides and felt the warm blood dripping from my knees. I trusted he'd send help. I don't know why but all it took was that one touch and I trusted him." I smile as I remember us as kids.

"I ran and I ran retracing my steps back home. My feet pounded the pavement of sub-one and eventually I felt the dirt path of my subdivision. I rounded the corner and flew up our walkway and was finally home. I opened the door and saw her lying with glassy eyes. Her chest was heaving like the baby bird I saw fall from its nest that spring. I remember cradling the bird as it lay broken but breathing. The shock from seeing mama's sick eyes and ragged breathing paled in comparison to the blood that covered her bed sheets. It was just as I'd seen it a week earlier in my vision. I went to her and could think of nothing but feeling her touch one last time. I slid my small hand into her cold damp palm. All I could think to do was sing and I made up a song just as she had done for me so many times before. When I came to the chorus I felt her squeeze my hand one final time. And just as it had with the bird, the breathing stopped. She was gone and there was nothing I could do. The healer burst through the door and sent me out but I already knew it was too late."

Ty squeezes my hand reminding me it was all in the past. "I went to the small room separating the sleeping quarters from the weatherworn door. I sat with papa in the only chair we owned and fixed my blue eyes on the tiny bundle he held. He rocked her as tears streamed down his face. I wanted to hate this thing that had taken mama from me. Eventually I decided I would face her and when I got close, she looked directly at me. All I could see was my mother's full green and gold-flecked eyes. I couldn't help but love her; she was already so much like mama." I smile remembering Emma like that.

"That's how the life of my family as we know it started. How my papa became a widower that was forced to work double shifts, how I fell in love with Emma, lost my mother, and met Garrett."

"I'm sorry Nessa. That must have been awful."

"It was but I got through it. I couldn't have done it without Garrett."

It's been a long time since I've let myself think of him. Ty filled the holes in my heart almost completely but now that I've let myself talk about him again, I realize a part of me still belongs to Garrett. Is it possible to ever let go of your first love? Can I ever find a way to give my heart away again? If not to Ty then I'll never be able to do it. I lift myself off the ground.

"It's time to rinse that stuff out of your hair."

We walk to the chilled river and rinse the dye from his soft hair. In no time he's transformed back to Eric. My heart aches as I try forcing it to choose its course. We walk back to the tent to finish packing, my heart still bound down.

Chapter 45: Nessa

Ty nudges me, "Nessa, time to get up. We should be headin' out." I throw my arms overhead stretching them out. "I made ya breakfast." He laughs putting a packaged nutrition bar beside me.

"I'm so sick of these things. I can't wait to get back to Jon's and get some real food," I groan.

Ty's voice trails off as he snaps off the corner of his bar, "Pancakes, eggs, sausage…" I shoot him a look of dissatisfied longing as I bite into my bar.

After breakfast we hardly move as we slowly condense our supplies into two hiking bags. He's carrying the explosives. I offered to take half but he refuses to let me carry something that could detonate at any given moment.

"So how many miles do we have to cover?" I ask.

"We're two hundred miles from the testin' facility and one hundred and thirty-four from your home."

The word home no longer conjures one specific location. There was the home I grew up in in sub-three, the one with the creaking blue door. Then there was the shelter I'd made that's now ash and char. But that's not all; home also feels like Jon's loft in the city and our tent in the woods. Home is an idea held loosely now, one tethered by so many strings they've become tangled and intertwined.

"I figure we can cover twenty miles a day. At that pace we'll be at the facility in ten days."

"Two days to spare." I smile.

We take a final look back at our tents before we push forward through the woods. The thick trees provide shelter from the whipping winds that cut through the air. The ground is frosted and crunches beneath our boots. The faintest dusting of snow fell yesterday and lingers in the deep woods. I hypnotize myself watching the endless impressions Ty's boots make in the snow as he walks ahead of me.

"Should we perfect our stories?" I ask.

"I thought you'd never ask Mrs. Barnal." He smiles as he continues picking his path through the frosted brush.

I give my best Central impression, "State your name and business." He turns laughing at my terrible impression.

"Eric Barnal, electronic surveillance coordinator. First day on the job."

"Credentials?" I ask in my 'official' voice.

"Citizen 99201, educated at MIFF." He swipes an imaginary card to imitate the card Zane made for him. "Who are you?" He asks in his usual husky voice.

"Excuse me?"

"What? Not official enough for you?" He teases. "Fine...State your name and purpose." His exaggerated voice makes me laugh. "Something funny, Miss?"

"No sir. Lindsay Barnal, reporting for duty sir."

"Duty?"

"Yes, first day on the job, tactical engineering."

"Credentials?" Ty barks.

"Citizen 99234, educated at MIFF where I met my husband." I smile emphasizing the word 'husband.'

"I've heard of your husband. He's a genius and very attractive."

"Shut up!"

"What? I was improvising." He looks back smiling before he stops, waiting for me to catch up. We kiss underneath a large dying tree, the ground crunches under our boots as I bring him closer to me.

I pull my head away. "He's alright. Not a genius though."

Chapter 46: Nessa

Days have passed since that kiss and we're twenty miles outside the testing facility now. The unpredictable weather nearly cost us the mission. On our seventh day snow fell like an endless white blanket caking the world with white flakes, heavy like glue. We were forced to stay under cover an entire day. We huddled together, every joint in my body trembled from cold. Without the gear Jon packed we would've died. Ty held me, his body virtually wrapped around mine as he tried warming me. I'm sure he was just as cold but he wouldn't show it, he covered me in all his gear, leaving him nearly bare.

After twenty-four hours of unrelenting snow the storm finally cleared enough for Ty and me to see where we were going. If we tried to travel in a storm like that we would've been turned around countless times and inevitably frozen to death. The two-day buffer has been reduced to one. Even that's closing in considering our speed has been severely cut by breaking trail through knee-deep powder.

Despite the arctic chill of winter I blaze like wildfire as I make my way through the snow and ice. Sweat collects on my brow and drips down my back. Cold can't touch me now that I'm up and moving. Ty and I move forward through the snow day and night. The closer we get to the city the more frantic I become.

It's almost as if my old home is calling to me, beckoning me to return. I can see Emma and papa eating in the pavilion. Emma looks taller, leaner, and dejected. She's been lonely without me; my stomach twists as I see her tucked in bed alone. I want to run to her and papa. I want to take my trail across the rotting log to the old oak by the river. I want to see our crystallized river and Garrett waiting for me. With each step my former life cries like a siren that's just out of reach.

I know Ty can tell something's changed in me; I'm distant and distracted. It kills me to hurt him. When I let myself focus on him my prattled brain clears and I'm happy. For a few fleeting moments a day he gets the old me, the Nessa he loves and the one that's starting to love him back. I wish I could stay in those moments forever but no matter what I do I keep getting pulled away. I don't understand how I can feel so right and so complete with him and then at a moment's notice, flat out question if it's true and real. Of course what we have is true and real, but is that enough? Wasn't what Garrett and I had true and real, but that wasn't enough. It wasn't enough to keep us together; it wasn't enough to keep me from falling for Ty. Ty's different though, I know that. We fit together, our lives, our pasts, and our futures. He knows me and I know him. Just by being the same, by being Prems, we have a bond stronger than I could have ever imagined. But then again, is that enough?

He lowers his atomic bag to the ground, hesitating before he speaks. "We can stop here for lunch. Did I do something to upset you?"

"No." Anger resonates in my voice. I'm mad at him for asking, for pointing out something I'm already sensitive about. "It's not you, it's me." I pause appreciating how stupid that sounds. "The closer we get to home the more I think about papa and Emma."

"And Garrett too. Right?" He asks, the pain obvious.

"I mean, I guess so, yeah." He turns away. "It's not like that. It's just sometimes I miss my old life. I don't necessarily want to go back with *him*. I'm not going to lie to you though, I think about a lot of things and one of them is him." Ty unzips his bag tossing me my bar.

"You don't have to explain."

"I'm sorry. I don't know what to say. The first seventeen years of my life were here and eleven of them were with him."

"I told you, I don't need you to explain."

We eat our bars in silence. Both of us hurting and internally licking our wounds. I wish I could make him understand how I feel but nothing I say or do ever gets the message across quite good enough.

My feelings for Ty are strong, probably stronger than I want to admit. I know I want to make him happy but I also know there's still a part of me I hold separate from him. It will be a year tomorrow that Garrett was ripped out of my hands by Central. A year since I fell across the cold stage and listened to his screams as they carried him away. Sometimes I think I'll need a lifetime to get over that one hurt. I know it isn't fair to Ty but I also know I can't let him go either. The thought of losing him only intensifies the pain.

"Ty I'm sorry. It's just hard for me to face my old life." He turns to look at me. His eyes are distant but at least he looks.

"We should get up; we need to make it to the facility tonight."

Half furious, half hurt, I get up hoisting my bag to my back. We push forward in silence, my mind racing a million miles an hour. I stare at the back of Ty as we move forward. The day's so long and almost uncomfortable. Finally Ty lifts his arm with his fist squeezed tight as he drops to the ground.

I follow with my heart hammering. He signals for me to stay low and move into position next to him. My pack sways left and right as I belly crawl toward him. His hand directs me to scan ahead over the small hill we're positioned behind. I slowly scramble to the top and see the idling hovercraft sitting in front of the massive wall of the testing facility.

I'm just about to lower myself back down to Ty when the black metal door carved into the wall opens and Natalie steps out. I drop my bag and fist the first rock my fingers find. I'm going to kill her. I watch her turn to the door and I make my move, pushing to my feet. I'm ready to run. I'm going to bash her skull in. I take my first step and then I feel Ty's hands clamping down on my ankle as he pulls me back.

"What the hell are you doing? Are you crazy?"

"Let me go, I'm gonna kill her!" I try yelling through his hands that muffle my mouth. I crash back to the ground.

"Nessa, stop it!" He's fighting to hold me down.

"Leave me alone! Let me do this!"

"No!" He's breathless laid out on top of my bucking body.

Just as quickly as she came she's gone, safe onboard the craft and taking off to Central. I'm furious. I wanted revenge. I wanted to see the snow painted red with her blood.

"What's your problem? You coulda got us both killed. You woulda blown the whole mission." He slams his head into the embankment, his breath spirals against the cold. "What good would that have done? Honestly! Where would we be? Dead in the snow and you know what they would've done? They would've gone after my family and yours. Emma would probably be killed just for sport."

He's right, it was stupid. I nod my head. I'm sure he won't forgive me and just then he reaches across taking my hand. I turn to look at him and I see the hurt I've caused him, it's written across his face. He's a good man, better than I deserve. He knows what I need and he's always there to give it to me.

"Nessa I'll fight for you till my last breath." I look down, ashamed. "Just don't make me take it today." He smiles weakly.

We sit together in the snow waiting for the shadows of night to fall around us. Finally night comes and we set up shelter.

"I'm due at the facility tomorrow at 0800." He's reviewing the plan for the hundredth time. "I'll go in first; you'll be able to see me with the binoculars. I'll get in and set the first bomb."

"Don't forget, you enter here." I use a stick to point to the entrance we traced into the snow. "You go down the tunnel and take a left at the fork." I'm mentally retracing my steps from the leap test. I veer my stick to the left. "You pass my target and continue to yours, it's about two hundred steps from the fork." He nods as I drag my stick through the snow.

"OS3-4," he says.

"Right, that's the room. At least it should be..." Now that the mission's upon us I'm beginning to doubt myself.

"It'll be the right room." He tries assuring me. "I'll assemble the bomb and sync it to be triggered at 2000."

"I'll be right behind you. The guards are expecting me to report to duty at 0900. I'll get in, plant the bomb in OS1-2 and coordinate it to detonate at 2000."

"I'll meet ya back here at the end of the day, 1900 at the latest." He's trying to sound confident but I hear his voice break at the end, betraying his ruse. "Well Lindsay, we have a big day ahead of us tomorrow. What do ya say we get some sleep?" I nod, lying down next to him.

Chapter 47: Nessa

I tossed and turned all night. I had a terrible dream that Central had captured Ty and Garrett. I had to choose which one lived. I looked at them both sitting bound and beaten to metal chairs in a cold sterile room.

The blood dripping from Ty's face ticked at a steady rhythm against the tile floor and Garrett's strained moans echoed throughout the room. I could only save one. I was utterly torn as I alternated back and forth between them. There was Garrett from my former life, from the naïve Nessa. We'd been dreamers together but it was more than just a dream.

And then there was Ty, the man I fell for since becoming enlightened to the deceitful ways of our nation. Two men pulling at two halves of me. I could feel my head just forming its decision, the haze was beginning to clear. I could almost see myself saving one and then clarity collapses as Ty's alarm goes off.

"Did you sleep at all? You were tossin' all night."

"Bad dreams." I pause hoping he won't push me to divulge any further.

"Yea, me too. They're just dreams, we'll be okay. We'll get through this together." He reaches for my elbow guiding me closer to him. His deep inhale pulls at my hair as he buries his head into my auburn locks. He exhales, "I need to start getting ready." He stands and moves across the tent toward his oversized bag.

He pulls out his white and black uniform. He changes quickly as the cold is biting, even inside the tent. He reaches down and fixes his hair before he covers his eyes with the contacts. When he turns to me with his white uniform and long white lab coat it's amazing how different he looks. He really could be one of them.

"Do I look the part?" He smiles as he does a slow spin holding the front of his jacket open.

"Without a doubt," I smile.

He leans down lacing his boots that have been stuffed with explosives. Hidden compartments inside the boots hold the bomb's components. "Well, I should be headin' out." I stand and look into his brown eyes, even though they aren't the deep green color I'm used to they're still the eyes of the man I trust. I can see his honesty.

"After today this will be all over and we can go back to our life across the wall," he says before he leans down to kiss me. It ignites the blood pulsing through my veins. My heart hammers as he pulls away. "I love you Nessa," he says and I smile weakly, still unable to bring myself to say those words back.

He turns to leave and I follow him with binoculars in hand. I watch his silhouette glide between the trees and over the frosted ground. As he drifts out of sight I pull the binoculars up, following him toward the entrance.

His steps are confident and his shoulders are square and strong. Closer and closer he gets until he's at the gate. I can tell from the way his hands are moving that he must be talking to someone or something. He reaches into the pocket of his lab coat pulling out his scan card, swiping it smoothly into the machine.

I hold my breath waiting for the next move. I'm not sure if I'm waiting for him to walk into the facility or be gunned down in front of me. The seconds tick by in what seems like an eternity. I hear a buzz echo from the gates as he disappears inside.

Now it's my turn. I put on my white uniform with my black belt that transects my body. I lace my heavy explosive laden boots and pull my hair onto my head as I struggle with my contacts. After my fifth attempt they're in and my eyes water in protest. I take down my hair and walk toward the gate.

My anxiety grows stronger and stronger with each step. A part of me wants to turn and go back into the woods and abandon the mission but I can't. I can't leave Ty and I can't abandon the one mission that could liberate my people.

The vines reach their threading spines towards the tops of the expansive wall and I follow their serpentine path much like I did on my first visit to the facility a year ago. Finally I reach the gate. I see the tower with the regulators cradling their guns. I stand and wait until at last the reader materializes in front of me.

"State your name and purpose of visit." A voice booms from the box.

"Lindsay Barnal reporting for duty; first day on the job, sir."

"Scan your card." I reach into my pocket and slide the invisible bar code under the red laser. The beam hovers for a moment and I wait for the beep. I try to distract him.

"Tactical engineer sir. You should be expecting me."

"Your card isn't working, stay right there." My heart drops straight into the depths of my stomach. I consciously try maintaining my composure while sweat starts collecting in my palms and across my forehead.

The doors open, there are two regulators standing at the ready. One with his gun nestled to his shoulder, pointing it straight at me while the other strides toward me.

"Scan card," he demands.

I hand over my badge. He immediately wipes it across his pressed white shirt and then positions it back under the reader. I force myself to breathe slow and controlled. The card hovers under the red beam. At last I hear the beep.

"All clear," he reports back to the machine. The gates swing open. "Sorry about that. It happens sometimes."

"Not a problem at all, I understand." I smile and make my way into the facility. I take the narrow sloping tunnel; it's so strange being back here and realizing how different my life is today compared to a year ago. I approach the fork veering to the left.

I work my way towards my target counting as I go. Finally I'm at the door labeled OS1-2. I swipe my badge across the reader and the door clicks open. I slide inside and see several machines spread out across the room. I recognize them from our training session. I find my target and begin assembly.

I kick off my boots and pull them apart, taking pieces of metal and wire from all the hidden spaces. Sweat covers my palms as I slide the pieces together like Hank instructed. I've only got two pieces left when I hear steps pounding down the hall toward me. The steps get closer as I frantically gather the pieces.

I can hear a man fumble in his pocket before finally pulling out his ID card. "This is OS1-2." Just as the door unlatches I grab the last component and scramble behind the giant black machine positioned in the corner. "We don't keep any surveillance equipment per se in here. But as you can probably tell from your training at MIFF, this room is one of the two tactical stations in the building.

Ty enters panicked. I'm sure he's half expecting to find me in the middle of the room with a bomb in hand. He scours the room until his eyes find me crouched in the corner.

"Your job will be to set up thermal surveillance alarms and cameras targeting this room. Central's decided to increase security to our most vital areas."

"I see, absolutely."

Just then Ty's boss, a short heavyset man turns toward my corner. I squeeze myself against the wall but it's not enough. Ty sees his move and reacts.

"Wow! Would you look at this?"

"What?" His boss turns to the machine at the opposite end of the room. I exhale.

"Oh never mind. For a second I thought it was the MT-19. Just something we learned about at MIFF but I was wrong."

His boss looks slightly confused but not wanting to sound ignorant he agrees that it looks similar to the MT-19. I laugh internally; Ty doesn't know the first thing about these machines let alone what their names are.

"Anyway, let me show you to your office and then it's time for orientation."

Ty leaves the room first. As soon as the door clicks I'm back to work. My boss will be expecting me in ten minutes. I feverishly assemble the last components and secure the bomb to the back of the towering machine. My watch beeps confirming a 2000 detonation. I slide out of the room with my heart drumming.

"Mrs. Barnal?"

"Yes?" I turn caught off guard.

"Hello, I'm Donna Estee, your supervisor. We've been looking all over for you."

"My apologies, I got turned around on my way to the restroom."

"No problem." She looks perturbed. I follow behind Donna's short blonde hair as she leads me through the winding and intricate maze that makes up the testing facility. "Today's orientation day, real simple. You'll be in the oval room reviewing protocol training with the other new recruits."

I make my way into the expansive oval room. Donna ushers me to a seat and turns to leave. I search dozens of faces looking for Ty. I find him sitting three aisles down.

Hours stretch on and on with orientation training dragging in the background of my mind. My head can't focus on anything but the mission. I keep replaying the operation over and over trying to calculate all the possible dangers. Finally the videos power down and the lights turn on in the expansive oval room.

The curtain framing the screen sways as a middle-aged man makes his way across the stage. His voice becomes amplified with the press of a button. "Ladies and gentleman that concludes your orientation to our facility. You have an hour to explore and further familiarize yourself before the craft arrives to take you back to Central."

I look down at the watch I concealed in my jacket, it's 1800. Right now all the leap participants are making their way to the banquet halls. Riding the shuttles in their uncomfortable clothes, getting ready to be tortured as they wait for the revealing of their results and what life they'll be forced to lead. Two hours until the video plays and our bombs detonate. Just two hours until freedom and I get to see Emma and papa.

Ty finds his way to me, "How was your first day?"

"It was good. Nearly a disaster but nothing my husband couldn't take care of."

"Oh is that what it takes to finally have you call me your husband? I had to save your ass for the tenth time before gainin' that status." He smiles as I reach for his hand.

"Let's get out of here."

We walk through the winding tunnels that spread beneath the facility and exit from the side door Natalie came from yesterday. We break into the cold and make our way across the field toward shelter.

"Did you have any problems?" I ask.

"Nope, in and out without a problem." He smirks.

"So now I guess we wait?"

He stops and pulls me toward him as we step through the cover of the tree line. "I can think of somethin' we could do."

He sweeps my legs out from under me laying me against the icy ground. His hands lace through my hair and make their way toward my face. He wraps around my hips pulling me on top of him. My legs straddle his. My hair falls around my face and before I can tie it up he's sweeping it away.

The intensity of his kiss and hands ignites something inside me that's wild and raw. I feel the pressure of his palm on my low back guiding my hips to his. He keeps his composure like always.

His breathing is calm and steady while mine races. I think about his control next to my wild desires and I blush.

We roll together in the snow; my back touches the icy ground as he pulls my shirt up and over my head. I arch my back from the cold. His mouth dances along my stomach and immediately warms me like fire. I take off his shirt and pull his muscled chest against mine. He works his way down making his way to my favorite place. I twist and turn under his touch. The intensity builds as my breath quickens. At last I get my release as I moan in bliss.

Our watches chime just as I hit my peak. "Shit, it's time already." He groans as he silences his watch and helps me from the ground, "Thirty minutes till detonation," he looks at me.

"It's scary isn't it? I mean it's exciting but scary." I can't find the right words to describe how it feels.

We pack our shelter and make our way to the hill with binoculars in hand. If everything goes as planned the bombs will detonate in fifteen minutes. Ty's watch begins beeping, counting down the fifteen minute mark. I pull mine out but nothing happens.

"You set it to 2000 right?"

"Yes of course!"

"Well it's supposed to beep. Shit." I ask my next question even though I already know.

"What's this mean?"

"Something went wrong durin' the sync. It's got to be done manually." He jumps to his feet tearing his bag open.

"What are you doing?" I ask frantically.

"Jon gave me a gun in case we got in a bind." His breath quickens. "I'll have to go sync it manually."

"No, you can't. It's too dangerous!" I cling to him.

"Nessa let me go. I gotta leave *now*."

He pushes my arms off and turns toward the facility. I crumble to the ground and watch his silhouette disappear into the darkness. Ty's watch continues to beep counting down the minutes, twelve more until detonation. I watch the seconds fly by as I mentally retrace my steps in OS1-2. I know I synched it, everything should be fine but my watch sits silent next to his beeping reminder that in eleven minutes the mission could have failed and he could be dead.

I feel nauseous thinking I could have jeopardized the operation and worse that Ty could die trying to fix my mistake. Ten minutes ticks on his watch and I hear gunshots ring out from the facility. My heart drops as I hear the popping of weapons firing. No way he'll make it, he's either captured or already dead.

Tears roll down my face and my throat heaves. I prop myself on my knees. I imagine him fighting his way through a group of regulators. I can see him gunned down, bleeding and dying alone.

The gunshots stop but his watch continues, a brutal reminder that time's running out. Six minutes left until I've failed the mission. Right now banquet halls across our nation are just about to award the leap winners. The video of Ty and I will be flashing across their screens. This is the moment Central will be revealed for the lying manipulative people they really are. In six minutes

Jake will be waiting for our bombs to explode and clear the airfield so he can swoop in to rescue us.

He and the other resistance pilots are sitting at our shelter beside the remains of the charred hill waiting to attack the walls that hold my people captive. So much depends on this mission. We're so close but I failed. I failed Jon and the others, I failed my people and family but what kills most is that I failed Ty. Five minutes until detonation. I push myself up and start running.

I can't let the mission fail, I can't let this all be in vain. I run through the trees and snow. I'm closing in on the facility with three minutes left when I hear another round of popping. More gunshots ring out from inside the building and just like that my watch begins ticking in time with Ty's. He did it. He synched the bomb and somehow he's still alive.

I wipe my card across my shirt and scan it under the reader. The doors open and I sprint through the tunnel into the facility. I hear screams and boots running as alarms begin sounding. I take the fork and nearly run into the first body, a regulator with blood staining his shirt crimson red. I leap across his lifeless body and keep moving. I hear more shots coming from the tunnel. I reach and grab a gun from the second regulators body.

I keep sprinting forward cradling the gun to my chest. The lights flicker off then back on and I see Ty kneeling. Blood pours from his thigh. His hands are steady as he holds them over his head in surrender.

"Who the hell are you?" The regulator shouts at him.

"Screw you Borg," he spits.

I hear the clicking of the gun as the regulator wraps his finger around the trigger. Without thinking I react. I raise my gun and pull the hammer back placing my finger around the trigger. It's Ty or him and I can't lose Ty. I squeeze down on the trigger and feel the kick as the bullet drives its way from the chamber. The shot lands right between the regulator's shoulders. He crumbles to the floor. Ty opens his eyes in disbelief as I sprint toward him.

"Nessa, what are you doin'?"

"We're partners, remember? I'll die for you." I pull him to his feet. "Let's not make me do it today though, okay?"

His left leg's gushing blood but there's no time to stop. We've only got one minute until detonation. I brace him across my shoulder pulling him down the hall.

"Forty seconds!" I scream over the alarms as we make our way to the fork. The gunshot's disabling him, he screams whenever his left leg touches down. "Keep going, we're almost there!" I yell. The watch beeps, "Thirty seconds!"

The lights flicker and dance in and out. I hear the echoing steps of regulators from somewhere in the maze of underground tunnels. Their boots get louder and louder as they close-in on us.

"Come on Ty we need to get out of here!" He fights for air as he stumbles headfirst.

Twenty seconds left until the facility explodes collapsing in on us. As we reach the final door I hear a regulator behind us. A bullet flies past me and Ty jumps in pain before I hear his screams. I turn aiming my gun at the regulator, this time there's no hesitation as I fire hitting him square in the chest.

"Ty!" I scream as I reach for his crumpled body. The bullet landed in his back.

Our watches frantically beep counting down the last ten seconds. I drop my gun and stoop over lifting Ty off the ground. My body shakes as I drag him across the threshold of the door. The watch screeches a continuous wail as we cross into the outside.

The explosions sound simultaneously. The ground shakes as fire and smoke barrel down the corridor racing toward the door. I throw the weight of my body against the solid metal sealing it shut just as the cloud of destruction reaches us. My body thrusts forward from the atomic power of the fiery wall but I resist. The ground underneath Ty turns crimson as blood and life pour out of him.

I reach into my jacket pulling out the beacon signal and press down on the buttons for five seconds, just like we'd been shown. I pray Jake can get here fast enough. I stumble to Ty and tear off my sleeve, tying it above his thigh. His breath is ragged and shallow, his skin's pale and white. I follow the warm blood to his back driving my hand into the pulsing wound.

I need Jake to get here now; he doesn't have much time. Ty's eyes flutter open and closed as his breathing begins to slow. With his slowing breath my heart frees itself and becomes his. I know that he is mine and I am his. So unfair and so wrong that my heart is just now ready to be given away. Ready to be taken by a man that might die in my arms. I press my head to his, "Don't leave me. I need you, I *love* you."

The corners of his mouth pull into a weak smile. I feel the pressure of air driving down on us. I look up to the massive belly of the craft. Jake lowers the basket and I drag Ty into it. I lay on top of him and imagine him doing the same for me back in the woods. We lift into the craft as the ramp seals shut.

"Nessa! Are you okay?"

"Kara, help! He's been shot." I crawl off Ty as we transfer him onto the gurney.

"I'll need your help," Kara demands. "Keep pressure," she guides my hands placing them over his gushing wounds. Kara begins administering fluids through his collapsing veins. "We need to get him to a hospital now!" She shouts to Jake. "I need to start a transfusion." She hangs a bag of fresh blood. The craft rockets forward as Jake tests his skills.

"ETA is thirty minutes Kara." Jake screams from the front. Kara gives no reply.

"Will he make it?" I ask.

"No telling, we're doing the best we can."

My hands are warm, more than warm, they're hot from his blood. Kara moves my hands around alternating from his gushing leg to his bleeding back. I can't help but feel like I'm in the way. Even if I am, I can't let go. I won't stop trying to staunch the bleeding.

Suddenly Ty's body arches, hanging in midair like he's being bent in two. I hold my breath, panicked. He crashes back to the table. The sound startles me, shaking me to my core. Kara's yelling orders and I do the best I can, but he looks so pale and now he's shaking. His whole body trembles as Kara tries hanging another bag of fresh blood. I hold pressure to his wounds but all I can think about are his eyes. Eyes that are rolling toward the back of his head.

Suddenly I get what I asked for as the bleeding stops. What if the bleeding stopped because he's gone? Maybe it meant he was still with me before and now he's not. His eyes roll one last time before they fall shut. He's still, this can't be right.

Jake veers the hovercraft to the side as he dodges our resistance fighters that are taking down the walls. The gurney slides across the craft as one of the bombs explodes close to us. Jake throttles forward. Without warning he careens the craft to the left, throwing it on its side. We aren't in a safe zone yet. The life line connecting to Ty's hand gets torn as the gurney slides across the floor of the craft.

"Jake you have to get control!" Kara shouts.

"Sorry but this isn't easy!" Jake yells from the cockpit.

Another explosion goes off, sending chills around my body.

"Brace yourselves!" Jake screams.

Debris from the exploding wall fly through the air, slamming into the side of the craft. Everything shakes and I watch in sickening horror as Kara tries to thread the IV back into Ty's hand. I keep my hands pressed to Ty's wounds, even though they aren't bleeding anymore.

"We've got to get there fast Jake, we're losing him!" Kara shouts as she threads the IV back into his vein.

Jake levels the craft and pushes forward, leaving the exploding walls of my former nation behind us. Finally we cross into safety but I know it might be too late. The craft slows and maintains its hover. Kara and I are at the ramp with Ty before Jake has the chance to release the latch.

"They're waiting for you!" Jake yells.

I can't tell if Ty's breathing. I want to collapse, my legs are trembling. Could I have lost him already? Was there a moment when he went from breathing and alive to suddenly gone, right under my touch? How didn't I feel the life leave him? I should have felt his spirit go. Right?

We're met by a team of doctors. They grab the gurney wheeling him through the doors. I collapse to my knees staring at my blood-covered hands in disbelief. The man I love could die tonight and it's my fault. I shake as I wipe the blood from my fingers.

Jake's hands feel foreign on my shoulders and do nothing to comfort me, "Nessa, I'm sorry. He's in the right place now. They'll take care of him."

In the distance the sounds of exploding bombs ring out over the wall. We completed our mission. My people can finally be free but was it worth it? Was Ty's life worth it? I can't answer that question; I don't even want to think about it.

"I need to be with him," I say looking at Jake.

Kara lifts me to my feet. "I'll go with you." She wraps me in her arms, leading me to the empty waiting room. I stare across the room at the yellow walls and wait as the hours pass. My mind's numbed to everything around me.

A doctor, probably in his early thirties startles me, "Miss. Hollins?" I shoot to my feet with Kara by my side. "He's out of surgery." He pauses and I want to kill him for making me wait. "He's going to make it."

I fall back into my chair on the verge of crying, "Can I see him?"

"Not yet, he's still in recovery but you'll see him soon enough." The doctor turns to leave.

Kara rubs my shoulders, "You saved his life, you know that right?"

I nod, "I'm staying here tonight, alright?"

"I'll stay with you then."

Chapter 48: Nessa

I wake startled by the blood covering my ripped uniform. Kara and I slept in the waiting room chairs. My neck aches in protest. "Kara wake up," I nudge her.

"Morning," she yawns shaking her head. "Let me go talk to the doctors, see if you can visit him yet."

She gets up and leaves. I watch her make her way to the nurse's station. My heart drums wildly as the anticipation builds. She turns with a smile, good news I'm hoping.

"We can see him now," she says.

I jump to my feet following her to his room. I hesitate outside his door, I'm nervous about what I'll see. Kara pulls the door open. There are alarms and machines hooked up everywhere but there he is, alive and awake.

"Nessa." His voice is weak.

"Ty! I thought I'd lost you." I reach for his hand squeezing it between mine.

"I didn't come this far makin' you fall for me just to die." He smiles, his eyes fighting to stay awake.

The nurse steps into the room, "He needs his rest. You can see him tomorrow."

Ty smiles, "She can stay."

My fingers trace along his hands, it's amazing how much better he looks already. I lose myself in his eyes, green ones that draw me into them. There's a gentle knock as Kara steps back in. I didn't even notice her leave.

"Nessa, we have your family. They're here to see you." I'd almost forgotten about that. A pit hits my stomach. Kara clears her throat, "They're in the lounge."

"Go see them. I'll wait for ya." Ty smiles. "I was thinkin' of going for a swim but I guess I can wait a blink." He grins.

"I'll be right back." My stomach twists and turns in excitement.

It's been a year since I've seen papa or Emma. I hope they recognize me. What if they're mad? Maybe they didn't want to be rescued. Maybe they would rather have stayed where they were. I shake my head, knowing they wouldn't have wanted to live a lie. I take the turn around the nurse's station and see them. My heart skips in my chest, throwing itself wildly as I get closer. Their backs are to me as they watch the news of last night's attacks stream across the TV.

"Papa…Emma?" I say. They turn, papa freezes and Emma runs.

"Nessa!" She clings to my waist as my heart races. She's grown so much in a year.

"Emma thank god you're safe!" Papa makes his way to me. His eyes are twisted with pain and confusion. "Papa, I'm sorry. I wanted to tell you but I couldn't. They would have taken Emma, they would have—" He cuts me off, pulling me into his arms.

His touch feels stronger than ever before, more comforting and honest than I remember. It feels so good to have them back.

"What happened to you? You look awful." Emma says.

"I've been through hell and back about three times. I'll tell you everything in time. All that matters is you're here. You're free and safe." I look at Kara and Jake. "These are good people. They'll help us." Emma's eyes give away her trepidation.

"What about the people we left behind?"

Jake chimes in from the corner, "We're not going to rest until we've freed everyone."

Emma looks back to me, "Did Garrett find you?"

"Garrett?" A pit settles deep in my stomach. "No Emma, they took him to Central after the banquet last year. He's probably still there."

Jake turns up the broadcast streaming from the massive television in the lobby. Images of the crafts bombing the walls flash and I see hundreds of refugees making their way through the rubble.

Emma takes a deep breath, "He escaped months ago."

It's like the air has been kicked out of me. "What?" I ask.

Papas rests his hand on Emma's shoulder, "A month ago he came to our house looking for you." The pit twists like a knife in my stomach. "He'd broken out of Central to find you. We told him what had happened, or at least what Central had told us." Papa speaks up, "He didn't believe the story. He knew you didn't accept any scout position, he knew it didn't exist. He left to find you."

My stomach hollows as I try catching my breath. The television blasts an emergency alarm and the screen flashes to static. Jake curses.

"Damn thing's broken."

The static stops as coverage begins again but it's different now. No more walls crumbling and refugees being rescued. Now it's a sterile white room with a single chair positioned dead center. There's a man tied to the seat. His body's limp as blood drips from the white bag covering his head.

Jake stares at the TV. "What the hell?" He looks back to Kara and me. I try focusing on the news. We all turn to the television as Jake dials up the volume.

The singsong voice begins, "Ladies and gentleman this is a message from behind the walls of Central. I'm here to inform you that one of the leaders of last night's rebellion has been captured." We all look to each other utterly confused. "He *will* be executed in one week from today unless his co-conspirator surrenders." Kara and I lock eyes. "Her name is Vanessa Hollins." A picture of my face flashes across the screen. "We're asking anyone with information regarding her whereabouts to contact us. We're prepared to initiate biological warfare on your people unless she's surrendered within one week's time."

The voice sounds so familiar and then it hits me, Natalie. Just then her long dark hair sashays as she walks in front of the camera towards the chair. My blood boils and I've never wanted to kill her more than I do now.

"One week Miss Hollins." She looks directly at the camera like she's staring into my soul. She pulls off the bag and I immediately drop to the floor. My knees hit as I feel myself in ruination. She lifts Garrett's chin, his swollen acorn-brown eyes look straight at the camera, straight at me.